LOVE IS ENOUGH

The Sisters of Rosefield Book 1

EMMA EASTER

Love is Enough
by Emma Easter

Paperback Edition

CKN Christian Publishing
An Imprint of Wolfpack Publishing

6032 Wheat Penny Avenue
Las Vegas, NV 89122

Paperback ISBN: 978-1-64734-486-3
Ebook ISBN: 978-1-64119-880-6
Library of Congress Control Number: 2019956422

LOVE IS ENOUGH

To my dear husband, Mike.

ONE

Sienna Gardner sat in front of the mirror and stared nervously at herself. Her heart skipped beats and her hands perspired. She could hear people talking and laughing outside her hotel room. The loud voices all sounded merry, waiting for her happy occasion to begin. But she wasn't happy. She was a nervous wreck, and it wasn't because of wedding jitters as Ben, her makeup artist, had assured her. It was due to the severe anxiety that had plagued her for months, which started with an explicit instruction from God. An instruction she had yet to obey.

Her long platinum blond hair had been straightened and styled into a classic chignon, and she was waiting for her makeup to be done. She turned as Ben came back into the room holding a bottle of face primer. He squeezed out a small amount into his palm and immediately started applying it on her face. Once he finished, he lifted two tubes of foundation and looked at her in the mirror, trying to decide.

"Which one do you want to use today, Sienna?

The dewy or matte foundation?" he asked quizzically.

She took a deep breath in an attempt to calm her heart, which had begun to pound again. She felt the anxiety attack getting worse and started to breathe in and out, in and out. But it didn't help.

Lord, please help me, she muttered under her breath. She pressed her lips together and forced a smile. "Use the dewy foundation, and Ben, you need to hurry up. I can't be late for my own wedding, can I?"

"Certainly not!" Ben chuckled.

As he did her makeup, her heart drummed faster and faster. She tried to pray, but the anxiety only increased. She kept telling herself to calm down, and avoided looking at herself in the mirror until Ben had finished. He smiled at her.

"Gorgeous as always, though you don't even need any makeup to look beautiful."

She tried, but her lips couldn't form a smile. Getting up quickly, she said, "When you leave, could you please tell my sisters that I need their help in here?"

"You didn't say anything about your makeup." He frowned. "Don't you like it? I know it's not usually what I do for your photo shoots, but I decided to keep it simple and go with a nude look today to let your natural beauty shine. I think you look amazing."

She inhaled and then exhaled slowly. "It's fine."

"Are you okay?" He frowned.

She shook her head. "Probably last-minute wedding jitters like you said."

"Maybe it's more than just wedding jitters." He

studied her face.

She walked away, unwilling to explain what was going on with her. He would not understand. What would she tell him—that God wanted her to quit her well-paid modeling job because it was immoral and vain? Or that God didn't want her to get married because He was trying to teach her to take a different life path?

Ben would definitely not understand. He would think she was just being ridiculous. She had told her fiancé, Derrick, about the panic attacks and the cause of it, but she didn't tell him she felt God wanted her to end their engagement. Just as she guessed, he didn't get it.

Ben left the room, and Sienna sat on the bed. She inhaled and exhaled again, and then stood up to put on her wedding dress. The dress was a heavily beaded ivory ball gown with an embroidered corset. When she had bought it almost a year ago, she'd been thrilled at how beautiful it was, and she couldn't wait to wear it on her wedding day. Now she could barely look at herself in it. It was an added reminder that she was disobeying God and choosing her own way.

Her oldest sister, Audrey, came into the room, dressed in a pale pink chiffon dress. Her short hair was pinned back with a silver pin, and she wore silver kitten heels. "Sienna, are you ready?"

"Umm, can you help me lace up my corset?"

Audrey looked around the room. "This is a gorgeous hotel room, but you didn't have to spend so much money on a hotel room when you could have just stayed with me at the house. If Mom and Dad were still alive, they would not be happy."

"You know the family house is small," Sienna sighed. The last thing she needed now was to feel even guiltier than she already did. "If I were staying there, Trish would have decided to stay as well until after the wedding. As much fun as that would be, I just wanted a little breathing space today. Besides, my wedding ceremony and reception are taking place here, so it's just convenient."

"I thought you would stay in the house since you decided to come back to Rosefield to get married," Audrey said. "I know it can't be compared to your luxury apartment in New York, but it's still our family home, where we all grew up."

"Just help me with my corset, please," she said and turned her back to Audrey. Audrey laced up the corset quickly and turned Sienna around

"What is wrong with you? And don't say it's 'nothing' because I know you. Something is definitely wrong."

Sienna pursed her lips. Audrey was pretty perceptive, but would even she understand?

Audrey sat down on the bed and patted the space beside her.

"I hate to see my baby sister this way. Sit and tell me what exactly is wrong with you."

Sienna looked down at Audrey and then sat beside her, her heart still beating rapidly.

"Is it cold feet?" Audrey asked. "You can back out of the wedding now, you know. It's not like that Derrick is even worthy of you. You are such a sweet, beautiful girl while he is a . . ."

"Audrey! Not again. Please, leave Derrick alone!"

"You know I always speak my mind, Sienna. I know you don't love him. You're only marrying him because he was like Dad's right-hand man when he was alive. You think you owe Dad that and that Dad would have wanted you to marry him. That's how he managed to weasel his way into your life."

"I'm having a tough time now, and I'd appreciate it if you didn't make it worse."

"I'm worried about you." Audrey frowned. "Please tell me what's wrong."

Sienna searched her sister's eyes. If only she could share everything with Audrey—the nightmares, the months of grueling dread and panic, the constant fear that she would die unless she canceled her wedding, quit her job, and did what she knew God wanted her to do right now. She wanted to obey God in all things, but canceling her wedding and quitting her job seemed way too much.

"Please, tell me," Audrey pleaded.

She sighed wearily and opened her mouth to speak just as someone opened the door. Trisha, her older sister, swayed into the room sheathed in a tight, pale pink dress. The dress was the same as Audrey's, but she'd fitted hers to hug her generous curves.

"Sienna, are you ready?" Trisha asked, and then gasped. She took Sienna's hand, lifted her off the bed and surveyed her. "You look stunning!"

"Thank you," Sienna said.

Trisha looked at Audrey and then focused on her again. "We have to go now before people start thinking you ran away from your own wedding."

Sienna's emotions roiled. It was precisely what she felt like doing right now.

"Sienna, are you okay?" Trisha asked with a concerned look on her face.

She nodded. "Just last-minute jitters."

You have to give in now, Sienna, or face the consequences of your disobedience to God, the now-familiar voice whispered in her heart.

She bit her lips and nudged the voice aside and went out of the room with her sisters. Audrey and Trisha held her hands as they made their way into the elevator and down to the last floor. She managed to hold back the anxiety and condemning voice, but as soon as she stood in front of the hall where her wedding ceremony was to take place, the voice came back, harsher than ever.

The wedding song began to play and she tried to suppress the taunting voice, but it wouldn't go away. She began to walk—or rather, tiptoe—down the aisle strewn with flowers. The hall was covered with white roses at her request as a symbol of purity, but she felt impure. Guilt threatened to suffocate her.

People watched as she made her way slowly down the aisle.

They must be thinking I'm the saddest looking bride they have ever seen.

She looked up at Derrick and mustered up a smile for him.

He smiled back, his eyes shining, clearly letting her know he couldn't wait to marry her. She started to hyperventilate and screamed at herself in her head. Get yourself together!

You know you shouldn't do it! You are clearly disobeying God! The voice shouted at her.

She reached the front of the hall and stood beside Derrick, with her heart still racing. She looked up at the pastor and suddenly, waves of intense anxiety like she had never felt before flooded her mind and soul. She began to tremble as what she dreaded took over her mind. She felt like she was dying. She started to hyperventilate and couldn't stop.

"Sienna, what's wrong?" Derrick held her hand and whispered.

The pastor stared curiously at her.

The pastor can see you're in rebellion, Sienna. You know what you must do!

People were beginning to murmur and whisper amongst themselves. She tried to breathe, but when she couldn't catch her next breath, she knew she had to end it now or die. She turned to Derrick with tears in her eyes. "I'm so sorry, I can't do this."

A hush fell over the crowd.

Derrick's eyes grew wide with confusion, and she felt terrible for what she had done. But she knew she had no choice. She turned and ran out of the hall.

She ran faster, spurred on by the sounds of determined footsteps behind her and the frustrated voices of dozens of people yelling her name. She kept running and didn't stop until she reached her hotel room. She quickly locked the door and then collapsed onto the bed.

She kept inhaling and exhaling hard until the intense panic began to subside. The suffocating guilt gradually subsided, and she heaved a sigh, exhausted. The only negative feeling that remained was the pain of loss.

Derrick was a good guy. He'd been in their lives for as long as she could remember. Dad and Mom had acted as foster parents to him for a few months when he was just twelve. He had been adopted by another family soon after, but Dad had kept in close contact with him, acting as his mentor. They had grown very close. Even when Derrick became an attorney, he was in the house frequently throughout her childhood.

Sienna pressed her lips together. Derrick had somehow found his way into her heart. Even though she'd been a little hesitant about dating him when he asked her out, she had known her father would give his full blessings. That had gotten her to agree to go out with him. She would miss him now, but he was better off without her. He would find someone better in no time.

A loud knock sounded at the door, but she ignored it.

She stood again, shed her dress, and began gathering her things to leave for New York. For months, she'd resisted God's call, but she was ready to give in now. Once she got to New York, she would pack up all her things, call her agent to tell him she was quitting modeling, and return here to Idaho. Before the end of the week, she would enroll in The Beulah Bible College and by month's end, she would be a Bible College student. Hopefully, once in Beulah, she would find total peace.

*****

Audrey returned home late after a day spent patrolling Rosefield. She went into her bedroom, shed her police uniform and changed into a pair of shorts and a tank top. For the umpteenth time that week, she checked her phone for any message from the mayor's office but found none.

As she headed to the kitchen to put together

something to eat, her phone vibrated in her pocket. She plucked it out and stared at it. And then she heaved a sigh of relief. It was the email for which she had been waiting.

Since the former chief of police retired a month ago, she'd been the acting police chief. She was eager to officially take over the position now. The mayor's office had let her know that an official email would be sent to her once they fully agreed on who would fill the position. As she had been assistant police chief for some years and now acting chief of police, she was confident she would be the one selected, but that didn't stop her from being a little bit anxious.

It's about time, she thought. She clicked on the email, a thread of excitement running through her, and then looked up as a loud knock at the door distracted her.

She frowned. It was almost ten o'clock. Who could it be?

She walked to the living room, opened the door and gasped when she saw who it was. Sienna was standing there with a large suitcase beside her.

"Sienna! What are you doing here? You didn't tell me you were coming to Rosefield."

"Can I come in?" Sienna sighed loudly. "I'm tired."

Audrey stepped aside so Sienna could enter the house. She shut the door again and sat beside her sister, gazing worriedly at her. Since Sienna had ran out on her wedding day more than a month ago, she'd become reclusive and had stopped answering her calls. Something was going on with her—something bizarre. Audrey needed to find out what it was. Audrey sat facing her.

"You look drained. What's up? I thought you were preparing for some designer's fashion campaign this week, so how come you're here?"

"My agent was negotiating a place for me in the campaign, but it doesn't even matter." Sienna took a deep breath and said, "I quit modeling."

"What?" Audrey stared at her in astonishment. "You quit your high-paying job? Why?"

"I've enrolled in a Bible college here in Idaho . . . near Rosefield."

Audrey stared at her baby sister in utter confusion and then shook her head. "What is going on with you, Sienna? First, you run out on your wedding day, and now you quit your job in New York and enroll in a Bible school in a small town?"

Sienna had always been slightly flighty, but her modeling job, apart from the financial success it had given her in just five years, had been perfect for her in every way. Quitting it was lunacy.

"I thought you were happy as a model. What went wrong?"

"It's a long story." Sienna wrung her hands and sighed again.

"Tell me. I have time . . . well at least for an hour, as I have to get to work early tomorrow."

"It started about eight months ago," Sienna said. She went on to tell an alarming story of nightmares, frequent panic attacks, and constant dread. She finally finished and said, "So you see why I have to go to a Bible school. I need to obey God so that all of it will stop."

"Frankly, I don't see it. You know I wasn't a big fan of Derrick, and even though I thought it was

pretty weird of you to leave him at the altar, ultimately, I didn't mind. However, suddenly quitting
the job you love, leaving New York, and enrolling
in a Bible school here in Rosefield sounds like madness to me."

"It's not madness. It's what God wants me to do."

"I just don't know, Sienna. Would the Lord use
all that anxiety and distress to get you to obey his
will? Surely, He can find better ways to do that."

"I didn't say the Lord used the anxiety, I said I've
had the panic attacks because I didn't obey God."

"And I don't think God would tell you to quit
your job!" She looked at Sienna. "I think you should
see someone, like a therapist or . . ."

"Please, Audrey! I just want to rest up today. I'll
be moving into the Bible College dormitory tomorrow."

"Where exactly is it?"

"It's actually on the outskirts of Rosefield, right
between Rosefield and Green Valley."

"Umm, I think I know it. What about Trisha?
Have you told her?"

"You know how Trish is. It's hard to reach her
because she's always busy with Stan and her friends.
Besides, I don't want to bother her, or anyone else,
especially after what happened at the wedding."

"Speaking about the wedding, have you seen
Derrick since then?"

"No. I haven't seen him, and I don't think I'll ever
be able to face him."

Audrey studied Sienna's face. She looked so
vulnerable. If only their parents were alive, they
would have had the perfect advice that she couldn't
provide. She pushed the depressing thought away.

"You know what? I don't really understand why you chose to do what you did, but I choose to support you, no matter what. It's your life, and you can live it the way you want to."

"Thank you, Audrey." Sienna smiled. "That's really why I chose to tell just you. I knew you would understand."

"I'm not saying I understand, but I will support your decision, even though I think it's crazy and thoughtless. Anyway, let's talk about something more uplifting. I'm getting a promotion soon. The mayor's office just sent me an email. Even though I haven't read it yet, I already know that's what it's about."

"Audrey! I'm so happy for you. At last, you finally get to live your dream of becoming the chief of police." She hugged Audrey and then beamed. "You've been the only female police officer for a while, and now you'll be the first female police chief in Rosefield. I'm so proud of you!"

"That's what I'm most excited about," Audrey said, smiling.

They changed topics, and Audrey told Sienna about the city parade they'd had a few days ago. After chatting for a few hours, Sienna yawned, then glanced at the clock.

"It's past midnight. I should go to bed. I leave very early tomorrow."

"And I'm supposed to be in bed now," Audrey said.

"Night, sis." Sienna got up and stretched. "I'll see you before I leave."

After Sienna went to sleep in the spare room, Audrey went into her bedroom and sat on the bed.

She took her laptop from the bedside table and placed it on her lap. Her palms were slightly damp with anticipation as she opened her email inbox. She clicked on the mail from the mayor and began to read it.

As she read, her heart began to sink, and all her dreams evaporated.

When she finished, she stared at the wall, confused. It had never occurred to her that she would be treated like this. Not after she'd given thirteen years of her life to the Police force.

She bit her lip and reread the mail, praying she had somehow misread it. But there was no mistake, she had read the mayor's message clearly. He was bringing in someone else to fill the position of police chief. From the words he used in his email, he didn't seem to care how she took it. It was as if he wanted her to resign if the message didn't sit well with her.

She narrowed her eyes as her disappointment turned to anger. There was no way she would let herself be treated this way. It was unjust, and she intended to fight it.

Her fingers flew over her keyboard as she typed out the most bile-filled email she'd ever written. After she was done writing, she sat back, read the email, and then smirked. There was no way she could send this email.

Sitting up again, she began to edit it. Once she was through, she reread it. It was now somewhat polite, protesting the mayor's oversight and asking him to reconsider.

Satisfied with the email she'd written, she clicked 'send,' folded her arms, and pushed down the rage-fueled words threatening to spill out of her mouth. Hopefully, the mayor would send for her as soon as possible so she could explain how much she'd personally contributed to the growth of the Rosefield Police Force and why she deserved to be the police chief now. Not that Mayor Stanley didn't know. Every time she met him since Chief Richardson retired, the mayor had told her that she was doing a great job. So, this email was surprising and hurtful.

She went into the bathroom to wash her face in preparation for bed. She splashed warm water on her face and then stared at her reflection in the mirror. People often told her she looked much younger than her age whenever she said she was thirty-two, but today she really felt old.

She changed into her pajamas and climbed into bed, still fuming. If there was no favorable reply to her email from the mayor's office before the end of the week, she would go there and personally fight for her rightful position. There was no way she would let some guy take the job for which she had spent years working.

Hopefully, I can convince the mayor that I'm the woman for the job.

Or I will quit.

TWO

Assistant Student Chaplain, Bryan Larson, hid behind the ornate altar of the Beulah Bible College chapel. He watched the beautiful new girl who lay prostrate on the floor, sobbing, with growing concern. He had been troubled since the first day he saw her here, and his concern had only increased as he saw her weeping on the floor every day.

As the school student chaplain, he'd seen many students do the same, and he'd done it himself. But what troubled him about her was not the regularity with which she sobbed on the chapel floor, but the devastated look on her face when she got up to leave. She came very early every day before the general morning prayers and classes started, and also after classes ended. Sometimes, a few other students were at the chapel, but most of the time, it was just her . . . and him. It didn't appear that she had ever noticed him watching, though, as she never looked his way.

He felt like one of the annoying self-proclaimed 'Watchers' in the school—students who were informally appointed by the new Provost to report any act of sin or what they perceived as sin. However, unlike them and their never-ending witch hunts, he wanted to help and comfort this girl. He couldn't go on watching her suffer. He had to approach her today and find out what was bothering her and see if he could be of any help.

He went back into his tiny office. He had previously shared an office with the Senior Chaplain, Dr. Lincoln, but the vestry had been converted for his use last year to give Dr. Lincoln his privacy. The senior chaplain, who was always away on one preaching engagement or another, had put him in charge of the morning and evening prayers. He needed to prepare for them now.

He picked up his Bible, sat behind the desk, and started to study for the morning prayers while waiting for her to finish. She usually spent quite some time praying and would probably be through in about an hour. Whenever he came to the chapel in the morning, he found her there. She went away after the general morning prayers, but by the time he returned from a class in the evenings, she was already back there. He left the chapel at about eight o'clock every evening while she was still praying. As he did, he always felt uneasy because he suspected she stayed late into the night, weeping on the hard floor.

About an hour later, he went to see if she had finished, but she was still there.

Ten minutes later, she stood up.

She had her back to him as he strode toward her, but before he reached her, a troubling thought stopped him. Am I doing this because I genuinely want to help her or because I'm attracted to her?

He sighed. He'd never admitted that to himself until now. However, it was true. He was utterly smitten by her. But that wasn't the only reason why he felt like he needed to help her. He was a chaplain and a student in his final year and therefore had a unique perspective which he hoped would enable him to help her spiritually or academically, whatever her problem was.

He watched her take a seat at the back and then turn to look out the window. He walked up to her, and she turned around just as he reached her. Her eyes grew big and then fear entered them.

He paused in concern. Do I look scary? Nobody had ever told him that he did. Why then was she afraid of him? She looked like she wanted to flee, and so he said quickly, "Hi, I'm the assistant chaplain. What's your name?"

She spoke so softly he had to listen carefully to catch her name. "My name is Sienna."

He repeated the name to confirm he'd heard it right, and when she nodded, he smiled at her. "I've noticed how troubled you look every time you come here to pray. Can I help you with anything?"

She started to shake her head, and he quickly added, "I do some counseling as well. If you tell me about it, I might be able to come up with a solution. If not," he smiled, "as they say, a problem shared . . ."

She got up, the expression on her face like that of a trapped rabbit looking for a way of escape. "Umm, there is no problem. I just come here to pray . . . that's all." She turned around and began to hurry away as if she feared he might ask her what it was she prayed about.

"Aren't you going to stay for morning prayers?" he called out and then sighed in frustration as she disappeared out the door. He sat down, his emotions churning.

Well done, Bryan. You've chased her off, and you probably won't be seeing her here any time soon.

He sat gazing out of the window while trying to figure out how he could help her if ever she came back. He was still slightly perturbed that she seemed to be somehow afraid of him. God knew he couldn't hurt a fly, but maybe the way he'd approached had been too aggressive.

Lord, if I can help reduce her burden in any way, please let her come back here soon, and show me how to help her.

He stood just as students started to enter the chapel and went to the office to get his Bible.

*****

Sienna entered her dorm room and flopped onto her bed. She glanced around the sparsely furnished room. Thankfully, her roommate was not around. She covered her face with her hands, bit her lip in distress, and for the umpteenth time, asked God to forgive her for her lustful thoughts.

Since she came to this school almost a month ago, she prayed fervently every day, asking God to cleanse her heart from all sin and take away the anxiety and guilt that plagued her. But instead of decreasing, her anxiety and panic attacks had somehow gotten worse. Because of that, she'd known not to keep going to the chapel after the day she saw that shockingly handsome chaplain.

However, she had continued to do so. The more she saw him, especially during the morning and evening prayers, the more taken with him she'd become. And not just for his good looks, but his assertiveness as he preached his sermonette and the strength in his voice as he led the prayers.

She had tried to keep her attraction to him in check and had managed to do so, until this morning, when he'd spoken to her.

He had never spoken to her. She mostly only saw him right before the morning and evening prayers. However, today, he had walked up to her and asked her name. She had been so flustered, now she could hardly remember what else he had asked, or how she had answered, for that matter. All she remembered was that he had actually spoken to her, and her insides had turned to mush. He looked even more handsome up close. She'd imagined running her fingers through his tousled blond hair and getting lost in those deep blue eyes. Since then, the anxiety and guilt had preyed on her more than usual. Speaking with him had spiked the guilt and made everything worse.

She felt like a reprobate who could never be clean the way God wanted her to be. It was not God's will for her to date or get married, she was sure of it. Wasn't that why she broke up with Derrick? To dedicate herself completely to God and be holy in everything?

She'd come here thinking she would finally be able to commit herself wholly to God and find complete peace of mind. But that had not happened. Instead, meeting so many people who seemed more in tune with God than she was, and constantly listening to lectures about living a consecrated life, had puzzlingly increased her guilt and shame. Her inappropriate feelings for that chaplain had now taken away the last shred of peace she possessed.

She whispered a prayer for forgiveness once more, gathered her textbooks, and stood to go to her next class. She paused for a minute, wondering whether to pray again before she left and then she looked up at the time. She was already late. She whispered a short prayer and then left the room. Tomorrow, she would definitely have to start a fast to utterly subdue her wayward thoughts. However, the chapel was out of bounds for now.

She reached the class and found that, despite her lateness, the lecturer hadn't arrived yet. She brought out her Church history textbook from her bag and took a front seat. She opened the textbook to read it but soon closed it again, distracted by the small group of people in the other row. They were holding some kind of meeting. She couldn't catch everything they were saying except for one phrase they kept repeating: "New campus rules."

She turned slightly to watch them. They all dressed like regular students, in jeans and sneakers, but they all had determined and somewhat angry looks on their faces. She knew now who they were. They were the students who called themselves, "The Watchers." She'd noticed them before but had never really given them much attention. But looking at them now and listening to bits of what they were saying, something about them intrigued and scared her at the same time.

She listened with fascinated dread as they talk-ed about fighting for total purity on campus and cleaning up the decay that was seeping into the school.

"The school authorities have given us the go-ahead to enforce the rules once they're made official," one of them said.

Sienna only mildly wondered what rules they were speaking about. The watchers themselves drew her. She envied them. They seemed like people who could stay on the straight and narrow without much effort. People like them never seemed to suffer the doubts that plagued her or people like her. They were confident in their spirituality and their place in God. They never questioned God's love for them, certainly never questioned their salvation. She wanted to ask if she could join them. Maybe being with them would help her. Maybe their spiritual confidence and moral elevation would rub off on her.

But something stopped her from going to them. Their talk about purity and decay still filled her with dread. She wasn't sure if associating with them would make her anxiety better, or make it worse.

She thought about it for some minutes and decided she would join them. She wanted their spiritual confidence. Her heart raced as she stood. Just as she left her seat, the Church History lecturer came into the room. She sat back down again.

World history was one of her favorite courses, and as the lecturer talked, she listened carefully. After the class, the lecturer gave them a class assignment to write an essay on "The Impact of the Early Church on the Roman Empire."

The next class, "Apologetics," wasn't one she

particularly enjoyed. She listened anyway and jotted down the points she wanted to read up on later. After the lecturer left, she breathed in and out as she felt a thread of worry go through her. Their next lecture was Church Missions, and the lecturer, Professor Cunningham, had told them they would be performing street evangelism soon, and she was dreading that. Her relationship with God wasn't stable enough for her to confidently share the gospel, let alone try to talk to someone about it. She sighed softly. There was nothing she could do, so she had to find a way to manage her apprehension before that day came. She turned in the direction the "watcher" leader had taken before the lectures had begun that morning. The boy was still there. Most of the members of the group were seated in the same row as he was. She decided that right after the next class, she would go and ask if she could join them.

A hush suddenly fell over the class, and she knew the lecturer had entered. The girl beside her giggled and whispered, "Hottie alert!" and Sienna turned. Her eyes grew round in shock. The gorgeous young chaplain was standing in front of the class.

No, please don't tell me he's our instructor for today. Where is Cunningham, for goodness' sake?

He looked over the class, his blue eyes moving from one end of the hall to the other. She began to hyperventilate, and then caught herself, forcing her lungs to breathe out, in, and out again. She lowered her head to avoid looking directly at him.

"Good afternoon, everyone," he said, "My name is Bryan Larson, and as many of you know, I am the assistant school chaplain. For now, I will be your sub-lecturer. Because of the shortage of lecturers lately and because of my major in Missions, I was chosen to stand in for Professor Cunningham. The professor had to have unexpected major surgery, but he is doing well now and is recuperating.

"So, now that I have introduced myself, let's get on with the class. I was told your street evangelism was coming up soon. As your lecturer for now, I've decided it will be this Saturday. I'll start by dividing everyone into groups of four."

Sienna raised her head slightly, unable to resist looking at him. Her heart skipped a beat as their eyes met, but she couldn't look away. His brows rose, and he seemed surprised to see her.

He turned his eyes away from her and said, "No, I'll be dividing the class into pairs instead." He walked to the back of the class, pointed at the two people nearest to the wall and told them they would be partners on that day.

He went on pairing everyone until he came to her. She sharply sucked in her breath as he looked at her. When he gave her a small smile, she trembled. She waited for him to pair her up with the girl next to her, but he didn't. He looked away, and instead, he paired the girl with the guy on her left and moved on to the next row.

He finished pairing up everyone except for her, and she wondered if he had forgotten her. But that was not possible. He'd smiled at her. It was a small smile, but a smile all the same.

He began a brief lecture on the "etiquettes of evangelism," and she looked down at her textbook.

Will I have to go tell him he skipped me after the class? She didn't want to do that. That would mean going to talk to him alone and she didn't want that. But what choice did she have?

The class ended about thirty minutes later, and everyone began to head out for the Hermeneutics class in Block B. She dallied, feeling nervous about going to talk to him.

As the last group of people made their way out of the hall, she decided against talking with him. She'd promised herself and the Lord that she would stay away from him. On the day of the street evangelism, she would merely attach herself to some people—maybe the guy and girl that she'd sat with today. If he asked, she would tell him she had joined them because he'd forgotten to pair her up with anyone.

She kept her head down as she made her way out of the hall. Lord, please help me get away.

"Hi, again."

She shut her eyes, blinking back tears of frustration. Lord, why? She stifled the urge to groan and turned to face him. "Hi," she said.

His eyes sparkled as he gazed into hers.

"You're probably wondering why I didn't pair you up with anyone."

She couldn't answer, mesmerized by his gaze.

"I didn't because we will be partners, you and I."

Her eyes fluttered and her insides tied up in knots. She immediately knew she was in trouble.

Lord, please help me.

As she left the class, she prayed for God's help over and over again.

*****

Audrey stepped out of the mayor's office, furious. He wasn't in town again. She'd come to the Town

Hall, prepared to state her case and get the job she'd worked so hard for. But she had met his absence. Most infuriating of all, he'd left a message for her through his secretary telling her that the new police chief he'd appointed was coming all the way from Florida in a week.

She entered her car and shut the door angrily. Imagine bypassing a dedicated officer here and bringing someone all the way from Florida to be the police chief of Rosefield. Shouldn't a police chief be from the town he was meant to serve, or at least from the same State? It was so annoying.

She drove home, feeling down. As soon as she got home, she called Trisha to tell her about the news from the mayor's office and how disappointed she was. Talking to Trisha might help her release some of the anger she felt at the injustice done to her.

Trisha's phone rang and rang, but she didn't pick up. Audrey sighed in frustration. Trisha hardly ever answered her calls these days. She was always busy with her husband when he was in town or occupied with running her bookstore when he wasn't.

Audrey ran her fingers through her short dark hair. She needed someone who would listen while she ranted.

She called Sienna's number, but the call didn't go through at all. She hadn't really expected Sienna to answer. After she'd left for her Bible College, like Trisha, she hardly ever answered her calls.

Audrey sat down on her living room couch and stared at the wall. An intense feeling of loneliness washed over her. She was usually self-sufficient and didn't mind being alone, but these days, she had noticed that she constantly had this feeling of loneliness. For someone like her, that was a very unpleasant feeling.

She thought about calling someone else, like a friend, but changed her mind. Almost everyone she knew was busy with a significant other, and by this time of the evening, most of them would not want to be disturbed.

She turned on the TV, wanting to distract herself from her anger and loneliness. It was days like these that she wished she had someone to share her life with—a husband. Not like Trish's Stan, though. Just someone loving and kind and funny who she could talk to when she got home.

At about ten o'clock that night, she got into bed, still feeling lonely. She covered herself with her duvet, cuddled her pillow and tried to shake the loneliness, but it didn't budge.

Maybe I'll go and spend the weekend at Trish's house, she thought. Tomorrow was Friday, so it was a perfect time to go to Trish's instead of staying home alone, moping. Hopefully, the weekend 'staycation' with her sister would take away little or all of the loneliness and sudden neediness.

*****

After work the next day, she went home, packed a few of her clothes, and drove to Trish's bookstore. Trisha usually stayed at the bookstore late on Fridays and then spent the entire weekend at home with her husband when he wasn't away on business. Audrey hoped that he was away this time so she could have Trish to herself for the whole weekend. Plus, she didn't want to have to deal with

Stan. They didn't get along too well, and neither of them liked the other very much.

She got to the bookstore and parked in front of the single-story building. Because of her love for books, which she had gotten from their late father, Trisha had decided to open a bookstore after she graduated from college. With the money she had saved from various jobs in school, she had started the store. At first, it had only been a few books, but now it was huge and the go-to store in Rosefield whenever someone wanted a good read—fiction or non-fiction.

Audrey slid open the glass door and entered. She looked around at the store filled with all kinds of books, from cookbooks to bestselling novels. Without thinking, she picked up a bridal magazine and flipped it open.

"Well, look who came to see me."

Audrey quickly put the magazine back on the shelf and turned. She smiled at Trisha. "Well, I decided to come because you didn't answer when I called you. Why is that, sis?"

"I didn't know you called." Trish shook her head. "I must have left my phone in my purse. I'm sorry."

"It's not just today." Audrey snorted. "You never pick up any of my calls these days. Anyway, I'm coming to spend the weekend with you. I hope Stan isn't home this time."

"He is home. Both of you have to learn to get along." Trish looked down at Audrey's duffel bag and squealed and clapped. "But it will be great having you at home for a girls' weekend. I just wish Sienna was also here."

"Won't I encroach on your lovey-dovey time

with Stan?" Audrey grinned and said in a teasing voice.

"I wish it was like that," Trish sighed. "Stan has been a little distant these days. And his business trips have increased. I'm a little worried."

"I wouldn't be surprised if he's having an affair," Audrey said. "That's probably why the business trips have increased and why he's now distant."

"Audrey! Oh, my goodness, how can you even say that?"

"You know what, I won't say anything anymore." Audrey shrugged. "I just want us to enjoy the weekend together without Stan's interference."

Trish sighed again, then smiled.

"Anyway, so have you found any 'special someone'?"

"Did I ever tell you I was looking for someone special?" Audrey blinked.

"Audrey, you don't have to keep pretending like you don't need anyone. Everybody needs someone, no matter how strong and independent they are." She smiled again, and her eyes searched Audrey's. "I know you get lonely being in that house all by yourself, every single day. I think it's high time you found someone."

"I don't need anyone, Trisha. I'm good on my own."

Trisha continued to speak as though she'd not heard Audrey. "I could ask one of my friends if they know someone suitable for a bull-headed but beautiful policewoman. There are tons of guys that would want to date someone like you." She grinned. "I just don't know if they can handle you."

"Very funny! And don't you dare try to set me up

with anyone!"

"Then find someone soon. Before the end of this year, if you haven't found someone yet, I promise you, I won't rest until I find someone for you."

Audrey narrowed her eyes, and then she exhaled. This was so typical of Trisha. She was preoccupied with romantic relationships and marriage and was the consummate matchmaker. If I hadn't warned her to stop setting me up someone years ago, I'd probably be going on dates every single weekend.

Or maybe you would have found someone by now, a voice whispered in her heart.

She pushed it aside. She had always been fiercely independent, and she needed no one. This feeling of loneliness was probably just a phase. But she hoped by God's grace, this weekend with Trisha would fix her.

She changed the subject and asked about Trisha's book sales. Soon, their conversation moved to Audrey's job, and she told Trisha about her visit to the mayor's. From time to time, customers came into the shop to purchase books, and Trisha got up to attend to them. After that, she came back and sat beside Audrey, and they continued chatting.

At about nine o'clock, Trisha closed up the bookstore and got into her car. Audrey got into her own vehicle and followed Trisha to her house. Stan was in the living room when they arrived, watching a football game on TV.

"Great, he's here!" Audrey groaned loudly.

"I heard that," Stan said as he scowled at her.

"You were meant to." She glowered at him. He was a slightly built man with a craftily groomed handsomeness which she thought was artificial and didn't care for. It had, however, gotten Trisha to go out with him when they were fifteen. Now she was married to him. Trisha looked between both of them.

"Please, don't start again, both of you. I want peace in this house this weekend."

"Then you shouldn't have brought your troublesome sister here," Stan said, and stood. "I'm going to my study."

He left, and Audrey sneered. "That guy has serious issues."

"Okay, Audrey. That's enough." Trisha shook a finger in her face. "Now that Stan has gone to his study, let's binge-watch our favorite show. I have a full new season recorded."

"You have a new season of Project Runway? Great!" Audrey rubbed her hands together.

"Isn't it strange how you're the one who likes fashion shows and yet isn't into fashion, while Sienna, who is, doesn't watch them and watches mostly crime dramas and cop shows?" Trisha laughed and shook her head. "You don't even like any cop shows."

"Maybe 'cause I'm a real cop, and I can't bear to watch those shows without criticizing every single thing I see." Audrey shrugged. "And those shows are pretty boring to me. Even though I don't particularly care about fashion, I love to see the end results of those creatively made clothes as the models walk down the runway."

"Same here." Trisha nodded and clapped. "So, it's decided. Throughout the weekend, we binge-watch Project Runway, and get mani-pedis."

It was Audrey's turn to laugh.

"My girliness ends with watching fashion shows

on TV. I'm not getting a mani-pedi, Trish. That's where I draw the line."

They curled up on the couch—or rather Trisha curled up—and binge-watched ten episodes of the show. Audrey felt herself being lulled to sleep, and soon she gave in. She woke up at night to find Trisha curled up beside her. She smiled and fell asleep again.

*****

Throughout the weekend, she and Stan stayed away from each other. She chatted with Trisha, stuffed herself with fast food as Trisha hardly ever cooked, and watched the remaining episodes of the TV show. On Sunday evening, after saying goodbye to Trisha, she carried her bag to the car and then sighed with contentment.

It had been a good weekend. She had been able to put her annoyance at the mayor's appointment of a new police chief behind her and also stave off her loneliness. Hopefully, she would remain in this positive mood for a while.

When she got home, she dropped her bag on the floor, flopped down on the sofa and exhaled. She felt renewed and ready for work and for the brand-new week.

But as she went to bed that night with the deafening silence around her, the lonely feeling returned, worse than ever. Along with the loneliness came a renewed anger about her job.

*****

Ken Baylor raised his brows as he looked around the room. A little over two dozen Rosefield police officers sat looking up at him. He'd asked them all in here for a meeting to introduce himself, get to know each of them better, and discuss ways to move the force forward.

He blinked in surprise as he realized that these were all the police officers in the town. There were about thirty police officers. So few, he thought. Compared to his Miami police department, this place was almost empty. However, the town they protected was also tiny and nearly crime-free. When he was told of the opportunity to be the po-lice chief of a small town of only three thousand people, he had initially refused. He loved his job at the Miami police department.

After attending the police academy sixteen years ago, he'd immediately joined the Miami police force and had risen in the ranks until he became deputy police chief. He didn't want to leave. Many people told him it was an excellent opportunity since he was going to be the police chief, even though it was just for a small town, but he'd been unmoved. What had swayed him, at last, was visiting Rose-field about a month ago. It was a beautiful, serene, and virtually crime-free town. Unlike the MPD, the only serious crime he'd heard the police had to solve here was a bank robbery that happened more than ten years ago.

He enjoyed solving crimes, but he valued peace more. And Rosefield was the embodiment of se-renity. It was the kind of place he imagined living whenever he thought of starting a family, which he hoped would be soon. Not that he had anyone to start it with, but he could dream. At thirty-four, it was constantly on his mind.

He glanced around the room once more and frowned. The assistant police chief—a strict-looking, abrasive woman, wasn't here. He had met her for all of two minutes when he'd arrived here two days ago. Apart from letting him know he wasn't welcome, she had ignored him. She wasn't present now, even though he had posted the details of this meeting on the general board as soon he'd set foot in the police station.

He already had plans to renovate the station and improve the way the officers carried out their duties. They might not have a lot of crimes to solve, but they were kept busy with other community duties almost as taxing. He needed all the officers on board to do this together, but his assistant chief of police wasn't here. That wasn't a good start.

He began to address them, telling them what his plans were. Someone asked if he planned to continue supporting the Youth Workshop that their ex-chief had started. He had already been briefed about it by the mayor. Apparently, its upkeep was one of the most essential duties of the police here. But he didn't get it.

"How come such a huge amount of police-allocated funds and manpower is being given to a youths' workshop?" he asked. He certainly had nothing against youth workshops, but from what the mayor had told him, it seemed it was a central duty of the whole police force here. As much as a youth workshop sounded great, he didn't think it was the police's main priority to oversee it.

"We know how lucky our town is to be almost crime-free," the officer answered. "We want it to stay that way, Chief. If the youths can be taught to use their time and talents wisely and for a fruitful cause, Rosefield will remain crime-free for years to come."

The officers in the room chorused their agreement.

One of them snorted. "We certainly don't want it to become like one of those big cities where criminals are bred daily." He looked knowingly at Ken, and everyone laughed. Ken chuckled.

"Okay, okay, you've had your laugh at my expense; now let's get on with the meeting."

The assistant police chief walked in with her eyebrows knit, and he inwardly cringed. She had this exact expression on her face the first day he saw her. Was she always this angry or was it just her default look? He watched as she sat in the back, and though he wanted to query her for her lateness, he decided against it. He would speak with her after the meeting. Maybe he could find out more about her then. Since they would be working closely together, they might as well get acquainted as soon as possible.

He started to talk about his plans to improve the entire department by upgrading certain important facilities that were now old—like the police cars, communication gear and the police station building. After that, he told them about his decision to send each of them to additional police training and conferences outside Rosefield every year. When he finished, he asked if they had questions or contributions. He listened to their ideas and took note of everything that sounded good. He answered all their questions as best as he could and asked a few himself.

At last, he rounded up the meeting, and they dispersed, but before they all left, he asked the assistant chief to stay. He walked up to her and asked to speak to her privately. She had not said a word while the meeting was going on.

She raised her brows and glared at him as though he had just asked her to do a hundred pushups. He turned around and began to walk to his office, hoping she would follow. She sighed loudly, then followed him to his office.

He sat down and motioned for her to take the seat across from his. She sat reluctantly.

"Assistant Chief Gardner," he said, "I called you in here just so we can get acquainted and also learn how we can work together to better serve the people of Rosefield. As my assistant, we will . . ."

"Let me stop you right there," she hissed. "I'm not your assistant. I am the assistant chief of police, and that will not be for long either. I have been a part of the Rosefield police force for over thirteen years and the only female officer for ten. This position you just took because you happen to be a man from the city. This was supposed to be mine after Chief Richardson retired!"

He raised his brows, completely taken aback. He wasn't expecting the tirade. She continued to glare at him while he stared at her for a full minute. At last, he took a deep breath.

"I just want to say I understand where you're coming from. I'd be ticked too if someone else took the position I had been working so hard to get for years. However, I can assure you that I was not appointed as chief of police because I am a man or from the city. I was given the position because I was qualified for the role."

He wanted to say more; to tell her about his years of service, his experience with the police force, but he quickly changed his mind. He added, "It's been done, and there's nothing either of us can do about it, so we might as well try to work together for the sake of Rosefield." He studied her face. It was a pretty one, if she lost the constant frown. "Can we do that?"

She frowned and folded her hands.

"I'm sorry, but I just can't." She shook her head. "I'm going to fight for what's mine. And contrary to what you just said, you were chosen because of your sex and where you come from."

His insides twisted up as she rose and left his office. He placed a hand on his forehead and sighed wearily. Lord, why do I have to deal with this now?

*****

Audrey stood up and glanced at the clock on the wall. It was three o'clock in the afternoon. She usually left the station much later than this, but today, she was going to see the mayor . . . again. Her recent email to the mayor's office had been ignored. Mayor Stanley had appointed someone else to fill the position that was meant to be hers. After her visit to the Town Hall, where she was informed that the mayor wasn't in town, she had called several times without getting a solid answer. Finally, she had gotten through to the mayor, and he'd asked her to come and see him today.

She grabbed her bag from the floor, walked out of her office, and nodded at a few of the officers who greeted her. She didn't feel like talking to anyone today. She quickly walked past the new chief's office so he wouldn't see her and then left the building. As she got into her police vehicle, her phone began to ring. She unzipped her bag and brought it out. Surprised when she saw it was Trisha calling, she answered.

"Hi, Trisha, what's up?"

"Audrey, can I come over to the station now? I need to talk to you about something."

"What is it?" Audrey frowned. Trisha sounded like she had been crying.

"It's Stan. I think he's cheating on me."

Audrey exhaled. This was why she wasn't keen on getting married or even being in a relationship. Most people she knew who were married or were in committed relationships had serious, never-ending problems with their spouses.

"Trisha, I'm not available now. I'm going to see the mayor. After that, I'll probably go to the Gibson's' house to see the new abuse victims they just took into their home. I'll be home before eight o'clock, though. Can you come to the house then?"

"Umm, Stan will be returning from his business trip this evening. I want to be home when he does. I'll come over to the house tomorrow evening." She sighed heavily and asked, "Have you spoken to Sienna? I've been trying to reach her for days."

Audrey pursed her lips. If Trisha's husband didn't so consume her time, she would have known their baby sister hadn't been available for a couple of weeks. Now that she'd confirmed that her dear husband had been cheating on her, she finally remembered there were other family members apart from him.

"I think she's fine. Give her time. She'll call you."

"I can . . ."

"Listen, Trish, I have to go," Audrey interrupted her. "I'll see you tomorrow. Okay?"

"Okay."

Audrey drove to the Town Hall, zooming past Hattie's popular Bed & Breakfast, and New Day Fellowship, the interdenominational church she attended. She arrived in five minutes, parked her car beside the mayor's black SUV and put on her police hat.

She looked up at the Town Hall, a brown and white brick building with a steeple, and began to climb the stairs. She entered the building with a firm determination to successfully state her case to the mayor. When she walked up to the receptionist, the young woman named Rita who had worked as a receptionist here for only about a year greeted her.

"I have an appointment with the mayor," Audrey told her. Rita made a quick call and then smiled at her.

"He'll see you now."

Audrey thanked her and quickly made her way to the mayor's office. She knocked and then entered. Mayor Stanley, a portly bald man of some fifty years of age, shook her hand and then asked her to sit. She sat in front of him and took a deep breath before she spoke.

"You're a hard man to reach, Mayor, but I know you've received my emails and messages." She paused for a few seconds, but when he said nothing, she continued speaking. "I've served in the Rose-field Police Force and risen to my present position through my own hard work. Every position I have risen to was all because I earned it."

She began to tell him about her contributions to the force, her passion for her job, and how well she had handled the role of acting chief of police. "That's why I was considerably disheartened when you ignored all that and appointed someone else the police chief." She ended her speech.

The mayor threaded his fingers together and looked her in the eye. "Assistant Chief Gardner, I reviewed your petitions and complaints, and I'm sorry to tell you this, but my decision stands. I appreciate your years of service, and I hope you will continue to faithfully serve the people of Rosefield beside the new chief of police."

"But I . . ."

"I am truly sorry," Mayor Stanley said with finality.

Anger wrapped itself around her, and she felt like screaming. She, however, suppressed the desire and asked, "Can you tell me why you appointed someone else when I've been so dedicated to the force?"

"We wanted someone with more experience in criminal investigations."

"But Rosefield is hardly that sort of place. We have very little crime here, and the few we've had have been quickly and efficiently handled by our officers."

What he was telling her didn't quite add up. She wanted to know the real reason why she'd been overlooked. He cleared his throat.

"As I said, we wanted a . . ."

"Is it because I'm a woman?"

"Of course not! Officer Gardner, I'm sorry, but

I have already appointed Ken Baylor as Rosefield's chief of police, so it's too late to do anything about it now." He stood, clearly indicating that their meeting was over. He held out his hand, and she stared at it for a few seconds before she shook it. When she got out of the building and entered her car, she screamed.

THREE

Trisha drove to Audrey's house with tears blinding her eyes. She ran over and over in her mind the shocking message she had found on her husband's phone two days ago. He'd just returned from a business conference in New York, and she thought he looked and sounded unusually chirpy. After kissing him, she'd teased him about it, asked if he had been given a happiness drug during the conference. He'd only given her a small smile and gone upstairs to their bedroom.

When she went up, he was showering in the bathroom. She sat on the bed just as his phone vibrated. Picking it up, she looked at it to know who it was. In her mind, they had always been the kind of couple who never hid stuff from each other, so she thought nothing of checking his messages. If only she had known.

She could hear him singing happily in the shower as she read the short message.

*****

Hi Stan,

I had a great time last night. When will you come to New York again? I can't wait to be in your arms once more.

Love you,

Carla

*****

She had reread the message a couple of times, refusing to believe what she was seeing. The text couldn't be for Stan, she thought. Maybe it was meant for someone else; some other guy named Stan. But what were the odds? She sat on the bed, her stomach queasy and her heart pounding. Was that why he was so happy? Had he been with another woman?

She felt an intense rage boiling in her stomach as she heard him whistling and singing loudly. How could he do this to me? She took a deep breath and told herself to calm down. There had to be an explanation for the message.

She glanced around their luxuriously furnished bedroom, with its ornate wood furniture, big poster bed, and expensive paintings. Stan had given her a more lavish lifestyle than most people in Rosefield, but she had never cared about that. In fact, she resented his many business trips that took away from the time they could spend together. But never had she imagined that those frequent trips included another woman.

She sat waiting patiently for him to come out of the bathroom. When he did five minutes later, she exhaled and handed him his phone.

"You have a new message," she said to him.

"From whom?" He frowned.

"Carla," she answered in a smooth voice. "She said she had a great time last night and wants to know when you will be in New York so she can be in your arms again."

Stan's eyes had widened with shock, and then he sat beside her.

"Listen, Trish, it's not what you think."

"Did you or did you not sleep with that woman, Stan?"

"I . . . did, but it meant nothing. She was just some girl I met at the hotel where . . ."

"Stop it!" Trisha had yelled at him. "So, I'm sharing you with some girl you met at a hotel?"

"I'm so sorry, what can I do to make it up to you?" He shook his head.

"Are you serious?" She glowered at him.

"Trisha, please forgive me. It will never happen again. I promise."

She was unable to resist as he drew her close and kissed her.

As she lay in his arms an hour later, her stomach boiled with anger. She wasn't mad at him, but at herself. Her ranting and raving had been for nothing. All Stan had done was take her in his arms and kiss her, and she had melted. She'd already forgiven him.

She turned around and studied his handsome face. He was sleeping soundly beside her, looking completely innocent and free from every care, while her heart ached because of his betrayal.

She watched him sleep for ten minutes more,

even as tears fell down her cheeks. There was nothing she could do but forgive him. It wasn't as if she was going to leave him. He was a part of her, and she loved him dearly.

She came out of her reverie as she arrived at Audrey's and parked beside her sister's police car. As she walked up the stairs of the two-bedroom bungalow that had been her childhood home, memories of her parents sitting together on the stairs, laughing and chatting, flooded her mind. They had loved each other so much. It was about seven years since they had passed away, but she still felt a sharp ache in her heart every time she thought of them.

She was eighteen and about to start college when they died. She had been dating Stan, who was her high-school sweetheart, for three years. Before they died, she remembered sitting beside her mother on the stairs and telling her that she couldn't wait to marry Stan.

Mom had said, "I don't know about Stan, honey. I don't think you should marry him, but that's just my personal opinion."

When her parents died shortly after that, she had married him later that year. Having him always with her had assuaged the pain of their death. She had always dreamt of a marriage like her parents'. Even though Stan had been somewhat distant for months, she'd thought she had a marriage like theirs.

But she was wrong.

She knocked on the door, and when Audrey opened it, she fell into her sister's arms and wept. Audrey pulled her in and shut the door.

"Trish, is it about Stan?"

Trish nodded as Audrey led her to the sofa. "I can't believe he would cheat on me after all we've been through together."

"I told you before you married Stan that he had it in him, Trish, but you didn't listen."

Trisha looked up at her sister. She should have known. Audrey was not exactly the nurturing type. She had no filter and spoke her mind always without caring how it made anyone feel. Trisha sighed. "He's never given me any cause to doubt his faithfulness until now."

"He's given you plenty, Trish; you just chose to ignore them all. Because of mom and dad, you've always had this dream of a perfect marriage. Even when the truth about yours had been staring you in the face for years, you've refused to see it because you didn't want anything to ruin your dream of a picture-perfect marriage."

"It's not true!" Trisha huffed.

Audrey went on as if she'd not heard her. "Remember that wedding we went to about five years ago—Kelly's wedding? He disappeared for almost thirty minutes, and that scantily dressed girl at our table was also missing for about that long. When he reappeared with that silly grin on his face and that girl came back five minutes later, I told you Stan had been with her. You vehemently protested, and we had that little fight."

"A little sympathy from you at this time would help, Audrey."

"You know me. I don't do sympathy that well; at least not at the expense of truth. If you come to me, I'll truthfully tell you what the reality of the situation is."

Trish groaned. So, Audrey had been right then. And she was right now. Stan had probably been cheating on her for some time without her knowledge. Her heart twisted.

"What am I going to do now, Audrey?"

"I don't know why you're asking me." Audrey shrugged. "You know my advice for you would be to kick him to the curb, but I already know what you're gonna do. You'll stay with him no matter what I say or what he does."

Trish hung her head. Audrey knew her well. Having already forgiven Stan, she had just come here to vent and not really to seek advice. In spite of herself, she smiled at her older sister. Audrey was very perceptive. She was like their mom in that way. Trish shut her eyes.

"Mom told me not to marry him."

She opened her eyes as Audrey chuckled. "I didn't bother because I knew it would be a waste of time to tell you anything."

"But I've put so many years into my marriage, and I still want a child . . . Stan's child." She exhaled. Audrey was looking at her as if she were insane, but she couldn't leave Stan at this time. He'd apologized once more this morning and promised he would never cheat again. And she had no choice but to believe him. She wanted to remain married and have the children she'd always wanted.

She remembered the pain she'd felt when she'd miscarried their child in the first year of their marriage. When it happened again, the second year, she'd been totally devastated. They stopped trying for some time and then started again.

If I can just have another child, maybe he'll be

faithful. Surely, a man with a newborn wouldn't have time to cheat on his . . .

"Earth to Trish," Audrey touched her shoulder. "Listen. To take your mind off this, why don't we go and visit Sienna? God knows I need the distraction, too, after my meeting with the mayor yesterday."

"Sienna . . . you know where she is?"

"Yes, she's at that Bible college between Rosefield and Green Valley."

"A Bible college? What about her modeling and her expensive apartment in New York?"

"She quit and has probably given the house up."

"What?" Trisha sat up. "She resigned? Why?"

"You'll have to ask her yourself when we get there. I don't understand it myself."

*****

"Sienna, I'm going to get something to eat. Do you want to come?"

Sienna shook her head and said to her room-mate, Veronica, "I'm fasting."

Veronica, a curvy brunette, regarded her with a confused expression on her face.

"You're always fasting and praying. I know this is a Bible college, so that's a given, but you never take a break. I don't know how you do it, fasting continuously. That cannot be healthy. You're already so skinny. If you go on like this, you might disappear."

Sienna forced a smile. If only Veronica would just go away and leave me alone. She shrugged. "I'll get something to eat later."

Veronica shook her head and left the room.

Sienna sat on her small bed. She had been fasting for the last few days, praying that God would cleanse her heart. She'd also been praying that her troubling attraction to Bryan, the chaplain, would disappear before it was time for the street evangelism.

Lord, it's in just a few days. Please help me, she prayed again. This was now her constant prayer. She said it at least a hundred times a day, but it didn't seem to be working. Bryan's face remained in her mind almost every minute of every day.

A knock sounded at her door, and she frowned. Who could it be? It couldn't be Veronica because she wouldn't knock. Sienna pursed her lips and stood. Whoever it was couldn't be visiting her either. She had no friends here who visited her as she kept mostly to herself. Maybe it was one of Veronica's friends. But then again, they never knocked. They just barged in.

She walked to the door and opened it.

"Audrey, Trisha!" she exclaimed and hugged both of them in excitement. "You guys are here!"

"Yes, we are!" they chorused.

She sat on her bed and patted the spaces beside her. "How did you guys find my room?" she asked when they sat. She couldn't stop smiling, thrilled that her sisters were here. Apart from the fact that she had not seen or spoken to them in a while, and she really missed them, their presence here gave her a much-needed break from her worries.

Audrey answered. "We asked around. It's not such a big place, and you're not exactly the kind of girl that can be hidden."

Sienna's heart pattered faintly. She knew what

Audrey was saying. Months ago, she would have smiled with pleasure at the compliment, but now, she felt guilty. She didn't want to attract any attention because of her looks. She quickly changed the subject.

"So, what have you guys been up to?"

Trisha shook her head.

"Sienna, I came here to find out what's really going on with you. Why did you quit your job and move away from New York?" Her eyes bored into Sienna's. "Does it have something to do with why you left Derrick at the altar?"

"I don't really know how to explain it." Sienna sighed wearily. "I already tried explaining it to Audrey, our resident know-it-all, and she didn't get it."

"Just tell me, Sienna," Trisha said. "You know Audrey isn't very patient with ideas she thinks are strange. I'll try to understand."

Audrey rolled her eyes.

"Okay, it started some months ago." Sienna's heart rate increased. "I had a strange dream that I was in hell . . ."

"Hell, literally in hell?"

"Yes. I dreamed that I was surrounded by these scary looking demons and that I was burning up. I couldn't get out no matter how hard I tried. When I finally woke up, I was covered in sweat. I began to pray about it, and I felt God was saying it was because of my lifestyle . . . you know . . . my job as a fashion model. I lived for myself and the vain things of this world."

"What are you talking about, Sienna?" Trisha asked, frowning. "You love God. I know very few people who love the Lord as much as you do. Why would you think that?"

"Before your nightmares began, did you ever think of your job as evil?" Audrey asked.

"Umm, not exactly evil, just vain and meaningless. Anyway, I felt like it wasn't God's will for me to continue modeling. But I continued anyway because I liked it."

"No, you didn't like it, you loved it," Audrey said.

"All the more reason why I had to give it up."

"And why did you abandon Derrick at the altar?" Trisha asked.

Sienna sharply sucked in her breath. The way Trisha had said "abandon" caused her already unmanageable guilt to shoot up. She answered quickly before she could be swallowed up by a mire of guilt.

"Because after that, I knew I had to be consecrated to God alone and marriage or a romantic relationship would rob me of that. I knew God didn't want me to get married."

Audrey looked accusingly at Trisha.

"I wasn't really bothered that you 'abandoned' Derrick at the altar," Audrey noted. "What has been troubling me is the fact that you quit your job."

"You don't have to look at me like that, Audrey." Trisha smirked. "I already know you don't think marriage and relationships are important."

"Did I say that?" Audrey scowled at her. "Anyway, just like I told you before, Sienna, I don't think God is behind any of it."

"Sienna, I think you should leave this place now. Come to Rosefield with us," Trisha said. "You can move in with Stan and me until you're ready to go back to New York."

Sienna clenched her jaw and shook her head.

"No, I think I'm exactly where God wants me," she said, determined.

Audrey snorted. "But Trisha, do you really want her to move in with you and Stan? With everything that's going on with both of you?"

"What's going on with them?" Sienna asked, looking pointedly at Audrey for answers.

Trisha narrowed her eyes at Audrey. "It's nothing," she gave Sienna a small smile. "There's no reason to trouble her, Audrey."

"No," Sienna said. "I want to know, Trish."

Tears shimmered in Trisha's eyes, and she didn't speak for a minute. Finally, she said, "Stan cheated . . ." She wrung her hands like a little girl and let out a sob. "Stan cheated on me."

"Oh Trish, I'm so sorry." Sienna wrapped her arm around Trisha's waist. "What are you doing now?"

"We've decided to see a marriage counselor."

Sienna nodded. She felt sorry for Trish, but her emotions were too unstable at this time to offer any advice.

Audrey's forehead creased.

"That's why I always told you guys to be careful when we were younger. Marriage isn't all it's made out to be. In fact, I think it's overrated."

Sienna smiled sadly, remembering Derrick. He was such a good guy. She remembered how he was so studious and kind. He'd looked heartbroken when she'd left him at the altar. Even though she had felt guilty about that, she was certain that what she did was what God wanted her to do. She nodded.

"You know, Audrey, I have to agree with you. I think everyone needs to focus entirely on their relationship with God."

"What about people who are married?" Trisha said. "Surely, God wants us to also treasure our marriages."

"I guess so." Sienna shrugged. "But I think people shouldn't get married unless they're sure their spouses won't take away the undivided attention that God requires."

"Way too many people have bad marriages that they conceal under a blanket of smugness," Audrey said. "I prefer to stay single."

"I like being married," Tricia crowed.

"No, you're afraid of being alone, that's all," Audrey replied tautly. "You give up everything that's important to you, including your dignity, just to stay married."

"I don't find the idea of coming home to an empty house every single night appealing!" Trisha's eyes flashed.

"And I don't find being married to someone who's warming up someone else at night appealing either!"

"Guys, stop it!" Sienna looked from Audrey to Trisha and back to Audrey. "Must you always be so brutally hone . . . umm . . . must you say everything that is in your head, Audrey?"

Trisha looked away. Audrey shrugged.

"All I'm saying is that you should learn to stay away from men, especially handsome men who seem way too nice."

Sienna saw something in Audrey's eyes that told her Audrey was thinking of a specific someone as she uttered those words. Bryan's face once again appeared clearly in her mind. His kind, bright blue eyes shone with concern for her, the way they had the last time she saw him. "Stay away from handsome men who seem way too nice," Audrey had said. Those words felt like a warning from God to her.

She prayed once more, Lord, please help me stay away from that chaplain.

FOUR

Audrey walked around the Rosefield Youth Center, smiling. The mayor had announced months ago that a sizeable amount of money would be going into renovating the place. As she'd been put in charge of the day-to-day running of the center by the mayor, she had been very pleased about that. The Youth Center was close to her heart.

It hadn't taken long for the renovations to start and most of the work had already been done. The sprawling single-story building, which had begun to look somewhat dilapidated with age, was now spanking new, with brand-new facilities and additional workshop spaces for the kids.

Teens were sitting and lying all around the well-manicured grounds, while others played basketball on the new basketball court. She went inside the building and found a group of kids taking piano lessons. She stopped to greet Jackie, the music instructor, and the redhead smiled at her.

"We love what they've done with this place," Jackie said. She had a wistful expression on her face as she added, "That handsome police officer also came here this morning."

Audrey nearly snorted. What was it with all these women, hankering after handsome men? Jackie beamed.

"He wants to start another workshop for the kids."

Audrey frowned. That guy took the position that belonged to me, now he also wants to hijack my kids' workshop. Can't I have one thing that's fully mine? She muttered, "He's not going to start another workshop? Not on my watch."

The woman looked confused "I thought you knew about it. He wants cooking and home management lessons for girls and a woodworking workshop for boys."

"What?" Audrey's eyes widened in shock.

"I said he . . ."

"I heard you." She marched away, furious. Of all the outrageous, sexist things she'd heard, this was the most ridiculous. She was going to give him a piece of her mind right now. If he fired her for insubordination, then so be it.

She walked all the way to the station feeling like her head was going to explode. Without knocking, she stormed into his office and gave him a death stare.

His eyes grew big.

"Really?" She stared down at him. "Cooking and home management lessons for girls and woodworking workshops for boys! You couldn't come up with something more sexist!" He opened his mouth to speak, but she cut him off. "And you had no right getting yourself involved with my kids' workshop in the first place!"

He looked up at her with a patient smile which made her even madder. "First of all, it's the police department's kids' workshop, not yours. Secondly, I didn't come up with the 'cooking lesson' thing. I don't know who did, but it wasn't me."

She said slightly less confident, "The music instructor at the Youth Center said you told her that this morning. Why would she lie?"

"I wasn't even at the Youth Center this morning," he said. "Did she mention my name ... Ken Baylor?" He smiled sweetly at her like she was a confused little girl who simply needed to be straightened out. "What exactly did that instructor say?"

Audrey answered reluctantly, "She didn't mention your name, but she said the handsome officer . . ." Her words suddenly dried up as she realized how absurd her thinking was. She'd assumed he was the one Jackie was talking about because of the words, "handsome officer." Was that all she had noted about him; that he was handsome?

His amused grin only added to her embarrassment. "Surely, there are other handsome police officers, or does it mean you find me 'particularly handsome,'" he teased. She harrumphed even as she asked herself the same question.

"Well, I guess Jackie was talking about some other officer. I'll go find out who it is."

His grin was still in place as he said, "That shouldn't be so hard. Maybe you'll finally discover another handsome officer apart from me."

She glared at him, then strode out of his office. Outside, she shut her eyes, mortified. She'd just made a total fool of herself, and he had enjoyed every minute of her humiliation.

Focus, Audrey. Forget about him and find the officer Jackie was talking about.

But as she asked each of the men about the kid's workshop and if they had spoken with the music instructor this morning, she admitted to herself that she did find Ken Baylor 'particularly' attractive. His piercing brown eyes, tanned complexion and general rugged look appealed to her. He was probably the most handsome man she'd ever seen. That didn't mean anything, though. She wasn't interested in dating anyone and certainly not the guy who took the job that was supposed to be hers.

At last, she found the officer who had said those ridiculous things to Jackie. His name was Officer Fred Draper, a dark-haired, bushy-browed, unruly, twenty-something-year-old. She had already given him several official warnings after he'd been caught a few times driving under the influence.

She gave him a piece of her mind and then made him eat his words.

*****

Trisha's jaw dropped as she gazed at the pregnancy test strip in her hand.

It can't be, or can it? She was scared of having her hopes dashed. But there were two clear lines on the strip rather than one. She took a deep breath and told herself to calm down and not get too excited. She checked for signs of pregnancy at least once a week, but she was never pregnant. Today, however, there were two lines. Unless her eyes were deceiving her, she was definitely pregnant.

Unparalleled joy rose in her, and she whooped, unable to contain her excitement any longer.

She took another deep breath to compose herself and did the test again. Again, it showed she was pregnant. She shrieked and then covered her mouth. She didn't want Stan to find out this way. She wanted to surprise him.

In her mind, she began to calculate the date of conception, and then realized it had to be the day she found out Stan was cheating on her. He had gone on another business trip after that and only just come back this evening. It was somehow fitting that this baby would be conceived on that day. Hopefully, it was a sign of what she wanted—a stronger bond between her and Stan through this child.

Lord, please let this baby stay this time.

Fear began to work its way through her heart and then she forcefully pushed it away. I will rejoice in the God of my salvation.

She took the pregnancy test strip, went to the bedroom she shared with Stan and found him still asleep. She sat on the bed, gently tapped his shoulders and said, "Wake up, baby."

He cracked opened his eyes and grumbled.

"Just a little more sleep."

She chuckled and held the stick above his head.

"What's this?"

"What does it look like, silly!" she declared, elated.

"No!" He blinked rapidly.

"Yes, yes we are pregnant!"

"Oh, Trish, are we really?" He stood and whisked her up.

"Yes, you're going to be a father."

"Wow!" He kissed her and then sobered slightly. "What, what if it happens this time again?"

She shook her head and put a finger to his lips.

"Shhh, it's not going to happen." She wouldn't allow him to entertain the idea. "We will take care and pray. I think this baby is going to stay, Stan." She smiled. "This time, we will have this bundle of joy and be stronger because of him or her."

*****

The students, about fifty of them, gathered at the parking lot of the Bible school. Bryan stood beside the big bus, discussing the route with the driver that would take them into the next town for their scheduled street evangelism. The weather was great today, a perfect blend of happy sunshine and refreshing coolness.

Bryan beckoned them to come nearer. He then led a short prayer, asking for God's grace as they went out to share the gospel and the bags of supplies each had donated. After the prayer, he addressed the group.

"So, we'll enter the bus now. You can all sit anywhere you want, next to whoever you want to. But once we get to our destination, you will each find the partner I paired you up with last week and then head out to share the word together. Do you all understand?"

They nodded.

From the corner of his eyes, he saw Sienna at the back of the group. Even though they could sit anywhere on the bus, he'd hoped that, as his partner today, she would choose to sit beside him. But he should have known she wouldn't. She avoided him at every turn.

And why do you need to sit beside her on the bus?

He thought about that. Maybe it was because he needed all the time he could get with her so he could find out exactly what was wrong with her. Since that day he asked if he could help her in any way, she had stopped coming to the chapel, even for the morning and evening prayers. Without a doubt, he knew it was his fault, and he wanted to change that.

Maybe she's found a solution to her problem.

But he doubted it. He watched her as she entered the bus. She still looked distressed, so fragile. He felt in his heart an overwhelming need to help her, to protect her. He got on the bus after everyone and sighed softly with longing as she sat beside someone else.

And then he chided himself. His intentions had become mixed up. He genuinely wanted to help her, but he could feel himself falling hopelessly for her. In his mind, he was already trying to figure out how to win her heart. But she didn't need a boyfriend now. What she needed was a person who would help her.

Another girl came to sit next to him and smiled cheerily at him. He smiled back and then looked out the window as the bus began to move. She looked a little gaunt today, Sienna. She was naturally thin and the prettiest girl he'd ever seen, but she did look extra thin. His heart flooded with worry.

He whispered a short prayer for her and then

tried to think of something less troubling. He watched cars speeding by, but her face remained in his mind.

They drove through Green Valley, the small town from which he came. He thought about his parents and the house he'd grown up in and smiled. It was a short distance from where they were now, his family house. He made a mental note to call his mom and dad as soon as they got back to the Bible school, and then his mind was back on Sienna again.

Soon, they entered the next town, Leedville, where they'd planned to share the Word and also hand out bags of daily supplies to people. The town had not yet fully recovered from the flooding that had happened two months ago, and many of the people could do with the groceries and supplies they were going to donate today.

They stopped in front of a church, climbed down from the bus, and without ceremony, divided into pairs. They all departed until it was just him and Sienna standing beside the bus. He walked up to her, knowing she wouldn't come to him.

"Are you okay?" he asked.

She nodded.

He smiled to try to put her at ease and then said, "We'll go in that direction," and pointed toward a diner. "I've been here before for street missions. The town is mostly safe. Some of the people can be a little prickly, but most of them are basically friendly."

She nodded. They began to carry the remaining bags of provisions from the trunk of the bus.

"Do we hand out the donations before or after

we share the gospel?" she asked.

He smiled in pleasure. This was the first time she had spoken to him without fear. The last time he'd spoken with her, she'd looked like she couldn't wait to scamper away. He held himself in check before she could notice he was staring and withdraw into her shell again.

"We'll hand out the food and then ask politely if they want us to pray for them. If they say they do, we can then share the gospel and pray for them. We'll let the Lord guide us," he replied.

She nodded without saying anything more.

He studied her face—how startlingly blue her eyes were and how smooth her skin was. His heart raced wildly. He wanted to reach out and caress her cheeks to see if they felt as soft as they looked, but he put his hands behind his back so he wouldn't give in to the temptation.

If only she didn't look so scared of me.

She was the kind of girl for whom he would give up everything; the kind with whom he wouldn't mind spending every waking moment.

He pushed the thoughts away. Remember why you wanted her to be your partner today. It was so you could try to help her in any way you can.

They walked past the diner and passed a barbershop. She kept a little distance between them as they walked. They saw a group of adolescents talking beside an old library, and they gave them some of the bags of groceries. He asked them if they had any prayer requests. Most of them shrugged, but three of them asked for prayers for different small ailments.

After he had prayed for them, he moved on with

Sienna.

He turned to her after they passed a train track.

"So, Sienna, I didn't get the chance to ask you in the class. I've been slightly worried about you since that day I spoke with you in the chapel."

She didn't look at him as she said, "I'm good."

"I wanted us to talk some more, but you haven't been coming to the chapel. How are you really doing? I've noticed you still look kinda depressed."

She shrugged and didn't answer.

They walked on while his emotions churned. He cried out to God in his heart. Lord, how can I help her when she won't even speak to me?

A man in a well-tailored, pin-striped suit began to walk in their direction, and Bryan felt a tug in his heart. He assessed the man. He certainly didn't look like he needed the food or provisions, but there was an air of poverty about him; soul poverty.

Bryan went up to him, and Sienna followed. He politely addressed the man.

"Hi, I was wondering if you would like us to pray for you?" He frowned in confusion as he heard something in his heart, and then quickly obeyed. He asked, "Do you want us to pray for . . . umm, a job as, umm . . . a budget analyst?" He looked sheepishly at the man. The word he'd just delivered, which he hoped was from the Lord, was very specific. If he were to be wrong, the man would definitely think he was nuts.

The man's face contorted and then tears began falling down his cheeks. He was trembling visibly as he said, "It's a miracle! I worked for years as a budget analyst for a software company in Boise. I loved my job, but I was let go some months ago. I've been trying to find another job since then. I lost my house, and almost everything I had, and someone suggested that I move to a small town because it's a lot cheaper to live in. I came here to see if I could make something of my life, but of course, the floods swept away the little things I had just acquired. I've been suicidal for a while now." He looked into Bryan's eyes, his own filled with tears.

"I was so miserable today that I prayed, even though I'm an agnostic. I said, 'God, if you are there, send someone to pray for me, because I can't go on,' and then I added, 'if you make that person pray for me to get a job as a budget analyst, then I will believe in you.' I knew my request was very specific and a little preposterous, but it was the hardest thing I could think of." He shook his head, his eyes wide. "I can't believe you actually asked me that. I'm not even from this town, and I told no one about my request."

Bryan smiled.

"We're not from this town either."

The man shook his head, his eyes full of awe.

Bryan whispered a prayer of thanksgiving and praise to the Lord. He asked for the man's name, and he told him it was Trevor.

"I'm going to pray that God gives you a job as a budget analyst, Trevor, and I'm sure He will." Bryan prayed for him, asking the Lord to grant him the job he desired and also provide for all his needs. Trevor wept as he prayed. After that, Bryan asked if he wanted to give his heart to Jesus.

He nodded vigorously, and Bryan whispered to Sienna, "Do you want to lead him in the prayer of salvation?"

She shook her head quickly and her eyes filled with fear.

Bryan silently sighed and then led Trevor to Christ. After they finished praying, Trevor hugged him and then Sienna.

"Thank you," he said. "I feel like a brand-new man."

"You are a brand-new man," Bryan said with a grin. "Jesus lives in you now." He handed Trevor a bag of groceries and chuckled as Trevor walked away, almost skipping as he went.

"That's our great God for you!" Bryan said and then turned to Sienna.

She was watching Trevor in wonder.

*****

Sienna watched Bryan as he handed out the re-maining bag of groceries to an old woman on the street. Her mind burned with questions she wanted to ask him. When that man was rejoicing in the fact that God had miraculously answered his prayer, she had shared in his joy and had been thrilled for him. She'd forgotten about her own anxiety, until Bryan had asked her to lead him in the prayer of salvation and then all her doubts returned and fear overwhelmed her. How could she pray for someone to get saved when she wasn't even sure she was?

She stood aside, waiting for Bryan to finish praying for someone else. As much as she'd been determined not to speak to him, a question kept running over and over in her mind, and she had to get the answer to it. And he was the only one she knew would have the answers she needed. He finally turned to her.

"We've given all the supplies out."

She nodded as her heart raced. They began to walk back to the bus, taking it slowly, and she asked, "Can I ask you a question?"

"Sure," he said, and his eyes lit up. "Anything."

"How come you hear God's voice so clearly?"

Bryan narrowed his eyes in thought and then looked at her.

"I've been practicing hearing his voice for some time now. It's about intimacy with the Lord first of all . . ."

"Intimacy, but I try to be intimate with God. I fast and pray and confess all my sins every day, but I never really feel God's presence, and I certainly don't hear His voice."

"Hearing His voice is not a reward for your many prayers. It's by His grace. You just come to Him and believe He'll speak to you because you belong to Him. As you spend time with Him and listen to Him carefully every day, His voice will become clearer and clearer."

"But doesn't it take a consecrated life to be able to hear His voice like you do?" She didn't wait for him to answer. "I envy people like you. Like those watchers. You're all so confident in your salvation."

"I'm not like the watchers, Sienna." He frowned and searched her eyes. "And about a consecrated life being the prerequisite to hearing God clearly, let me ask you a question. If you had a child who wasn't very well behaved, would you stop speaking to her, or do you speak even more clearly, knowing how much she needs to hear your voice in order to change?"

She looked at him, feeling slightly confused.

"I guess I'll speak to that child more, but are you saying that rebellious people hear God's voice more clearly?"

"No, I'm saying we all do if we are His."

"And me, can I hear Him clearly too, just like you do?" she asked in a small voice.

"You belong to Him, don't you? Yes, you can hear Him just like I do. You just haven't practiced listening by faith."

Her excitement suddenly waned as the familiar condemning voice filled her thoughts. She took a deep breath to try to calm her growing anxiety.

"I'd like to hear him speak clearly, but," she sighed, "I don't know if . . ."

He looked into her eyes, and she lowered her head.

"What?" he asked.

"I've been so full of doubts."

"In what way?"

She looked up again, wondering if she should tell him about her panic attacks, her doubts about her salvation, her constant feeling of impurity.

They reached the bus and stood some distance away. Some of her classmates had returned, but some had yet to arrive. She searched his eyes and the sincerity in them drew her in. Without considering it any further, she told him the whole story. How she started having nightmares about going to hell months ago, how she had left Derrick at the altar. She told him about quitting her job and coming here. With her hands sweating, she talked about the continuous fasting and prayers that had yielded nothing, and her constant depression.

He looked terribly concerned when she finished. His brows were knit as he said, "That's a lot for someone to go through, Sienna. I know one thing, though. God isn't the one behind all this."

"Then who is?" She grimaced.

He looked away for a second and then focused his gaze on her again. "I might be wrong, but I think you have religious OCD, also called scrupulosity."

"I've heard of OCD, but not religious OCD or scrupulosity." She blinked. He nodded.

"Everything you've told me seems to point to it." He put his hands on her shoulders, and she sharply sucked in her breath. "Tell you what, Sienna, I'll find out everything I can about it and let you know what solutions I can come up with. Does that sound good?"

She nodded, her heart soaring. "Yes. Thanks, Bryan."

"You're welcome." He beamed. "It's my pleasure." He looked away, but she thought she saw a shy expression creep into his face before he did.

All the students finally came back, and they all got on the bus. All the way back to the Bible College, her heart brimmed with hope from what Bryan had told her. From time to time, she surreptitiously glanced back at him. Their eyes met once, and when he smiled at her, she smiled back and then quickly turned away.

On campus, as she entered her room, she felt certain that her face glowed from spending half the day with Bryan Larson.

FIVE

Audrey took a sip of her coffee as she drove to work. She turned on her car radio, but the channel that came on the radio was playing blues, which made her sullen. She turned it off.

She'd been wondering what to do since the mayor basically told her there was no chance of becoming police chief any time soon. She wanted to quit, had sworn she would if she wasn't promoted to her rightful position, but three things stopped her.

First was her undying love for the police force, especially the Rosefield police department. The same reason she'd been angry—that she had given thirteen years of her life to the police—was the one reason that gave her pause. She wouldn't have given that many years to the police force if she didn't genuinely love it.

The second thing that stopped her from resigning was the youth center, managed by her as assistant police chief. She loved that place and how the workshops helped to keep the youth of Rosefield out of trouble. Because of initiatives like the youth center, Rosefield was free from the serious crimes that plagued many towns.

The last reason she put off quitting was a troubling one. She had refused to admit it to herself until very recently. Even though she still resented the fact that she'd been overlooked for the position of police chief, she'd grown to like and respect the new chief, Ken Baylor. There weren't very many people she liked and respected at the same time, but he was one of them.

She'd respected her old boss, but she had not liked him. Ken was different. With all the officers at work, he had a playful, carefree disposition that sometimes annoyed her; but he was also firm when he needed to be. He was a good leader, and everyone liked him. He never bossed it over her the way her former supervisor had. Every day, she found she chafed less and less under his leadership. She still wanted the position that had been given to him, but perhaps she could wait until Ken moved someplace else, and she was sure he would soon enough; knowing he was a city boy through and through, she didn't think he could bear living in a small town for too long.

Then she would take over.

She stopped at an intersection and waited until the traffic light turned green. As she began moving again, her two-way radio came alive. The voice on the other end belonged to Patrick, a young police officer who had joined the force two years ago. When she answered, he told her someone had broken into the youth center and stolen a number of things.

Audrey's heart sank. No, not the youth center.

". . . One of the volunteers came in this morning and found that a lot of the new equipment had been taken," he said.

Audrey turned her car around and drove to the center. En route, she asked Patrick if the security guard was hurt and was told he didn't appear to be seriously injured. He'd just passed out when he was hit on the head.

"Roger that!" Audrey said, glad the guy was okay. He would be the first one she questioned once she got there.

As she approached the youth center, she saw that it had already been cordoned off with yellow tape. Quite a number of people stood outside the tape, watching. She wasn't surprised by that. Burglaries on this scale were almost unheard-of in the town.

A few police officers were already on the premises. They removed the tape just enough for her to drive inside it, and then put it back again. She parked in front of the building and got out of the car.

Ken was standing at the corner of the art and design room when she walked into the building. He turned to her with a grim look on his face.

"Who could have burgled this kid's center? They stole most of the computers here and some instruments in the music room. They even stole the art supplies here."

She shook her head as she looked around at the place. Many of the paintings the children had hung on the walls were scattered on the ground, and some chairs were broken. So not only did they burglarize it, they also vandalized the place. The window had been shattered, probably where the thief—or most likely thieves—entered.

We need better security for this place, but who would have thought?

Ken left the room to check the other parts of the building while she searched for clues as to who the perpetrator was. She met him outside the building again, and they questioned the security guard. They looked at each other in concealed amusement when he told them he was asleep during the burglary and had only gotten up to use the restroom when he was hit on the head and passed out.

When they got to the station, Ken called her into his office.

"I think one or a few of the teens did it," he said to her.

"No," she shook her head. "None of the kids in Rosefield are capable of this."

"Then who do you think did it?"

"I have a hunch."

"Share," he said.

For a minute, she shared her suspicions. When she finished, she rapped her knuckles on the table.

"I've gotta get back to work." She started to get up, but sat back down when Ken said to her, "You have a quick mind, Gardner."

She nodded and blurted out, "You have a great smile, Baylor," and then she shrank. When he raised his eyebrows, she almost groaned.

Why did I say that? What was I thinking?

As usual, she had spoken whatever came to her mind. Most of the time, she didn't care what she said, but this was the second time she'd spoken something that had thoroughly embarrassed her. The first time had also been to him . . . and about the way he looked. She stood, mortified, and walked to the door.

"Audrey," he said as she turned the knob.

She turned.

"You have a beautiful smile too. I only wish I saw more of it."

She turned around and walked out of his office with a big smile on her face.

*****

Ken continued to look at the door minutes after Audrey had left his office. Their little flirting had been completely unexpected. He wasn't sure what to do now, but he had enjoyed it, and he wanted more. The problem was that he didn't know why she'd spoken those words to him. Was it because she liked him, or was it just said in her blunt I'll-say-whatever-is-on-my-mind manner?

He looked down at the files on his desk. Apart from the burglary case today, he had a mountain of work, projects he had planned to take on when he was appointed the chief of police. He had started on some of them already, but a lot of it, he hadn't even looked at yet.

He opened a file on his proposed officers' training and then shut it again. He just couldn't concentrate on work right now.

Is it professional to ask out a fellow police officer? Is it wrong? There were quite a few pretty female officers at the MPD, but he'd never been attracted to any of them. What was it about Audrey that made his heart pound every time he saw her?

He wearily ran his fingers through his hair.

Maybe it was her frank brutality mixed with feminine vulnerability.

He put his head down. What was he thinking, wondering if he should ask her out? He had to put that idea out of his mind.

But he couldn't.

Why can't I ask her out? I should.

But he knew he wouldn't. The truth was, he was afraid of rejection. In spite of his foolish speculations about her true feelings for him, he knew without a doubt that she would reject him. She didn't come across as the kind of woman who wanted or needed a man. And after what Lauren had done to him the year before, he'd become wary and overly protective of his heart.

He sighed and forced himself to continue working. They would have to remain the way they were now. The best he could hope for was her friendship. That was it.

*****

Sienna turned around after class and saw a group of watchers, gathered together, talking. She wanted to speak to the leader before she talked to Bryan. She listened as they sat discussing the new rules to help promote purity and holiness on campus. It sounded like what she needed right now.

She stood and walked up to them. "Can I join your meeting?" she asked, looking at each of them, and praying silently that they wouldn't refuse. If there was one thing she needed to help her be totally pure, this was it.

"Sure, anybody can join in."

She sat beside a girl in a red hoodie and listened as they talked.

"So," the leader said, "for our new member," he looked at her, "we were discussing what to do about the increasing decay on campus."

A boy with freckles said, "Since the Provost asked us to come up with some ideas and recommendations, we've put our heads together and have come up with a list of rules. They aren't complete yet, but we're hoping that by the time they are, the school authorities will approve them and make them official."

He began to read the rules and Sienna listened with growing anxiety. ". . . No hugging, no dating, no kissing or holding hands. Guys are not allowed in the girls' dorm and vice versa. Anybody who displays any form of disobedience will be suspended. Sex and other forms of it are strictly prohibited and any student caught or reported will be expelled immediately."

He went on reading while Sienna felt increasingly agitated. She knew these things were right and she felt ashamed. What if someone thought about these things, were they also guilty? Didn't the Bible say if you looked at someone with lust in your heart, you were also guilty of adultery?

She felt totally exposed; like everyone in this group could see her lustful thoughts about Bryan. She wanted him to ask her out. She constantly thought about kissing him. That meant she was utterly guilty and deserved to be punished.

Lord, I promise to stay away from him.

She continued to listen as they talked about other topics from subjecting the flesh to fasting in order to cleanse the soul. She was already doing most of what they said, but still, she didn't feel clean.

Maybe she wasn't like them, she thought. Maybe she wasn't even a Christian? That might explain why she never felt clean no matter what she did. And if she wasn't a Christian, did that mean she didn't have the Holy Spirit and therefore had a demon?

Her mind kept tormenting her the more she listened to them.

At last, they finished the meeting and dispersed, leaving her with her torturous thoughts.

God, are You there? Can You even hear me?

She felt and heard total silence, and terror came over her. Maybe He wasn't even listening to her. What if she had committed the unpardonable sin and He'd turned His back on her?

Her thoughts grew drearier and drearier until she closed her eyes and cried out.

"Sienna?"

She opened her eyes. Bryan was in front of her, gazing at her with a troubled expression on his face.

"Are you okay?"

She started to hyperventilate, and he took her hand. He stared intently at her. "What is it?"

She looked at their joined hands and grimaced. This wasn't right. Snatching her hand away, she got up and ran out of the class.

*****

Bryan sat on the seat Sienna had just vacated, worry spreading through him. He'd been studying about Scrupulosity since he'd left her after the street evangelism. The more he'd read, the more certain he was that she had it.

He knew the only solution was to help her focus on God's love and grace. However, how could he tell her that and help her if she ran away every time she saw him?

He felt the familiar tug in his heart. He had to go help her now. But he didn't know where to start. He didn't even know her room number. He stood as the urgency to go find her grew. He began to fear that she might be in physical danger.

I need to find out her room number. But from whom?

Lord, where do I find her? He prayed. He'd never seen her with any friend.

He decided to ask all her female classmates until he found out where her room was. He hurried out of the class. Now, where do I begin?

Students milled around the hallways, and he looked around until he saw a girl he knew was in Sienna's class because he remembered sitting behind her in the bus on the way back from the street evangelism. He politely stopped her and asked if she knew Sienna's room number in the girls' dormitory.

"You mean that model-looking girl?"

Bryan nodded.

"I don't know, but you can wait until tomorrow. She'll definitely be in class."

He held back a groan and thanked the girl. When she walked away, he thought, if I wanted to wait until tomorrow, I wouldn't be asking, would I?

He sighed loudly and began to make his way to the girls' dormitory.

SIX

Sienna reached her room and flopped down on the bed. She was grateful her roommate wasn't here. Veronica's inquisitiveness would be even harder to bear now. She looked up at the ceiling, feeling like her soul was empty and bereft of God's presence. Fear gripped her and tears ran down her face. She got up and then knelt down on the floor. She started to pray in earnest, asking God to forgive her sins. The more desperately she prayed, the worst she felt. There was no feeling of God's light in her heart, not even a flicker.

She reached for her Bible under her pillow and randomly opened it, just to hear something from God. She read the passage aloud, "For if we sin willfully after that we have received the knowledge of the truth, there remaineth no more sacrifice for sins, but a certain fearful looking for of judgment and fiery indignation, which shall devour the adversaries."

She got up and took a deep breath. It was a lost cause then. She had lost her salvation and wouldn't get it back. If God had turned His back on her, she would turn her back on Him. If He didn't want her anymore, then there was nothing left to do but to live it up from now on.

First, she needed to leave this place.

She packed her things into her suitcase, locked it, and rolled it to the door. Before she left, she glanced around the room. She'd come here looking for peace and a stronger relationship with God, but she was leaving here wholly cut off from Him.

She walked out of the room with her suitcase, went down the stairs of the dorm, and strode to the college back gate. Outside the gate, she found a taxi and said to the driver, "The airport, please." She entered the cab and exhaled. She'd already made up her mind to go back to New York. It would be difficult to get back into modeling there, but she would find a way somehow, no matter what she had to do. She'd had a good relationship with her former agent, and there were some other industry people she could call. This time, there would be no boundaries the way there had been when her focus was on pleasing God. She had rejected so many jobs because of that. Now, she would do whatever it took to get to the top.

About an hour and a half later, she was on the plane flying back to New York City. She made a mental note to call Audrey and Trisha once she landed and tell them she had gone back. She would not do anything other than that. They would be happy for her.

When the plane landed hours later, she took a cab to the Peninsula Hotel on Fifth Avenue, knowing she had to find an apartment soon. Thankfully, the money she had made from previous modeling jobs would more than keep her going until she could get more jobs.

She called Trish, who was as happy for her as she'd guessed. After that, she called Audrey. Surprisingly, Audrey was a little skeptical and wondered why she had abruptly left the Bible school. However, after convincing her it was what she wanted this time, Audrey wished her well. After the calls, she ordered room service and took a long bath. When the food arrived, she clapped in delight at the sumptuous spread. There was a surf and turf platter, a plate of caviar carbonara, a huge cheeseburger and a decadent-looking chocolate cream pie.

She stuffed herself with relish. She'd mostly starved herself, fasting regularly while in the Bible College. Even when she had eaten, it had been sparingly. This type of food, she'd not had in quite a while.

After eating she called her agent.

"I want back in," she said immediately when he answered the call.

"Sienna! How are you? It's been a while."

"It has," she said.

"Where did you go, Sienna?"

She sighed wearily as a thread of pain went through her. "I don't want to talk about it."

"You sound different," he said. "I thought you had quit for good. You do know many of our former clients won't hire you anymore. You canceled all the photo shoots I had lined up for you and quit, just like that."

She sighed again. "I know, but find anything."

"Anything," he sounded unsure. "You know what? I can ask Surge Model agency if they will sign you on exclusively as you've worked with them a couple of times. Obviously, they have some of your pictures, but I'll show them your full portfolio."

"Anything, Zack."

"You know a lot of their clients are lingerie and swimwear designers. Are you ready for those sorts of photo shoots? You never took those types of jobs before."

She shrugged. "I don't care anymore."

He paused for a few seconds and then said, "Okay, let's cross our fingers and hope that Surge agrees. I do think there is a good chance that they will."

After he promised he would get back to her, she ended the call.

She felt a prick in her conscience, but she brushed the guilty feeling away. She was starting a new life, free from all that exhausting demand for moral perfection. Hopefully, the agency would agree to sign her on exclusively. If they did, modeling lingerie and swimwear would be a regular part of her life.

She glanced around her lavish hotel room with its cream and gold décor and wondered what she was going to do now. She was bored. Months ago, she would have turned on the TV to find some 'clean' entertainment, but she'd promised herself she was going to 'live it up' now. Sitting in a hotel room alone, watching TV, definitely wasn't living it up.

She remembered the nightclub in Manhattan where some of the models she'd worked with went regularly. She passed by it on her way to go-sees and photo shoots, and she'd always glanced at it with a slight feeling of disgust. But apparently, there was something about that place that had made an impression on her because she pictured herself there now, gyrating to some upbeat music.

She would go there tonight, and it would probably become somewhere for her to go when she wanted to have fun. She went out to shop at a boutique close to the hotel. She bought a skimpy sequined dress and sky-high heels for her night out.

At about ten p.m. she left the hotel in the dress, hailed a cab and entered.

As the driver drove to the nightclub, her mind wandered to Bryan, and she shut her eyes as an excruciating pain ripped through her heart. Pressing her lips tightly together, she groaned softly. She had fallen hard for him, and she would miss him terribly.

She opened her eyes and wiped away the tears on her cheeks with her fingers. If only they could be together. From the way he looked at her every time she saw him, she knew he liked her too. But it wasn't possible for them to be together. Like the watchers, his purity shone bright like the sun, condemning her, constantly reminding her of her shortcomings. He belonged to God while she didn't.

He would find out in Church Missions class tomorrow that she wasn't on campus anymore. Before long, he would forget about her. But she knew it wasn't going to be so for her with her obsessive thoughts. Unless she could find a way to expunge his face from her mind, it would remain etched there. The memory of what could have been between them would torment her forever.

The taxi driver stopped in front of the club, and she got out. The club called Gold Nile was a white nondescript building with troops of people entering. She walked up, and a burly man she guessed was the bouncer looked her over and let her in.

Inside, she looked around. The club was packed with people dancing, Smoke filled the air. The pulsating music, effervescent multicolored lights and general unfamiliar rhythm of the place slightly unnerved her. She took a deep breath, let it out slowly, and told herself to calm down.

I'll have to get used to it to enjoy it.

She climbed up a flight of stairs to the spherical sitting area and found an empty seat. A huge artificial palm tree stood next to her, and she turned to admire it before she ordered a mocktail.

Just as she finished sipping her drink, a man approached her and asked if he could sit with her. She assessed him. He was handsome and refined-looking in a fitted blazer and white button-down shirt.

She smiled and said, "Yes."

He sat beside her, nodded to a waiter and ordered himself a hot toddy. "Can I buy you another drink?" he asked her.

She thought about it. Most people were drinking alcohol here, and today she felt adventurous. She had never had alcohol before, but there was always a first time. She nodded. Since she wasn't sure what kind of drink to order, she asked the waiter to bring her what he had requested.

He smiled. "Good choice."

He asked her name. When she told him, he told her his and asked what she did for a living.

"I'm a model," she said.

He sat up on his seat and smiled. "That's an interesting job to have."

The waiter came back with their drinks, and he immediately lifted his to his lips. He drank his while she stared at hers nervously. She exhaled and forced herself to drink the cocktail and then coughed as she swallowed it. "Hot," she said, shaking her head.

"You've never drunk alcohol before, have you?" He smiled sympathetically at her.

She shook her head. She took a deep breath again and took a sip of the drink. She forced herself to savor the bittersweet taste and then swallowed carefully. It warmed her inside, and she took another careful sip.

He smiled at her and then asked what it felt like being a model. At first, she gave him a brief answer, but as she took sip after sip of her drink, she felt herself getting mellower and more and more talkative.

He asked if she wanted to dance and she nodded. She got up but stumbled. When he caught her in his arms, she sat again and giggled, "Guess I can't . . . dance."

He grinned. "Do you want to get out of this place . . . with me?"

She looked at him, fully understanding what he was asking. A warning bell went off in her, but she ignored it. She focused on the fascination she felt. He was handsome, and people went home with strangers from the bar all the time. It meant nothing. If she was going to free herself from her religious shackle and expel Bryan from her mind, this was a good way to start.

"Why not?" she said to him. As she got up and followed him out, her stomach quivered with a strange mix of uneasiness and excitement.

After being with the man in his hotel room for a night, she knew without a doubt that she'd totally expunged God from her heart. Bryan's face, however, remained. An intense feeling of desolation came over her as she left the hotel room in the morning and stayed with her throughout the day.

*****

Audrey opened the brown envelopes containing the photographs from the burglary scene. She scattered the pictures on her desk and stared at them. The images didn't reveal much. One of them showed the back lawn of the youth center covered with huge tire marks. It meant the burglars had entered the premises with a big vehicle. But she already knew that from the surveillance cameras. The footage from the CCTV camera in the front and at the back of the building had shown two hooded individuals in all black outfits carting away items from the building into a waiting van. She and Ken would watch the footage again to see if they could find anything else that would help them with the case.

Audrey pushed the pictures aside, leaned back in her chair, and sighed worriedly. Sienna had called again yesterday to tell her she'd been signed into a new modeling agency. Even though Audrey was happy for her, there was something about the way she sounded that troubled her. She'd sounded like she was reciting her words from a script.

"Are you okay?" Audrey had asked, gripping her cell phone.

"I'm good. I thought you would be happy that I've gone back to modeling."

"I am. It's just that you sound a little off."

"Nah, I'm good. I've gotta run, but I'll talk to you soon." She had ended the call before Audrey could ask any more questions. Audrey had sighed wearily and prayed that Sienna would tell her if something was really wrong.

A knock sounded at her office door, distracting her from her thoughts, and she looked up. Her heart skipped a beat when she saw it was Ken.

He said, "Have you discovered anything else about the burglary case?"

"Not yet, but I want us to watch the footage from the CCTV camera again."

He came and sat across from her, and she inhaled. As usual, he had that grin on his handsome face that took her breath away.

Easy girl, breathe, she said to herself, and stood to turn on the DVR.

As they watched the footage again, she pointed at one of the hooded burglars. That's a woman right there. The baggy clothes didn't do enough to hide her curves. We just assumed they were both men."

"I don't know why I didn't notice the first time we watched it," Ken said. "That means your hunch was . . ."

He stopped mid-sentence as a sudden commotion outside her office drew their attention. She stood to go check what it was and Ken closely followed. The musky fragrance of his cologne filled her senses and without thinking she inhaled it deeply. And then she chided herself.

"What's happening out here?" Ken asked.

A man who had been arrested for a DUI brandished a small pocket knife. Police officers surrounded him, laughing.

Ken shook his head.

"What does he think he can do with that in a room full of cops?" Will, a gangly officer, roared.

Lieutenant Burns chuckled. "Maybe he wants to whittle us nice wooden presents. After all, we saved his life by arresting him."

They all laughed again.

Audrey watched them in amusement as they mocked the man. And then she noticed something that none of them had seen. The guy's hand was inching slowly toward Will's gun on his hips. Audrey dived for the man just as he drew out the weapon from the holster. She tackled him to the floor and wrestled the gun from his hand.

Everyone watched with eyes wide and mouths agape. She hurled the guy up with her and then shook her head as the others rushed him. She left them and then went back to her office. Ken came to sit across from her as she took her seat. He studied her face.

She raised her eyebrows. "What?"

"That was impressive out there," he said. "But I'm not surprised."

"Really?" she asked, slightly shocked.

"Yeah, you are kinda like Wonder Woman!"

She snorted, but couldn't hold back her smile.

"I love how your eyes light up when I compliment you."

"And I love the cute things you say to me."

They were constantly flirting these days. She knew nothing more would come out of it. It was not like they would get married and ride off into the sunset.

She grimaced at her thoughts. Get married? How did her thoughts suddenly move from their light-hearted flirting to marriage?

He tilted his head toward her, his eyes studying her. "What are you thinking about?" he asked.

"'Bout marrying you," she blurted out and then groaned in embarrassment. "I . . . did not mean . . ." She stopped trying to speak. Always with this man, she said the most ludicrous things. She sighed. "I'm sorry."

She expected to see his usual silly grin, but he did not smile. He looked serious. I've offended him this time.

"You don't need to apologize," he said gruffly. "I like you too . . . very much."

Her jaw dropped, and she stared at him, unable to say a word.

He finally smiled and said, "I don't know if dating a fellow police officer is discouraged here, but I can't help myself, Audrey. I want to get to know you better. Would you like to have dinner with me Friday evening?"

"Yes," she said quickly, and then cringed inwardly at the eagerness in her voice. She felt suddenly shy as she looked at him and said more slowly, "Yes, I will have dinner with you."

SEVEN

Audrey rifled through her closet in a sort of panicky mode looking for something to wear for her date with Ken. None of the outfits she'd looked at seemed appropriate for the date. She stood back wearily, huffed and then continued searching. Most of her clothes were either outdated or too casual for a date. She couldn't remember the last time she'd gone on one, and so she hadn't stocked up on any dressy outfits. The closest thing she had were her church outfits—usually dark jeans and a few simple tops. Somehow, they seemed unsuitable today.

She pulled out a designer dress that Sienna had given her for Christmas last year. She had never had the guts or desire to wear it. This time, she forced herself to put it on and then regarded herself in the mirror. The strapless fitted white dress hugged her every curve. She sighed. This looked like she was trying way too hard.

She took the dress off and finally selected another—a knee-length black gown. She looked at herself in the mirror after she put it on. It looked nice, but simple-nice.

As she put on her black kitten heels, she could hear Sienna's and Trisha's voices in her mind scolding her, saying her outfit looked too plain. "You are going on a date, not to church," they would say if they saw her now. But she wasn't like them. That white dress just wasn't her.

She glanced at the mirror again. This was her—simple and practical.

She thought about wearing some makeup for the first time in years, but her mind rebelled. Makeup also wasn't her. A makeup kit sat on the edge of her dressing table. She stared at it for a long moment. It was a gift from Trish for her last birthday. It had sat in the same spot for a year without being touched.

She could see a trend now. Her sisters were telling her through their gifts that she needed to try harder with her appearance.

She picked it up and then decided to use some. Ken was definitely worth the effort. She tentatively applied pink gloss on her lips and fought the urge to wipe it off. She could see Ken's handsome face in her mind, and she wanted to look pretty for him. She swiped on some mascara and then decided she'd applied more than enough makeup.

The doorbell rang, and her stomach quivered.

He's here.

She took a deep breath and shook her hands to try to calm her nerves.

You have to watch what you say to him today. I know you really like him, but that doesn't mean you have to blurt it out. Grabbing her purse, she went down the stairs and eagerly opened the door.

But it wasn't him. Trisha came in, tears running

down her cheeks. She had a travel bag in her hand. She dropped her bag on the floor and flopped down onto the sofa.

Audrey frowned in alarm and walked over to her. "What's wrong, Trish?"

"It's Stan. He cheated on me . . . again."

Audrey sighed with relief, sat beside Trish and put her hand on Trish's shoulder. "I told you, Trish, but you still decided to stay with him."

Trisha stared at her through her tears. "You don't know what happened. Some weeks ago, I found out I was pregnant and . . ."

"What! And you didn't tell me!" She looked down at Trisha's stomach. It was still flat but not as flat as it usually was. "How come I didn't notice? As a cop, I'm supposed to be able to pick up on these things."

"You've been busy with your life. And I didn't tell you because Stan and I decided to wait for a few months before we told anyone; because of our last two miscarriages, you know. Anyway, I was over-the-moon happy, and I thought he was too because he started coming home early and he cut back on his business trips. I told myself that he wouldn't spend this much time at home if he were still cheating on me. But I was wrong. I don't know why, but this morning, before he woke up to go to work, I decided to check his phone. I found another message . . . this time from him to a girl called Samantha. Another girl. I even saw the girl's picture on his phone."

She bent her head and broke down.

Audrey held her as she cried. She looked up with her cheeks streaked with mascara and eyeliner. "You were going out?"

Audrey nodded and opened her mouth to speak just as the doorbell rang. "That's probably my date."

Trisha groaned. "So, you can't stay here with me? I really need you now. Is there any way you can postpone?"

Audrey sighed. "I like this guy a lot and you know I haven't had a date in a while . . ."

Trisha nodded and started to stand up. "Okay, this distressed pregnant woman will get out of your hair."

"Way to pile on the guilt." Audrey held her hand. "Wait, Trish, don't go." She went and opened the door. "Ken." Her heart pattered as she gazed at him. He looked so handsome dressed in a navy jacket and pinstripe button-down shirt.

He gave her a once-over, and his eyes lit up in admiration. "You look beautiful."

"Thank you," she said and smiled at him. Now how to explain the situation with Trisha? This was going to be hard. She opened the door wide so he could come in and pointed in Trisha's direction. "Ken, this is my sister, Trisha. Trish, this is Ken, my date, and my boss."

Ken lifted his brows, a silly grin on his face. "Boss ugh! Today I'm your date."

Trish quickly wiped her tears and smiled brightly at him. "Hi, Police Chief Baylor. I haven't spoken to you in person. Pleased to meet you."

"And you."

Audrey said to him, "I'll be right back." She led Trisha away into the kitchen.

Trisha chuckled. "You didn't tell me your date was the police chief. He's gorgeous. No wonder you agreed to go out with him. You usually don't care about dating."

"Stop it, Trish! I'm not going out with him because of his looks. He's smart and funny. Most of all, he's a great human being. That's why I agreed to go on this date."

"You are totally smitten with this guy!" Trisha teased in exclamation, and then she scrunched up her face. "Stan is handsome too." She put her hand on Audrey's shoulder with tears running down her cheeks and said, "I'll repeat your own words back to you, Audrey. Be careful of handsome men who seem too nice." She sniffed and looked away. "I guess you can go. I'll be fine."

"No, I'm not leaving you like this," Audrey said. She really wanted to go out with Ken, but Trish needed her. She couldn't bring herself to leave her pregnant sister in such a miserable state. An idea came to her, and she said to Trisha, "I'll be right back."

Walking to the small living room, she found Ken sitting on the couch, riffling through the Police Academy magazine that had been on the coffee table. She came and sat next to him. "Ken, what if we had dinner here instead of some expensive restaurant. My sister is depressed right now, and I don't want to leave her. I could order something for us to eat or you could have my famous lasagna. I made it yesterday and it's really nice."

She held her breath, hoping he would agree.

He smiled. "Sure, I wouldn't want you to leave your sister, and I would love to have your lasagna. Do you want me to help with anything?"

"No," she said, relieved that he'd agreed to stay. She winked at him and gave him a naughty grin.

"Just sit and look pretty."

He laughed as she left for the kitchen.

Trisha was still there munching on chips. Audrey brought out the pan of lasagna from the fridge, covered it with foil and put it in the oven to reheat it. She turned to Trisha and asked, "So now that he's cheated on you while you are pregnant, what are you going to do?"

"I don't know. I know you want me to leave him, but it's not that easy. When you get married to that hunk out there, you'll know."

Audrey's stomach flipped, but she pressed her lips together and shook her head. "Who said we were going to get married?" Even as she said the words, she knew she didn't believe them, because she still imagined herself in a wedding dress in front of a church, holding Ken's hands and saying marriage vows.

"From the longing expression on your face, I would definitely say you're thinking about that. Anyway, I can't just leave Stan. We've been through so much together."

"Well, it's your life, but as someone who truly cares about you, I'll advise you to get rid of him. He's a jerk!"

Trisha looked like she was going to cry again. She shut her eyes and said, "I don't think I can do that, especially now that we are both expecting this child."

Audrey put her arms around her and drew her close. "Don't cry, Trish. You can come and eat with Ken and me once I dish out the food."

"No, I think I'll go to bed in Mom and Dad's room."

Audrey smiled sadly. They still called their old parents' bedroom, "Mom and Dad's room." She slept in the other bedroom she had shared with her sisters growing up and hardly went into that room.

Trisha stopped at the kitchen door and turned around. "You guys have a good time." She gave Audrey a half smile and walked out the door.

Audrey took the lasagna from the oven and carried it to the dining table. She quickly dished it out onto square white plates. Ken turned his face to her, and she smiled at him before going back to the kitchen. She brought out a bottle of non-alcoholic Sangria from the fridge, took out two glasses from the cabinet and went to set them on the dining table.

As they ate, they talked about work until Ken shook his head. "We need to stop talking about work, Audrey." He smiled at her. "Tell me about yourself."

"What do you want to know?"

He leaned forward and stared into her eyes. "I want to know everything about you, except for your job, of course."

She gazed at him for a minute, captivated by how his eyes danced as they studied her face. She finally shook herself out of her entrancement and sighed softly. "Okay. I'm the oldest of three girls."

She told him about growing up in this house. "I had a happy childhood." She folded her hands on the table and talked about choosing to join the police force after she went with her high-school senior class to an excursion at the police station. The sights, sounds, and the uniforms had fascinated her. "I went to the police academy when I was eighteen, wanting to make a difference in my small town. I joined the Rosefield Force officially at nineteen." Tears suddenly filled her eyes. "We lost our parents six years later. It's been seven years since they died in a car crash."

"I'm so sorry."

"Even though it was very sad, it somehow didn't surprise any of us that they died together. They loved each other so much, and neither of them would have wanted to live without the other." She looked up wistfully. "Thankfully all of us were financially stable by then. My sister Trisha was dating her now husband and got married soon after. Though my baby sister, Sienna, was just fifteen at the time, she'd been scouted as a model the year before." Her heart grew heavy as she said, "We were all devastated by our parents' death, and the emotional trauma stayed with us for a while. However, through God's help, and our love for each other, we eventually got through it."

He looked sad, and she smiled to lighten the mood. She said to him, "It's your turn."

He told her about being the youngest of five siblings. "My family lives in Tampa, and I had a normal-ish childhood," he said. "Like you, I joined the academy because I wanted to make a difference. I moved to Miami after the academy to join the MPD. And I've also lived in Boise, just for a few months, before I became a cop."

He paused for a minute, as she scrutinized his face. He looked a little distressed. "I was once engaged to be married, but she called it off a month before the wedding. She's married to someone else now."

His expression was so wistful that Audrey felt a sting of jealousy. She, however, pushed the jealous feeling away. Being jealous of a girl who was in his past and now married was ridiculous. She smiled sympathetically at him. "You have something in common with my sister, Sienna, but at least your story is better than hers. She left her fiancé at the altar."

"Wow! That's rough!"

Audrey nodded.

Soon they moved to the living room and settled side by side on the couch. They talked about everything from their love of old movies to the most interesting places they've each visited. Audrey kicked off her shoes and placed her feet on the coffee table as she told him about her best friend growing up and the silly antics they got into. She howled with laughter as he shared childhood story after story, and she teased him about being a very naughty child.

Sometime later, his eyes grew round as he stared at the clock on the wall. "Wow! It's past midnight! I was having so much fun I didn't even look at the time." He stood up. "I guess I have to get going, Audrey."

She stood up reluctantly, walked him to the door and said, "I had a great time." If only this night didn't have to end, she thought. It felt like it had just begun.

"I did too." His eyes searched hers. "I love the way your lashes flutter when you're lost in thought."

She knew what he was doing. It was now their usual flirty banter. She couldn't resist teasing him and said, smiling, "I love your shoes."

"My shoes?"

She laughed at the look on his face.

"Surely you can do better than that," he said.

"Okay," she replied, and then lost the smile. "I love the cute dimples that appear on your cheeks when you smile. I love the way your eyes sparkle when you're saying something funny." She fingered his beard. "And I love how this feels . . . just the way I imagined it would."

His eyes were as round as saucers when she finished. He shook his head and exclaimed, "Wow! Okay; and I only said something lame." So, let me really say what I want." He caressed her cheeks. "I love how smooth this is," he said, and kissed each of them." Her heart thudded as he ran his fingers through her hair and cupped her face. He kissed her nose and said, "I love your nose; it's as cute as a button." She trembled as he smoothed his thumb over her lips and said, "I love how soft your lips feel, and I can't wait to kiss them."

Her heart raced as he drew her close and kissed her chin and the corner of her lips. But just before their lips met, Trisha came into the room, screaming.

"Audrey! I think I'm about to lose my baby. Help me!"

Audrey gasped and pulled away from Ken. There was blood on Trisha's legs."

Ken sprang to action. "I'll call 911."

Audrey went to hold Trisha as she howled. "I don't want to lose my baby again. Please help me!"

"It's okay, Trish," Audrey rubbed her sister's back comfortingly while her heart pounded. "Ken is calling for help. The paramedics will be here soon."

*****

Trisha bit her lips worriedly as she looked up at the doctor. She was lying on her back in the hospital bed. The doctor stood beside her, pressing his stethoscope to her uterus. She waited impatiently as he kept probing and listening, and then asked for the third time since he started examining her if her baby was okay.

He gave her a small smile, but he didn't answer. She wanted to scream at him, to insist that he immediately tell her if her baby was fine, but she held herself in check. When she saw Stan enter the room, she held back a sob and held out her hands to him.

Stan came rushing up to her.

"Trisha, are you okay?" he asked.

She looked up at the doctor and then shook her head. "I don't know yet."

The waiting felt excruciating, but at last, the doctor smiled at her and Stan. "Your baby is fine."

"What about the bleeding?" she asked.

"It happens sometimes, but your baby's heartbeat is strong. There is no need to worry. However, I would advise you to stay away from any strenuous physical activity and stress until your baby is born."

She exhaled, relieved.

Stan hugged her. "Thank God the baby is fine."

The doctor left, and Stan sat beside her on the bed. She looked at him, the man she had married and still loved in spite of his continual betrayal. She had asked Audrey to call him as the ambulance took her to the hospital, but Audrey had been hesitant.

"He's the father of this baby, Audrey. I have to call him. What if something has happened to our child?"

"Trish, stop it! Your baby will be fine."

"Please, just call Stan. He deserves to know what is happening."

Audrey had snorted but called. Thank God he was here now. But once they got home, they would have to have a serious heart to heart.

He looked at her as if he wanted to cry and said, "I know you are angry with me, Trish, but please come back home. I need you."

"No, you don't. You need other women. Not me."

At this point, she wasn't sure what she would do. Sometimes, she was certain that she wanted to leave him, but at other times, she couldn't bear the thought of being separated from him.

"I love you, Trish. Please come back to me. Besides, you know our baby deserves to have both a mother and a father."

She looked up at him, and for the first time in their marriage, she felt a deep sense of loathing for him. "Can you tell me one thing, Stan?"

"What?"

"Why can't you stop cheating? Is it something I have or don't have, or is it a sickness that you have?"

He looked taken aback, like what she had just asked him was the last thing he expected her to ask. He did not answer for a full minute, and then he said in a shaky voice, "I don't know, I don't know what it is, but I know I love you. The affairs meant nothing. I think I get lonely when I'm away."

She eyed him with disgust. "You get lonely! You think I don't get lonely when you leave on your many business trips? Why are you the only one who gets to act out when you are lonely?" She glowered at him. "I could cheat as well, Stan. I just choose not to."

He bowed his head. "I'm sorry. It won't happen again. I promise."

"You can't promise anything." She sighed. "I told Audrey to call you because I was afraid something had happened to our baby. I'm not ready to come home yet. I'm going to remain in her house, until I can sort out my emotions."

He nodded. "I understand."

"And Stan, if I so much as hear that you looked at another woman a minute longer than you should, this marriage will be over."

He nodded again. "That's fair. I promise to be faithful from now on."

She looked at him, wanting with all her heart to believe him, but knowing he could fail to keep his promise now, just as he'd failed before. She said, "If you can't do it for me, at least do it for our child. You just said that a child is better off with both parents. Ours will have only one if you fall off the wagon again."

"I promise I won't." He bent his head and kissed her.

She smiled. "I choose to believe you."

Thirty minutes later, while he was asleep on the seat facing her, Audrey came in. She'd probably been in the reception area waiting and was still in the black dress she had worn for her date.

Trisha smiled at her. "My baby is fine, Audrey."

Audrey sighed audibly and then hugged her. "I'm so glad."

Trisha said, "I'm so sorry I ruined your date."

"No," Audrey replied, "it was already over by the time you came out." She touched Trisha's hair. "I'm just glad your baby is fine, and you are good too."

Trisha nodded and leaned her head back on the pillow.

Audrey looked over at Stan with a disgusted look on her face. "He's still here. What did you tell him?"

"I told him that I think I'll stay in your house for a little longer, until I know what I'm going to do."

"I know you say you still love him, but does he love you? He wouldn't be cheating on you constantly if he did."

Trisha sighed. "Audrey, please let it go for now, I just want to rest." She held out her hand, and Audrey took it. "I hope you don't mind me staying at your place until I can sort out my emotions."

"No, you can stay for as long as you want."

"Thanks." She squeezed Audrey's hand. "So, how did your date go?"

"Great, it went great."

"That's good." She laughed. "Imagine, you are now dating your boss! Isn't that something?"

Audrey smiled, but didn't say anything more about it. A minute later, she scrunched up her face and asked, "Have you heard from Sienna?"

"No, I haven't spoken to her in a while."

"I'm worried about her. Even though she has gone back to New York and to her modeling, something isn't right."

"I think she'll be fine," Trisha said. "Now that she's moved back and her life is back on track, she'll need time to settle down and get into the rhythm of things again. She'll be back to her former self in no time, you'll see."

"I hope so."

Trisha nodded and then turned to watch Stan as he slept. She could feel tears threatening to spill down from her eyes again, but she blinked them back. Hopefully, Stan would get back to his former self; to the husband she'd married when they were just teenagers. That boy only had eyes for her and had promised to love her forever.

EIGHT

Sienna rolled out of bed and held her head in her hand. She had a terrible hangover from partying all night with some other models. The clock beside her bed showed the time was a little past ten a.m. Staggering to the bathroom, she stood in front of the mirror and looked at herself. She looked comical. Her hair was messy and having slept without wiping off her makeup, her face looked like she'd had it painted by a three-year-old. She partly did look like a clown.

She had a bikini shoot this morning. The designer, Alessio, would be waiting at the location of the shoot. She had modeled for him before. He usually arrived before anyone else did. She smiled. Though middle-aged, he was cute. She'd partied hard, drinking and dancing throughout the night with other models at his house yesterday. Still, he would expect her to be at her best today.

She called a cab, not feeling up to driving this morning, and then quickly brushed her teeth, took a shower, and went downstairs to get something

to eat. She sat at the dining table hastily munching a turkey sandwich and looked around her.
Her new apartment was still unfamiliar. It was a
fully furnished two-bedroom duplex-apartment in
SoHo with a gorgeous view of lower Manhattan.
She loved the all-white décor with gold accents
as it gave her some measure of the tranquility she
craved.

After eating, she took some aspirin for her
headache. She pulled on a floor-length floral dress
and put her hair in a high bun. She packed another
change of clothes into a small bag, wore a pair of
flat sandals, and grabbed her purse.

Once she exited her apartment building, she
entered her waiting cab and leaned back on the
seat while the driver drove her to Long Beach—the
location of the shoot.

The cab driver stopped at an intersection, and
Sienna looked out the window. A new building at
the side of the road caught her attention, and she
craned her neck to see what kind of structure it
was.

The instant she saw it was a church, an intense
panic took hold of her. Her heart began to palpi-
tate, and her hands grew damp. A voice whispered
harshly in her heart, You are going to hell!

She clenched her fists and then unclenched
them. She began to breathe in and out, in and out.
They finally started moving again, and the panic
gradually passed. She took a deep breath and shut
her eyes, both relieved and worried. She'd not had
an attack this serious since she came back to New
York.

Since she started modeling lingerie and swimsuits, the anxiety and panic attacks seemed to have lessened. Also, her ever-busy schedule helped. Her days were filled with shoots, fittings, auditions, parties and more parties, so she had no time for anxiety. From this experience just now and those back in the Bible College, she knew what to do henceforth. As long as she stayed away from any form of exposure to religious texts, places, and people, she would be fine.

When they got to the beach, it was empty except for the photographer and, of course, Alessio. The photographer had already set up his props and equipment and was checking his cameras when she walked by him. He greeted her and then Alessio came up to her. Today, he'd put his long hair in a bun similar to hers.

"You are a little late," he said in his strong Italian accent. He kissed her cheeks and then pointed her toward a makeshift tent a few feet from where they stood. It had been set up as a temporary hair, make-up, and changing area.

She strolled to the tent and sat down in front of a mirror to get her hair and makeup done. Alessio came into the tent just as the makeup artist started working on her face. "Are you ready for the shoot today?" he asked her.

Sienna smiled. "I'll be ready once I have my hair and makeup done."

Alessio said, "Talking about hair and makeup, I think we should go for something totally different from the last time." He gave the hairdresser and makeup artist directions on what he specifically wanted.

For the next two hours, her hair was stretched

and curled while her makeup was being done. After they finished, she stood and stared intently in the mirror. The final hair and makeup look was a low ponytail and a dewy nude face.

The wrangler came into the tent and handed her a sheer beige bikini. She almost gasped at how skimpy it was, but she plastered a smile on her face and went into a private part of the tent to change into it. A condemning voice immediately arose in her, but she pushed it away.

She walked out to where the photographer was waiting and stepped lightly into the water while the wind blew in her face. As usual, she felt slightly self-conscious as she stood in front of the camera. A tiny voice whispered in her head, Are you sure you want to appear on the front cover of a magazine looking like this?

She ignored the voice and told the photographer she was ready.

He gave her directions on how to pose for the pictures, while Alessio stood behind him watching her.

"Too girl-next-door," the photographer said to her as she struck her favorite pose.

She adjusted it to appear more alluring.

He smiled. "Good. Really good!"

The shoot lasted for four hours. After it was finally over, she flopped down on the sand, exhausted. Alessio walked up to her, bent down and said, "There is a party at my place tonight. Do you want to come?"

She wanted to tell him she needed a break, a chance to just rest in her apartment, but she nodded. She'd promised herself to live it up and saying no to party invites wasn't living it up, so she said she would come.

She went into the tent and changed into a pair of distressed jeans and a white T-shirt. Slinging her bag over her shoulder, she made her way to her cab.

Alessio came again and stood beside her window. His smile was as bright as the sun. "I would like you to come as my date, Sienna," he said.

She thought about it for a few seconds. He was handsome and charming. Most of all, he was a regular client. To indulge him was guaranteed to get her more gigs like this one. They paid well enough for her to afford her great apartment and BMW. She nodded and told him she would love to be his date.

He beamed, obviously pleased.

When she got back to her apartment, she set her alarm, collapsed on the bed, and immediately fell asleep. She didn't stir until her alarm began to ring, letting her know it was time to prepare for the party. She groaned. All she wanted to do was lie down and sleep until tomorrow, but it was essential for her to go. She would get to schmooze there and book more high-paying jobs.

She wore a pink slip dress, brushed her hair and put on minimal makeup. She left her apartment and drove to Alessio's home. Once there, she parked beside a blue Mercedes and got out. A long line of expensive cars was already parked in front of the Spanish villa.

The music, loud and throbbing reached her ears as she climbed up the stairs leading to the entrance of the house. She pulled on the party face and boisterous personality she often reserved for parties like this before she entered. The villa was packed with guests drinking, chatting and laughing loudly. A waiter carrying a tray of cocktail drinks walked by, and she took one.

She took a sip of the drink and carefully made her way through the house to the gazebo. A group of models from her agency stood there, chattering and giggling. She joined them for a few minutes and then spotted Alessio near the pool. He was dressed in his usual flamboyant style—a fitted white suit, red tie and red pocket square with a gold necklace and multiple rings on his fingers. He was talking to a man who was dressed in a similar fashion.

Their eyes met, and he smiled at her and yelled in his usual manner, "Sienna! You are here! Good. Come! Let me introduce you to someone who you'll definitely want to meet!"

She began to make her way toward him while her heart raced loudly in her chest. The man he was talking to had his back to her but still looked familiar. She wondered who it was as she reached Alessio and then gasped when the man turned. It was Orlando Costa, one of the most famous designers in the world.

She felt nervous as Alessio made the introductions, but she tried not to let her nervousness show.

Orlando Costa was a talker. He gave her a lengthy account of his humble beginnings and how he grew his fashion empire to where it was now. She already knew the story, everyone did, but she listened politely. She kept hoping he would mention something about booking her for one of his fashion shows. So far, she had done print and commercial modeling. She wanted to do runway badly. That was her ultimate career dream. Also, modeling for Orlando would open a lot of doors she could only dream about.

At last, he stopped talking about himself and said to her, "Have you done any runway shows?"

She shook her head. "Not yet."

He gave her his business card and pointed at a phone number on it. "Have your agent call me tomorrow so we can set a date for you to come to my office." He pointed at an address on the card. "Do you know where it is?"

She wasn't sure, but she would find it. She nodded. "I do."

"This is where you'll come when we agree on a date. Once the contracts have been signed, you'll be booked for my show at fashion week."

She sharply sucked in her breath. Fashion week! I'll get to model for Orlando Costa during fashion week?

Her stomach fluttered with excitement, and she felt like she was in a dream.

Orlando Costa left a minute later to talk with someone else, and Sienna whooped. "I don't know how to thank you, Alessio," she said, kissing his cheek.

He gave her a sly smile. "I know one way you can thank me."

She looked at him and immediately knew what he wanted. Her heart sank, and she looked down at the cobbled floor.

He said to her, "I'm going to Belize for a weekend getaway with a few other models. I want you to come."

She took a deep breath, feeling slightly nauseated, and then exhaled slowly. She looked up at him and finally made her decision. This sort of opportunity with Orlando Costa only came by once in a lifetime. Alessio had just made it happen for her. Besides, Alessio was hardly repulsive. He was rich and handsome.

She nodded. "Okay, I'll come."

*****

Audrey took a deep breath and then walked into the youth center with Ken. They went straight to the music room and found the instructor, Jackie, standing next to a child who was playing the piano.

Audrey smiled at the boy and then asked to speak with Jackie outside the music room. They stepped out together, and Jackie sighed wearily. "Do you have any leads yet on the thief who stole our musical instruments? Fortunately, they didn't take the piano, but the guitars, microphones, and cellos are gone. I want to see the person who did this in jail."

Ken said, "We've just discovered who the person is and we are about to make our arrest."

Jackie's face lit up. "You have? Who?"

"You, Jackie," Audrey answered. "You are the thief."

Jackie harrumphed. "Is that a joke? Because it's not very funny!"

Audrey looked at Ken and then faced Jackie again. "We know it was you, Jackie. Give it up!"

Jackie shook her head. "It wasn't . . . me," she stammered. "Besides, didn't you say the faces of the burglars were covered? How then can you tell exactly who it is?"

Ken smiled. "First, we never said there was more than one burglar. How did you know that?"

"Of course there was more than one person. A single person could not have stolen all those things."

Audrey said, "Yes, you are right, but we never said the faces of the burglars were covered. We know you did it."

"You can't prove it," she blustered.

"Yes, we can. When you broke in through the window, you cut your finger, didn't you? We found traces of your DNA there."

Her eyes widened with shock, and then she huffed. "That still doesn't prove . . ."

"Your accomplice, Officer Fred Draper, confessed everything. You are dating, aren't you?"

Jackie shut her eyes, groaned and then said, "We did it to protest Fred's dismissal from the police force. That was unjust."

Audrey smiled coldly. "You do know he had been given several chances to change, but he didn't. Constantly driving while intoxicated is not the way a law enforcement agent is supposed to conduct himself." She shrugged. "Anyway, you are under arrest."

They cuffed her and led her away while the kids strained their necks to catch a glimpse of what was happening.

*****

Ken stood on the balcony of the Symposium in Boise where the national police convention was being held. He turned and stared at Audrey who was standing beside him, looking into the distance. She'd removed her police hat, and strands of her dark hair sailed carelessly in the wind, having escaped her tight bun. He felt an intense urge to tuck them behind her ears but resisted. The hall was full of police officers. At any minute, one of them would come out here. If he were seen touching her hair or touching her in any way, it would raise eyebrows. He smiled and asked, "What's on your mind, Audrey? I can see you're deep in thought."

She sighed audibly and turned to face him. "I was just thinking about you."

He smiled amusingly. He'd gotten used to hearing her say whatever was on her mind. He was certainly glad that she was thinking about him right now. From her expression, he knew there was more, but he waited for her to come out with it on her own. She would tell him without his encouragement.

She finally said, "When you first came to Rosefield as Police Chief, I wanted to get you out by any means. I sent petitions and messages to the mayor and even went to his office." Her eyes searched his, and she smiled tenderly at him. "I don't feel that way anymore."

It wasn't what he was expecting her to say, but he wasn't surprised by what she told him. He smiled sadly, remembering how she had fought him. She'd been at his throat then and hated his guts, and he didn't blame her for it. He had been given the position she'd dreamed of for years. He felt a wave of guilt come over him and he sighed wearily. He'd tried to make it right.

When she finds out what I did, will she understand, or will she be mad at me?

She put her hand on his shoulder. "Stop it, Ken!"

"Stop what?" He looked quizzically at her.

"Stop feeling guilty for my sake. I know you've been feeling this way for some time, but just as I said now, I don't feel bad anymore. As a matter of fact, I really like the new police chief."

He smiled and then he couldn't resist anymore. He tucked a stray strand of her hair behind her ears and said, "I love the way you look right now. You take my breath away."

Her eyes softened, and she placed her palm on his cheek. "I love how you love everything about me."

He kissed her palm, his pulse quickening. Since their date at her house, their usual flirting had evolved to deep-hearted confessions of their feelings for one other. Unfortunately, they'd not had time to do more than that. Their work schedules had been hectic. They'd been working hard to solve the youth center case, to plan this conference which half the Rosefield police officers attended, as well as a host of other things. Now that their schedules had calmed down a bit, he wanted to move forward with a relationship with her and see where it took them.

He gazed at her lips, and his heart raced with desire. He'd been dreaming of kissing them every day. He couldn't hold back anymore. He pulled her close with his eyes planted on her lips and leaned down to kiss her the way he had been longing to.

Just then, someone walked onto the balcony, and they reluctantly pulled away from each other. She groaned softly, and he caught the look of regret in her eyes. He smiled ruefully at her.

"Baylor, they are about to start," Nolan, one of his buddies from the MPD said. Nolan looked at him and Audrey and then added, "Everyone should go in now."

Ken nodded, and he left.

"Do you want to go on a date with me after the conference?"

The smile she gave him melted his heart. "I would love that. Where do you suggest?"

"A cozy restaurant, somewhere we can talk and," he smiled and focused on her lips, "maybe continue where we stopped." He heard footsteps approaching and said, "We'd better go in."

They went in together but sat in different parts of the room to avoid speculations about their relationship.

A man stood in front of the hall, a police and public safety instructor. He talked about new techniques for public safety. After a while, when he started repeating himself, Ken lightly drummed his fingers on the desk, feeling bored. He looked across the room, caught Audrey's eyes, and smiled discreetly at her.

She smiled back; a smile that clearly told him she couldn't wait for their date.

*****

Audrey looked up to thank the driver as he opened the car door for her. She stepped down and then smiled as she took Ken's hand. Ken had hired a chauffeured limo for their date, and she felt special. She was glad that she had decided to bring along the outfit she was wearing now -- a floral skater dress with open-toe heels. She had brought it hoping he would ask her out again, and thankfully he had.

They threaded their fingers together as they walked into a restaurant that was barely visible as it was covered with flowers. Inside, she smiled. It was dimly but pleasantly lit. The soft blue lighting and marine-inspired décor made it appear as if they were floating in water and gave off a romantic ambiance. The place was quiet, as there were only a few guests.

Ken grinned. "Do you like this place? When I lived in Boise, every time I drove past this restaurant, I always told myself I would bring a special woman here one day . . . once I found her."

Her pulse raced, and she breathed, "I love it."

"I knew you would," he said.

A host showed them to a table at the far end of the restaurant. They sat facing each other and Audrey smiled. "This is a fancy place."

The waiter came to take their orders and then she turned back to him. "I love the way you make me feel special every day."

He took her hand, kissed it and beamed at her. "I love the look in your eyes . . ." He suddenly stopped mid-sentence and looked up. "Did you hear that?"

She shook her head and then her eyes widened. "Was that a gunshot?"

They stood and went out cautiously. Neither of them had their weapons, but they were eager to get out and find out what or who was causing the loud bangs. The evening sky was alighted with sparks of multihued lights, and people stood on the road, looking up at the sky. It was probably from a wedding or some other party. It was the most beautiful fireworks display Audrey had ever seen, and she smiled widely at Ken. "It's gorgeous," she said.

Ken smiled back. "Not as gorgeous as you."

Her heart lit up like the fireworks in the sky when he cupped her face, looked into her eyes, and said, "What better time for a kiss than now."

Jolts of electricity ran through her body as he claimed her lips and kissed her passionately. She pulled him closer and returned his kiss with fervor. She trembled, relishing the feel of his lips on hers.

When they finally came up for air, her heart thudded in her chest.

He gazed at her and said softly, "I've fallen in love with you, Audrey. I love everything about you."

She smiled up at him. "And I have fallen in love with you too, Ken. Every inch of you."

He held her in his arms again and kissed her softly, filling her with a sweet sensation. They held on tightly to each other while they watched the fireworks. After a minute, Ken said, "I wish we could stay here forever."

She laughed. "Who knew a date on the street would be more romantic than in an expensive restaurant?"

He kissed her hair. "I guess we have to start heading back. We have an early day tomorrow."

"Yes, we do, but not before this. "She ran her fingers through his hair and kissed him again and again until she was sated.

*****

On the third and final day of the conference, Audrey entered the hall early. She took a seat in the front row, near the window. A few minutes later, police officers began to troop in. Ken entered, and his eyes went around the conference hall. When he saw her, he smiled before heading in the other direction to find a seat. She sighed wistfully, touched by his gesture. It was as if he wanted to be sure she was okay before he could relax and find a seat for himself. They were staying at the same hotel, but they'd both decided to keep their room numbers from each other to avoid temptation.

The conference soon started. A firearms instructor talked about new methods of police combat and marksmanship skills. After that another talked about criminal investigations. The Boise police chief then spoke about the national police budget and general police welfare for what seemed like an eternity.

The entire conference took nearly three hours. When it finally ended, Audrey remained at her seat, waiting for everyone to disperse so she and Ken could head out of the hall together. They had made plans yesterday to spend today together. First, they would have lunch at a café near the conference hall. After that, he'd promised to show her around the city he'd lived in for years. She felt giddy with excitement. I get to spend a full day with him, she thought.

When the hall was nearly empty, she looked back, saw Ken, and walked toward him.

A booming voice behind caught her off guard, and her eyes widened in surprise. She turned around, already knowing who it was.

"Chief Baylor and Assistant Chief Gardner! I'm glad I caught you two at the same time. I have something important to tell both of you."

"Mayor Stanley!" Audrey exclaimed. "What are you doing here?" He was standing beside the Miami police chief, looking from her to Ken.

Audrey's heart drummed as she walked toward both men. She glanced discreetly at Ken who was right beside her. She wanted to ask if he knew what the mayor was doing here, but she couldn't. Not with the mayor so near.

Maybe the mayor found out about our relationship, she thought guiltily. There was a rule about not dating fellow officers in the Rosefield Police Department, but surely no one took it seriously, she thought. She'd never heard anyone get into trouble for breaking that rule.

That's because apart from you, the Rosefield Police Department is populated with only male officers. She thinned her lips. As the only female officer, she had never been attracted to any of the men, until now. Were she and Ken in trouble?

She shook off the thought as she reached both men. She was being silly. Even if the mayor knew they were dating, it wasn't like he could fire them because of that. And he definitely couldn't stop them from seeing each other.

She squared her shoulders. Being in a relationship had not affected her and Ken's jobs or productivity in any way, nor would it ever. Besides, that didn't explain why the mayor was here.

Ken shook hands with his former boss, and then the mayor cleared his throat. He looked between her and Ken and said, "Well you both look pretty friendly." He smiled. "You are probably wondering why I'm here at your police conference in Boise." He faced Audrey. "After the case of the burglary was solved, I called Chief Baylor to my office to thank him, but he clearly made me know that you were the one who actually discovered the identity of the burglars. Amongst other things, he told me what a fine officer you were, which I already know."

Audrey glanced at Ken and faced the Mayor again.

He turned to Ken. "I know you love your former job and weren't initially keen on coming to Rose-field. I came here to make everything right. I just finished talking with Police Chief Renner here, and we came to the same conclusion."

Audrey bit her lips. Please, don't say what I think you are about to say.

"I'm going to honor both your requests. I'm appointing you chief of police, Gardner. And you, Baylor, can go back to your old job." He looked at Audrey and Ken with a triumphant expression, as though he had just announced that they'd won the lottery.

Audrey pressed her lips together, trying to feign off the dizziness coming over her. Her heart cried out as she turned to look at Ken. Some months ago, she would have been thrilled, but now, all she felt was terrified. She didn't want Ken to move away from Rosefield. He was the only man she'd ever loved, and she wanted him close.

She couldn't bring herself to look at Ken.

Mayor Stanley frowned. "Did you both hear what I just said now? I've just given you both what you wanted. Why then are you looking at me as if I just fired you?"

Ken spoke. "Thank you so much, Mayor. I am excited, and I know Assistant Chief Gardner is too.

She just needs to let the news sink in."

Audrey's eyes widened in shock. "What are you saying, Ken?" she blurted out as she stared at him. She turned to the mayor. "I don't want him to leave anymore! I'm good with being the assistant chief of police for now."

The mayor shook his head. "I'm sorry. The paperwork has already started, and Chief Baylor has already stated his desire to return to his old job here." He turned to Ken. "Am I right, or do you want to remain in Rosefield?"

"No, I want to come back here."

Audrey stared at him in horror, her head pounding.

"Well, it's decided then," The Miami police chief said. "Congratulations Chief Gardner, and it will be great to have you back, Ken."

Mayor Stanley and Police Chief Renner left together, and Ken faced her.

"How could you, Ken! You told the mayor you wanted to go back to Miami, and you didn't tell me?"

"I knew you would resist, Audrey."

Tears filled her eyes, and her heart ached. "Yesterday, you told me you loved me. Now, you can't wait to leave?"

He gazed into her eyes. "I do love you, Audrey. I love you with everything in me. That's why I am leaving. I know how much you've wanted to be police chief; how much work you put into fulfilling that dream. I just couldn't go on living with myself, knowing I took that away from you. I had to let the mayor know you deserved to be police chief and not me. There is only one thing I want more than to stay in Rosefield with you."

"She sniffed as the tears fell down her face. "What?"

"I want you to have your dreams."

Audrey shook her head. "I don't want to live without you."

He held her hand. "You are not going to."

"But we won't get to see each other again."

"We will call and text each other every day. Besides, it'll be great, you'll see. You can come and visit me at any time. And when I'm able to get away, I'll come to Rosefield, and we will spend whole days together."

Audrey felt drained. She bowed her head, her emotions mixed up. On the one hand, she was moved by his selfless act, but on the other, she was mad at him for it. At last, she raised her eyes to his and said, "You are the kindest person I know. I'm really grateful for what you've done for me . . . it's just that I don't want to be apart from you."

He took her in his arms. "We won't be apart. You'll be in my heart, and I will be in yours."

She smiled sadly, and he wiped the tears from her face with his thumb. "We still have a week to spend together," he said. "Let's make it the best week of our lives."

NINE

Trisha smoothed down her red dress and opened the door to let her husband in for their date. As usual, he looked handsome, dressed in a plaid shirt and black denim. He'd suggested this date. "So we can try to fix our relationship," he had said. Since Audrey wasn't in town and she didn't feel up to going out with him yet, she had decided to invite him to the house. Today, she would let him know if she was coming back to him or filing for a divorce.

"Take a seat, Stan. I'll be right back."

He looked around the living room. "Where is your sister?"

"She is in Boise for a police conference, but she will be back tomorrow."

"I'm glad she's not around, Trish. She doesn't like me, and she's been against our relationship from the beginning. I know she's hoping we get divorced."

Trisha shook her head. "It's not that she doesn't like you. She just doesn't trust that you are good for me, and you have managed to prove her right time after time."

"I told you I have changed, Trish. I'm not that guy anymore."

She shrugged and went to the kitchen to serve their food on a plate. She had already decided on what to do about their marriage. This dinner date was only a formality.

She dished out the food onto ornate oval plates that had been her mom's pride and joy. She smiled to herself as she remembered her mother scolding her for breaking one of them. After placing the plates of food on a silver tray, she carried it to the dining table.

"The food is ready!" she called to him.

As they ate, they talked about the early days of their relationship, and Stan was quick to remind her how they had loved each other and stood through every test.

"Remember when your parents died, how we clung to each other. You made it through . . . we both did because our love was so strong. I still love you so much, Trish. I don't want our marriage to end."

She looked at him and said, "Stan, you don't have to say all these things to make me feel good. I've already decided to come back home to you."

He gave a jubilant shout, stood and lifted her into a tight hug. "Thank you, Trish. Thank you."

She smiled at him, and then they talked about their unborn baby. They dreamt about baby names, and she howled with laughter as he suggested the silliest names she'd ever heard.

She shook her head. "I'm not naming my baby boy Wednesday just because you think that's the day he'll be born! Besides, I think it's a girl."

He gazed tenderly at her. "Whatever the sex of our baby is, I know we'll love him or her very much."

His phone began to vibrate, and he ignored it.

She said to him, "Won't you answer that?"

"No, there is no need."

She shrugged, and they went back to their conversation. A minute later, his phone started to vibrate again.

"Just answer it, Stan."

He glanced at it and then turned it on its face, but not before she saw the small guilt that passed through his eyes. She shut her eyes as her heart sank. He's still cheating.

"Who is that?" She asked angrily, pointing to the phone.

He picked it up from the table. "It's no one important."

She narrowed her eyes and grabbed the phone from him. Quickly, she checked his call log and found the call was from Carla. She smiled coldly. "You are still seeing that girl."

"It's nothing. She just wanted . . ."

"Don't lie to me!" She scrolled down the screen and found recent calls from him to the girl. "You're a compulsive liar!" She glared at him, fire blazing in her eyes. "I want you to leave. Right now!"

"Please, Trish! It's not what it looks like."

"Go now!" she screamed. "Now!"

He stood and scrambled out the door.

She put her head down on the table and bawled.

*****

After his classes, Bryan carried his textbooks and went out of the hall with the other final year students. He walked back to the chapel and went into his tiny office. He sat at his desk, his emotions roiled, and as usual, his mind raced with troubling thoughts about Sienna.

He shut his eyes and sighed wearily as her face appeared in his mind. He saw her eyes, sad and full of fear, the way they had been the last time he'd seen her. Almost every night, her face filled his dreams. Always, her eyes looked haunted. She opened her mouth to scream, but no sound ever came out.

For the past two months, he'd been trying to find her. A girl he asked about her near the girl's dorm had said she saw Sienna leave with her suitcase, but didn't know where she'd gone.

He'd continuously prayed, asking the Lord to protect her, but still, he feared for her safety. It wasn't like he could go to the police and say she was a missing person. She was an adult who had left the college of her own volition. He didn't know if she was in physical or spiritual danger, but he knew that what he felt was real. She was in some type of trouble, and he didn't know how to help her. And that alone left him heartbroken. In spite of all he'd done to avoid falling for her, he had fallen hard, just in the short time he'd known her. Her face would continue to haunt him for a long, long time.

Lord, why did you bring her my way if you weren't going to keep her in my life?

He put his hand on his head and groaned. If only he'd found a way to get the solution she needed across her path before she'd suddenly left the school. He stood again, feeling restless, and went out of his office. He stepped out of the chapel and began to walk toward the school gate. Students milled around the hallway and the grassy path leading to the front gate.

He reached the gate, leaned on it and took a deep breath. Lord, where is she?

He groaned and then started to turn.

Look to your left.

He blinked. That was the Lord's voice. He faced the gate fully again and turned his head to his left. "What is it, Lord?" he asked.

The salon across the road.

There was a shabby building across from where he was standing with the words "Royal Palace Salon" emblazoned on the top of it in gaudy gold letters. He'd seen it many times before, but it had never registered much in his mind, and he'd certainly never entered the building. He crossed the road, curious as to why the Lord was sending him there. He didn't often hear the Lord's voice audibly, but when he did, he hardly ever questioned it. He knew enough to simply obey. He'd had lots of strange and wonderful things happen when he did.

He reached the building and entered. There were rows of old padded red chairs facing a long mirror stretching from one end of the salon to the other. Two middle-aged women sat having their hair done by two female spiky-haired hairdressers. They all turned as he entered.

One of the hairdressers, who looked slightly orange, said, "Hi handsome, what can we do you for?"

He smiled, not knowing what to say, while he prayed fervently in his heart. Lord, why am I here. He didn't hear anything, so he said the only thing that came to his mind, "Do you cut men's hair here?"

His mind rebelled. Are you actually going to let

one of these girls cut your hair?

He brushed away his concerns and waited.

The girl didn't say anything. She craned her neck to the side and called out, "Dan, someone is here for a cut!"

A thin boy who looked about seventeen or eighteen came out. He didn't speak to Bryan, only indicated for him to follow. Bryan followed him as he opened a door and stepped into another room. An old swivel chair, a single mirror and a wooden desk stacked with magazines were the only furniture in the room.

"You can sit here," the boy said.

Bryan sat on the swivel chair and decided the Lord had brought him here to share the gospel with the boy.

The boy put a cape around him and went to get the clippers. He glanced at himself in the mirror, and then something caught his attention. A single magazine was lying beside the stack, and on the cover was a familiar-looking face. He couldn't see it properly, but the face looked like someone he knew.

The boy came back to start cutting his hair, but he turned around. "Can you excuse me?" he asked and stood up. He went and picked up the magazine, and then took a sharp breath.

It couldn't be.

The face on the front cover looked like Sienna's, but it couldn't be her. The girl in this picture was scantily clad in black lacy lingerie that left little to the imagination. His face grew hot.

He looked closely at the picture, ignoring the boy who was smirking at him. Unless Sienna had a twin sister, this was definitely her.

He checked the date and found it was published yesterday. Which meant it might be a new photograph. Lord, please let it be someone else and not Sienna.

But he already knew it was her, and it was a recent photo. This was why the Lord had brought him here. He flipped the magazine to the back, looking for some kind of contact number or address. He found not only an address for the magazine but a phone number also. He asked the teenage boy for a pen and paper, and when the boy brought him what he asked for, he wrote down the address and phone number. After that, he let the boy cut his hair and then strode out of the salon.

He knew now why the Lord had brought him here and what the Lord wanted him to do. He wanted him to bring his prodigal child home.

*****

Sienna pushed her front door open and flung aside her duffel bag. She'd just returned from the weekend getaway with Alessio, and she felt like throwing up.

She collapsed to the floor as her body began to tremble. Her chest felt like an elephant was sitting on it. She took a deep breath, but there was no relief.

The stench of the debauchery she'd seen and experienced at the getaway clung to her. Self-loathing wrapped a firm hand around her throat, strangling her. She writhed on the floor as she felt a dark presence clasp her wrist. She cried out as she felt herself being literarily dragged into the flames of hell. Her chest felt like it was about to explode. Dread, unlike anything she'd ever known, overwhelmed her. It was as if the fiery wrath of God was being poured down on her.

She cried out again, but there was no relief. Instead, scenes from the weekend getaway played through her mind, taunting her. She had shut off her conscience and descended into moral degradation, convincing herself that her career was at stake. But her conscience couldn't be shut off for too long. The sight of a man at the airport holding a Bible and some gospel tracts had begun her unraveling. Now, she felt like she was going to die.

She took deep breaths, but her chest still felt constricted. "Help," she cried weakly. An overwhelming sadness settled on her, and she sobbed. "I can't keep living like this." She was tired of the constant dread, the panic, the hopelessness; all of it. She got up and staggered to the bathroom. "Please forgive me, God," she said.

She opened the cabinet where she put all her medicine. She grabbed a bottle of pills without reading the label and emptied it into her palms. Taking a deep breath, she swallowed it all. With tears trailing down her cheeks, she said again, "Forgive me."

Her vision began to blur and a horrible pain stabbed at her stomach. She grabbed hold of the sink as she began to sway and then collapsed on the floor, writhing in pain. She knew she was going to die and cried out one more time, "Please forgive me," before everything went black.

*****

Bryan jumped into a yellow cab at JFK airport, his heart beating fast in his chest. For some reason, intense fear had gripped him immediately as he landed at the airport. He knew he had to get to Sienna as fast as possible.

"Lord, please protect her," he prayed.

He had already given the cab driver a written address of the Paragon magazine. As the man wove through traffic on the way there, Bryan kept on praying, asking for protection for Sienna. He could sense it now more than ever that she was in trouble. In between prayers, he craned his neck out the window, wishing the taxi could move faster.

They came to a traffic jam, and for the first time in years, he felt like swearing. He held his head in his hand and whispered harshly, "Lord, please help us get out of this!"

He tapped his feet continuously while looking outside his window.

If only I could get out of this car and run to the magazine's office. But he knew that would be unwise, so he kept praying.

Fifteen minutes later, the cars in front of them started to move, and he breathed a sigh of relief.

The driver soon stopped in front of a large building, and Bryan quickly paid his fare. He got out, entered the building, and rode the elevator to the thirteenth floor. He stepped out of the elevator and immediately rushed to the reception area where a young blond woman was standing. The words, 'Paragon Magazine' were engraved on a silver panel above her head. People hurried back and forth, oblivious to the terror in his heart.

"Please, I'm looking for a model named Sienna Gardner. She was on the cover page of your latest edition. She's a friend of mine, and I think she's in trouble."

The receptionist stared at him like he was vag-abond who had wandered off the streets into her sanctuary.

He pleaded, "Please, do you know where I can find her?"

She shook her head. "Models don't work here. You need to contact the agency she's signed to if you don't know where she lives."

"Isn't there a way you can find out what agency she works . . ."

"Signed to!"

"Yes, signed to. Please. I need to know that she's fine."

"I'm sorry, I can't help you. I'm not allowed to disclose that info to just anyone."

He wanted to scream at her. Hadn't she heard what he just said? One of their models was proba-bly in trouble, and she didn't even care. He opened his mouth to plead with her again, but she held up her hand. "I have a call."

He huffed away and exhaled. "Lord, please help me." He glanced around, wondering who he could approach that would actually be able to help him. And then someone tapped his shoulder. He turned around.

A man in a tight blue suit said, "Young man, are you looking for Sienna?"

"Yes, do you know where she lives?"

The man looked at him as if trying to figure out what sort of relationship he could possibly have with Sienna. He finally asked, "Are you, family or friend?"

"Umm . . . I'm a friend from her Bible college."

"Oh, yes, the religious school she ran away to months ago." He said grimly, "I'm Zack, her agent. Sienna was taken to the hospital this morning. She was found by one of the maids at the apartment building she lives in. I think she tried to kill herself."

Bryan's heart stopped beating. Lord, no!

He felt guilty. If only he had been more proactive about helping her maybe she wouldn't have tried to take her own life. He shut his eyes as his vision began to blur.

"Are you okay?" Zack placed his hand on his shoulder.

He nodded and shook the dizziness off. "Can you give me the address of the hospital she was taken to?"

"Sure, I plan on going to see her this evening, but I'm glad someone is here for her now. I've been hoping a family member or friend would show up, but I didn't have anyone's contact." He took a pen and paper from the reception desk and quickly wrote down the hospital address. He looked relieved as he said, "Please take care of her."

After thanking the man, Bryan again took the lift to the bottom floor and raced out of the building. He quickly found a taxi to take him to the hospital.

He raced into the large Benedict Memorial Hospital with his heart in his mouth. Walking up to the reception desk, he said to the nurse standing there, "I'm looking for a patient named Sienna . . . Sienna Gardner." He quickly added.

The nurse asked, "What's your name?"

He told her.

She gave him a visitor's form.

He filled the form quickly while her fingers flew over her computer's keyboard. Taking deep breaths to try to calm down, he prayed silently, Lord, please let her be okay.

She looked up at him. "She's in room four-oh-four."

He sighed in relief. At least she was still alive.

He took the stairs and found the room quickly. Before he entered, he whispered a quick prayer again. He opened the door and saw her lying in the bed. Her eyes were closed, and her blond hair was splayed out on the pillow. He walked up to the bed, and as he looked down at her, his heart flooded with regret. She looked so pale.

If only I had found a way to help you sooner.

He resisted the urge to run his fingers through her hair. Instead, he gently laid his hand on her forehead. He blinked, totally caught off guard when she opened her eyes.

Her eyes grew big as she stared at him. She looked astonished. "Bryan," she said weakly and then tried to sit up.

He touched her shoulder. "Don't. Try to rest."

"How come you are here?" she asked hoarsely.

He smiled down at her. "The Lord told me how to find you."

She moaned, and then turned her face away.

He kept his hand on her forehead and whispered a prayer for her. The doctor came in just as he ended the prayer.

"Hello," the bearded doctor said. "Are you her husband or boyfriend?"

His pulse raced, and he said, "Umm . . . no . . . I'm

only a friend."

The man said to her, "I can discharge you this evening if you have someone to take you home. You need plenty of bed rest and lots of healthy food to regain your strength. Do you have anyone who can get you home?"

She shook her head, but Bryan spoke up. "I'll get her home."

"And does she have anyone to take care of her when she gets home?"

Bryan looked at Sienna. She bit her lips and shook her head.

"Then I'll take care of her," Bryan said to the doctor.

The doctor looked at him. "First of all, she needs to be watched constantly, so she doesn't try to hurt herself again. For now, I'll suggest she doesn't get up much for a few days. Because of the number of pills she swallowed and how much we had to pump out, she's a little weak now. She'll need someone to get her food, maybe help her bathe and change into clean clothes. Can you do that?"

Bryan's eyes widened with panic. "I'll have to bathe her?" he asked in apprehension. He didn't mind caring for her at all. That was why he was here. But he wasn't sure how he was going to handle seeing her undressed while bathing and changing her. Lord, please help me!

Sienna shook her head. "No," she said weakly. "My sister Audrey, she'll come and care for me. Bryan, please call her. Also call my other sister, Trish, and tell her I'm at the hospital, but that I'm fine now."

The doctor smiled. "When you have that sorted

out, we can discharge her." He left after he gave a few other instructions.

Sienna turned to Bryan. "Can you call them now?"

He nodded. "I'll call them right away." He brought out his phone from his pocket.

"Call Audrey first," she said. She sat up slightly and called out the numbers for him.

He dialed the numbers and waited as the phone rang. He could feel Sienna's eyes on him, and he looked up at her. He smiled, but she didn't smile back. She looked at him the way she did when she first saw him—with fear and anxiety.

Why is she scared of me again?

Troubled, he turned away. A confident-sounding female voice came on the line, "Hello, who is this?"

"Is this Audrey?"

"Yes, who is this?"

My name is Bryan. I'm a friend of your sister, Sienna." He considered telling her that Sienna had tried to kill herself but changed his mind. It wasn't his place. Instead, he said, "She overdosed on some pills and had to be rushed to the hospital."

The woman cried out, but he immediately added, "She's fine now. She just needs someone to take care of her."

"Can I speak to her?" the woman asked.

He looked back at Sienna. She was lying on her back again, looking exhausted. "She wants to speak with you," he said.

Sienna shook her head. "I'm not up to speaking on the phone right now."

He told the woman Sienna was resting. After the woman told him she would be coming immediately, he ended the call and called her other sister. He told her basically the same thing, and she also promised she was coming down soon.

He walked back to the bed and tentatively touched Sienna's hand. Her eyes were shut now. "I'll go sign the discharge papers, and then I'll come right back to take you home," he said.

She nodded without opening her eyes.

As he went away to make the arrangements for her discharge, he lifted up a prayer of thanksgiving to God for saving her life.

TEN

Audrey's heart pounded with fear as she looked at Ken.

"What is it, Audrey?" he asked and leaned forward on his desk.

"It's my sister, Sienna. She overdosed on something and had to be rushed to the hospital."

Ken gasped. "Oh no! I'm so sorry." he replied, looking so concerned and worried.

Audrey removed her police hat and shut her eyes. The man who called hadn't said anything about it, but she had a suspicion that the overdose had been intentional. That broke her heart.

If only I had trusted my intuition. She had known something was off about Sienna after she went back to New York, but she'd let Trisha convince her that their baby sister was fine.

Audrey stood up. She'd come into Ken's office to tell him about her plans for their special date this evening. They had only five days left together, and they had planned to go on dates every one of those days, even though they were mostly working days.

He had planned yesterday's date and had taken her to Blue Water, the only proper restaurant in town. Today's date had been hers to plan. She'd wanted it to be special, an unforgettable experience for both of them before they said their goodbyes. Now it would not be possible. Worse—he might be gone by the time she came back from New York. She felt like crying, but that would do no good. She had no choice but to go to Sienna now.

She told Ken.

"Go . . . go. It's what you have to do."

She bent and kissed him. "I'll try my best to come back before you leave." She couldn't hold back her tears anymore. Tears fell down her cheeks, tears for him and for Sienna. "If I'm not back by the time you leave, know that I love you dearly and I'll miss you terribly."

He stood and gathered her in his arms. "It's okay, baby. We'll talk on the phone and Skype as well. It'll be fine. Our love will only grow stronger. You'll see." He kissed her and then pulled away.

She grabbed her knapsack from her office and hurried out of the station.

Trish was out when she got home, probably at the hospital for her prenatal appointment. She packed a few clothes, unsure of how long she would spend in New York. If she needed more, she would buy cheap new clothes. Sienna's would be too small for her.

On the flight to New York, she looked out the window at the fluffy white clouds and prayed that God would protect Sienna. After praying, she thought about Trisha and wondered if she'd been informed. Worry had been her constant companion since she got the phone call about Sienna. It had not crossed her mind to call Trish and find out if she knew.

She slept on and off throughout the trip. It was about eight o'clock in the evening when the plane landed. She immediately called Sienna's phone. It rang and rang, but Sienna didn't answer.

Sienna, come on sis. Pick up!

It stopped ringing, and she called again. This time the phone clicked and a male voice said, "Hello?"

The same voice. "Hi, is Sienna there? Can I speak to her?"

"She's asleep right now."

Audrey frowned. "Okay, if she wakes up, let her know I'll be at her apartment in about an hour."

After the call ended, she took a taxi from the airport and gave the driver the address to Sienna's apartment in SoHo. She'd been to Sienna's old apartment in East Village but not this new one. Siena had only just given her the address a few weeks ago. She'd dictated the address over the phone and then said, "For when you are ready to come to New York."

As the cab driver wove in and out of traffic, Audrey tried to calm her nerves. He finally stopped in front of a white brick and steel apartment building.

She entered the building, took a deep breath and prayed again. She walked into a glass elevator, rode it to the seventh floor and stepped out into an interlocking black and white tiled hallway. She quickly strode through a row of flats until she found Sienna's apartment number.

She rang the bell, and the door opened almost

immediately. A guy in his mid-twenties, with messy blond hair and boyish good looks, stared at her.

"You must be Audrey," he said.

"Yes."

He opened the door wide, and she entered. She followed him up a spiral staircase, and he pointed at a door at the end of the short-carpeted hallway. "That's her room."

She walked to the door, opened it and entered the spacious room. Sienna was on the bed with her back turned. Audrey hurried to her and sat on the bed. "Sienna, are you okay?"

Sienna turned her head, and Audrey hugged her tightly.

"I'm okay," Sienna answered. She pulled back and smiled at Audrey. "I'm so glad you are here. The doctor said I need a few days of bed rest and plenty of food. So sorry I made you leave your job. I would have hired someone, but I just wanted my older sister." She started to cry.

Audrey hugged her again and patted her hair. Her emotions roiled as she held on to Sienna. After a minute, she drew back and studied Sienna's face. "What really happened? How did you overdose on a drug?"

Sienna shook her head and started to sob.

Audrey felt the tears swimming in her own eyes. Seeing her little sister like this and not knowing how she could help her was killing her. With her fingers, she wiped away Sienna's tears. Looking her in the eyes, she asked softly, "Sienna, did you try to kill yourself?"

Sienna didn't answer.

Audrey felt like breaking down, but instead, she

exhaled. She had to be strong for her sister. But most of all, she needed to understand why Sienna had tried to take her own life. "What's happening to you? Please help me understand." She couldn't hold it back anymore, and the tears flowed down her cheeks.

Sienna sighed softly. "I've already told you what I understand." She muttered, "Except for Bryan, no one really gets what I'm going through . . . not even me."

"Who is Bryan?" In spite of herself, Audrey smiled through her tears and said, "Is he the hottie downstairs?"

Sienna laughed weakly. "Yes, he's the one." She grew serious again. "It's been terrible, Audrey, but I don't want to talk about it anymore. Tell me about you." She smiled. "Trish told me you have a cute boyfriend now."

Audrey sighed. Sienna was avoiding the real issue. They needed to talk about it. She searched Sienna's eyes and saw how world-weary they looked.

Maybe Sienna didn't need to talk about it right now. Perhaps, what she needed now was some cheering up and not a re-immersion into the darkness that had caused her to attempt suicide. Even though there was nothing more Audrey wanted than to get to the bottom of this, she would humor her sister.

She put on a smile. "There is someone. I hope you can meet him soon. He's going back to Miami in a few days, though, and I don't know when I'll see him again." She grew somber as she thought about Ken's departure to Florida. And then she brushed the feeling away and focused once more on cheering Sienna up. She took Sienna's hand, "I'm glad I'm here now to take care of you."

She jerked her head up when she heard Trisha's voice.

Sienna smiled.

"Trish is here!" Audrey grinned. "Good, it'll take the two of us to get you out of this funk."

Trisha rushed into the room with a strangled cry. She reached out and pulled Sienna into a tight hug. After a long moment, she pulled back and said through her tears, "Oh Sienna, I'm so glad you are fine. I was told you OD'd on some pills. How did that happen?"

Sienna looked away.

Audrey pressed her lips together and then to deflect Trisha's questions, she said, "You weren't home when I came back and packed my things to come here. I'm assuming you went for your prenatal appointment. I hope the baby is doing well."

Sienna sat up. "Baby?" She moaned. "You didn't tell me you were pregnant!" She reached out and caressed Trisha's bump, her eyes wide with excitement.

"You've not exactly been the easiest person to reach," Trisha said. "Besides, I thought Audrey would have told you by now."

Audrey shook her head. "Nuh uh! You told me you were going to tell her yourself, remember?"

Trisha sat beside Audrey on the bed. "I'm so sorry, Sienna. After I told Audrey about the baby, I wanted to tell you too." She took Sienna's hand. "Apart from the fact that I couldn't reach you the first two times I tried, a lot has been going on with me." She bit her lips and then shook her head.

"Enough about me, though. Now that you know you're going to be an aunt soon, please take care of yourself. My baby will need her model-aunty to teach her about fashion."

Audrey gasped. "It's a girl?"

"Yes, I just found out. Unfortunately, I'll only be able to spend a few days here. I have to get back for my prenatal appointments. I'm really glad I came, though."

Audrey said, "I'll only be able to stay for a few days also." She told them about her appointment as chief of police. Trisha squealed with joy while Sienna told her she was truly happy for her.

Audrey took Sienna's hand. "But I'll make sure you're totally able to start taking care of yourself before I leave."

Trisha smiled at Sienna. "Who brought you home from the hospital?"

"Bryan."

"You mean the hottie downstairs?"

Audrey burst out laughing. "That's what I just said to her now."

"He is super cute," Trisha said. "Is he your boy-friend, Sienna?"

Sienna mumbled. "He's just a friend."

"I can see from your eyes that you like him," Audrey said. "Maybe you should tell him that you want to be more than 'just friends'." She said making air quotes.

Sienna shook her head vigorously. "No, no!"

Trisha giggled and said, "If you don't scoop him up right now, I will!"

For a few seconds, Sienna stared at Trisha with huge round eyes, and then she burst out laughing.

Audrey and Trisha stared at her and then they both joined in.

Audrey heaved a sigh of relief. Seeing Sienna laughing now felt so good. This was exactly what their baby sister needed from them—lots of humor and laughter. They had to do more of this, she and Trisha. That would be the goal for the next few days before they both returned to Rosefield.

*****

Bryan sat in Sienna's elegantly furnished living room, flipping through the TV channels. From time to time bits of the sisters' conversation drifted to him. He looked at the clock on the wall again. It was almost eleven o'clock at night. He'd been ready to leave for a motel for two hours now, but he couldn't without telling Sienna, and he didn't want to intrude on the ladies' conversation.

He continued waiting for another thirty minutes, and then he stood. He had to get to a motel now. He hadn't even decided on one yet.

He started to make his way toward the stairs but backed up when they exited the room. He was surprised to see the older sisters holding Sienna by both arms and leading her down the stairs. The doctor had given clear instructions that she remain on bed rest for some days.

They reached the bottom of the stairs and began to lead her out to the porch. He wanted to tell them what the doctor had said, but he changed his mind. She was with people who cared for her, and they would make sure she was just fine.

He followed them to the porch. The fluorescent

light was on, illuminating the place. They set her down on a wicker sofa with white cushions and sat beside her.

He said to Sienna, "I'll have to leave now, but I'll be back tomorrow. I haven't even booked a motel to stay in yet. Is there any affordable one near here?"

She gave him a look that screamed what she thought about his question —that he'd completely lost his mind.

Her older sister, Trisha, chuckled. "Why would you want to go and stay in some motel when you can stay here?" She grinned up at him. "I know we" she pointed at herself and their oldest, Audrey, "sorta look like cougars, but I promise you that we are harmless."

He found her comment hilarious and roared with laughter.

Audrey shook her head. "Stop it, Trisha! Maybe he feels uncomfortable in a house full of women. Sienna said he was a chaplain."

He smiled, partly embarrassed and partly amused. The thought of staying with them didn't make him uncomfortable. It was the thought of staying with their sister that did.

Sienna said faintly, "Please, Bryan, you don't have to go. Stay here. Besides, it's late."

"Don't worry," Trisha gave him a teasing smile. "We will be gone before you know it. Both of you can then have the house all to yourselves."

His heart jumped into his mouth. That was exactly what he was afraid of. He didn't want to be all alone with her. He trusted God to keep him on the straight and narrow, but he just didn't need that sort of temptation at all. He started to shake his head, but Sienna pleaded, "Please stay."

Trisha added, "Audrey and I will stay with Sienna in her room. You can take the other room."

He shut his eyes, exhaled and then nodded. "Okay, I will."

He sat on the chaise lounge and half listened as Audrey talked about her boyfriend, a guy named Ken who was the police chief of Rosefield. After that, Trisha spoke about her plans for her unborn child. Bryan mostly spent the time gazing between the striking night Manhattan skyline and Sienna. Under the bright fluorescent lamp, she looked like an angel with her light blond hair and delicate features.

Trisha soon stood up. She placed her hand on her stomach and yawned. "I'm tired. I have to go in."

Audrey also stood. "I'll go start dinner."

"It's past mid-night, Audrey," Sienna said.

"I know it's late, but we can't go to bed on an empty stomach. At least I can't."

When they left, Bryan looked at Sienna. She was staring into the distance, lost in her thoughts. He wondered if it was the right time to speak his mind. After a few minutes, he decided to and asked, "What happened Sienna? Why did you try to take your life? Can you tell me?"

She didn't look at him. She just shrugged and said, "I can't."

He sighed softly. "Well, that's okay. You can tell me whenever you are ready."

"I don't think I'm ever going to tell you."

He shut his eyes, feeling a mixture of misery and frustration. Lord, how can I help her if she doesn't tell me what happened?

He exhaled in an attempt to put his emotions in check. Staring again at the night sky speckled with bright twinkling stars and a half moon, he said, "New York's skyline is gorgeous, but nothing compares to the breathtaking beauty of God's natural creation. And they speak of His love and grace."

"I don't know about that!" she said tartly. He blinked in surprise and turned to look at her just as she yawned. "I think I will go inside now," she said and stood up. She reached the sliding glass door and then turned around. "Bryan?"

"Yes, Sienna?"

"Thank you for coming to help me today."

He smiled and said softly, "As I said before, God told me to come here and help you." The Spirit whispered to him, and he added, "He wants you to know that He loves you very much."

She turned around and went into the house.

He remained in the porch, looking at the stars while still trying to calm his raging emotions. The more time he spent with her, the deeper he fell for her. She was irresistible, but she was also very troubled. The last thing she needed now was a romantic relationship.

Half an hour later he went back into the house. Audrey was placing plates of delicious-looking lasagna on the dining table.

"This looks and smells so good," he said, his mouth watering. He sat at the table and ate with Audrey and Trisha. Sienna ate on the sofa so she could stretch out her legs.

After dinner, Trisha said to him, "So, Bryan, tell me, what do you do as a chaplain? Do you give advice, because I need some right now?"

"Sometimes I do," he said.

"Okay. So, I've been wondering if I should file for a divorce from my husband. I still love him, and I know God said He hates divorce, but I am tired of his ways."

He wanted to tell her that it depended on the specific situation, but Audrey spoke first.

"You know what the right thing to do is," Audrey said. "I'm glad you are considering it, though."

Trisha laughed harshly and then began to tell Audrey about finding her husband's mistress's message on his phone. "I didn't want to tell you about this latest one, Audrey," Trisha said. "I was too ashamed to."

Bryan listened for a while, wondering why their lives sounded so much like a script from a soap opera. He looked over at Sienna who had now curled up on the sofa with her eyes closed. What the sisters were talking about seemed like a private discussion. He excused himself, got up with his food and went to sit next to Sienna.

"Are you okay?" he asked her.

She didn't answer.

He took a deep breath and said, "I'm praying for you, Sienna."

She opened her eyes, gave him a half smile and then stood. "I need to go to bed," she said, stretching.

He watched her as she left, his heart aching for her.

*****

Sienna jerked up, her heart racing and her body trembling. Her bed was covered in sweat in spite of the air-conditioning. She could hear Audrey and Trisha's soft snoring from the other end of the room. She threw off her duvet and hurried out of her room to find Bryan, panic spurring her on.

She'd just had another terrifying nightmare—that she'd been thrown into a horrible flaming hell and monsters surrounded her. It had seemed so real that even now she felt as if those ugly beasts were chasing after her.

A loud voice mocked her as she hastened down the stairs, You deserve to go to hellfire for your sins. And she knew she did. But she had to find Bryan. He was the only one who could help her now. He always talked about God's love and grace, and he heard God's voice clearly. Maybe God would listen to him on her behalf and have mercy upon her—if it wasn't already too late for her.

She reached the bottom of the stairs and hurried on to the guest room. The depression and despair that had caused her to swallow a bottle of pills were taking hold of her again. The doctor had told her to see a shrink to help her deal with her anxiety, but she wasn't sure she would survive this night.

She pushed open the guest room door and saw a form spring out of the bed. She turned on the light, and Bryan's eyes widened. He was in his boxers, and so she understood why he looked embarrassed. However, she was too scared to care. "I need your help, Bryan."

His expression turned to one of concern, and he said, "Okay. Can you give me a minute to put something on?"

"Okay," she whimpered. She quickly exited his room, but just halfway. She pressed her face against the door and held the handle tight, her heart racing in fear."

He came out a minute later dressed in the green T-shirt and jeans he was wearing earlier. He led her to the sofa. "What happened?"

She sat close beside him, drawing comfort from his calm masculine presence. "I had a terrible nightmare but, I don't even know if it was just that. It seemed so real." She couldn't hold it in anymore and told him about everything. The meeting with the watchers at the Bible College, how she fled the school since God had turned his back on her and how she'd decided to live it up. She felt incredible shame as confessed about going home with the guy at the club, and most of all about the weekend with Alessio. When she finished, she bowed her head and sobbed.

He is going to push me away now and tell me I am disgusting for doing all those things. And I'll deserve it. She felt completely broken.

He placed a hand on her shoulder and then he wrapped her in his arms. She looked up at him in shock. There was no judgment on his face. She wept even louder, overcome by the love and acceptance she saw in his eyes. "Aren't you repulsed by me? Because of the terrible things I have done?"

He rubbed her back soothingly and then held her and looked into her eyes. "Sienna, when you were trying your best to be good and please God, you still felt unclean, didn't you?"

She studied his face, wondering where he was going. And then she nodded.

"Your nightmares, panic attacks, and feeling of condemnation did not start because you did these things you just confessed. Remember what I told you in school? About scrupulosity or religious OCD?"

She nodded.

"I looked it up and wanted to tell you about it the day you left school. It's a debilitating disorder characterized by moral obsession and pathological guilt."

He began to tell her all he knew about it and how it had even affected some of the early church fathers like Martin Luther.

That surprised her. The more he talked, the more it all made sense. When he told her that it wasn't from God, she let out a sigh of relief.

"The solution is not trying to please God with more and more religious rituals like you did in Bible school, or running away from God just like you've done lately. The only solution is to believe in God's perfect, unconditional love for you. God's word says that perfect love casts out all fear! That is what will take away all these fears and give you total peace."

She wept as she listened to him, her heart growing lighter and lighter. The more he talked about how much God loved her, the more at peace she felt until finally, a supernatural peace settled over her. For the first time in more than a year, she felt no trace of anxiety or fear.

He took her hand. "Never forget he loves you and that you are his no matter what your mind tells you."

She nodded and smiled. "Thank you, Bryan!" Tears filled her eyes; tears of gratitude to God, and to this precious man He'd sent her way, who had gone to such great lengths to help her. Her heart flooded with all that she felt for him, and she stared deep into his eyes.

He looked away all of a sudden and then said, "Will you go back to your room or do you want me to stay here with you until you fall asleep?"

She felt completely at peace and knew she wouldn't have any more nightmares. Still, she didn't want him to leave. She said, "Can you stay with me for a while?"

He nodded. "Sure."

She grinned in gratitude and lay on the couch with her feet on his lap. She felt somewhat giddy having him so close beside her. She sighed in contentment, closed her eyes, and gave in to the sweet sleep wooing her.

*****

Sienna watched closely as Bryan counted his cards. The wind blew his hair across his face, and he brushed it back with his fingers. He groaned and threw his cards on the table. "I have only ten cards." He turned to face Audrey, who sat next to him near the porch railing. "How many do you have, Audrey?"

Audrey thinned her lips and placed all her cards beside his. "Sienna and Trisha took them all. I have just eight."

Trisha laughed as she counted out her pack of cards and threw them on the table. "I have the most cards," she said. "Sienna, how many do you have?"

Sienna rolled her eyes. "Twelve." She chuckled as Trisha gave a triumphant yell. "We know you've won, Trisha. You don't have to rub it in."

Trisha got up to do a little dance, and they all laughed.

"Okay, sit down, Trish," Audrey said. "I'm going to beat you this time."

They all played another round of the card game, and Trisha won again.

Everybody groaned.

Audrey shook her head and said, "You guys are blessed. I'm the unlucky one who will have to listen to Trish gloat night and day when we get back to Rosefield."

They laughed again, and Sienna gave a contented sigh. She hadn't been this happy in such a long time. With her heart steeped in peace and her sisters and Bryan in the house, she almost felt like she was in heaven. Since her talk with Bryan three days ago, she'd not experienced a single symptom of the panic attacks. "We should play again," she said.

"Not me," Trisha said. "I'm hungry." She started walking toward the kitchen. "I'm going to make fried rice. Who wants some?"

Audrey shook her head. "You're pregnant, Trish, you should rest. Let me make my special lasagna."

"Audrey, I'm pregnant, not sick! We can make it together."

Bryan chuckled. "You guys have a special lasagna? I can't wait to taste that."

"It'll blow your mind," Audrey bragged.

They left for the kitchen, and Sienna turned to face Bryan. She grinned. "You are not tired of my sisters yet? They are a handful."

He got up and came to sit beside her. "What are you saying? I love your sisters! They are so entertaining."

She nodded, and then sharply sucked in her breath at the look in his eye. It was the way he always looked at her whenever he thought no one was watching—like she was a rare gem he'd just discovered.

He looked away toward the kitchen and said, "Since you are better now, I think I'll leave for school tomorrow."

She gasped, and a thin thread of fear went through her. She blurted out, "You can't go."

"Why not?"

"Umm . . . Audrey and Trisha will be leaving tomorrow. Who will stay with me?" She knew he wouldn't buy the reason she just gave. She was completely well now and didn't need anyone to care for her again. She searched her mind for something else to say and added, "I need you."

He sighed, and then he looked her in the eye. The softness in his eyes caused a lump to form in her throat. He said, "I don't know if my staying here will be good for either of us. Cause it's not what you need."

"What do you mean?"

He sighed and then said huskily, "I'm deeply in love with you, Sienna."

Her jaw dropped, and her heart pounded. She knew he liked her a lot. But he'd just confessed that he loved her. She shut her mouth and then cried, "Then why won't you stay with me if you love me?"

"I think it might hinder your complete healing. I'm way too attracted to you to stay here alone with you." He moaned. "Besides, I need to get back to school now."

An anguished sob rose up in her. She wanted to

tell him she liked him. That she loved him too—because she did, even though she was just now admitting it to herself.

But she held back.

He was right. He was always right. If he said it would be better if he left, then that was the right thing to do. That, however, did not alleviate the sadness that had settled in her heart. She said to him, "What if I have a panic attack?"

"Just remember what I've been telling you about God's love and grace. Choose to believe that God loves you and that you are his even when you don't feel that way."

She smiled sadly and nodded. "Is there any way I can convince you to stay?"

"I have to go, Sienna. I've done what the Lord brought me here to do. You've rededicated your life to Him, and your fears are gone."

Except for the fear of losing you.

Reining in her emotions, she said, "I'll miss you." She added, "If only I could return to the Bible school, but I already signed a three-year contract with my agency."

They had given her time off to recuperate, but she wasn't sure how she would continue with them. Most of their clients were lingerie and swimwear designers. She didn't want to keep doing that kind of modeling.

Bryan shook his head. "You can't just come back to the Bible school, Sienna. From what you've told me, it was fear and that anxiety that brought you there and not God."

She bit her lips. One more thing to keep us away from each other.

Brushing the sad thought away, she decided to share her dilemma with him. "I don't know what to do about the contract I signed with my agency. I don't want to keep modeling lingerie and teeny tiny bikinis. I don't even want to think about going back to work right now."

"Just pray about it, Sienna," he said. "God will show you what to do."

"He will?"

"Yes, just the way he showed me his will for my life."

She smiled sadly. "I've been wondering how you came to the Bible College and became assistant chaplain even as a student."

He looked into the distance and then said, "I gave my heart to Christ almost nine years ago. That same year, I felt like the Lord was calling me to carry his message of love and grace to the world. I knew then that God wanted me to go to a Bible college."

His eyes took on a faraway look. "I thought I was going to a Bible college immediately I graduated from high school, but God told me it wasn't time. I went to college, and on the day I graduated, God told me it was time to go to a Bible college. However, He said He wanted me to go to a specific one where they needed to hear about His grace and love."

She said, "Beulah."

"Yes. I thought he would lead me to a big Bible school in a big city, but instead, he told me to go to the outskirts of my town. When I drove out of Green Valley, driving toward Rosefield, I saw a building with the words, 'Beulah College' emblazoned on it. He told me that was where I was to go.

That's how I came to attend Beulah."

"And how did you become a student chaplain?"

"In my second year, the senior chaplain, Dr. Lincoln, started to teach my Biblical Theology class. Every time he gave a test or asked questions, I had the answers when others didn't. It wasn't me, though, it was the Lord." He smiled. "Anyway, he said I was his favorite student."

"One day, he asked if I would like to be his assistant and serve as a chaplain. Even though I didn't know the first thing about it, I knew it was what God wanted me to do. So, without hesitation, I accepted to assist him, and I have learned a lot about what being a chaplain meant in these years. Soon, he left me with a lot of his duties, and that is it. That's how I became the assistant chaplain in school."

She said, "I always get inspired by your stories." Her eyes watered as she thought about him leaving. "I wish you could stay."

She took his hand and was glad when he didn't pull it away. As she gazed at him, she considered telling him that she loved him too, but Trisha yelled out, "Food is ready!"

Audrey set the food on the dining table while Trisha set down glasses of iced tea.

As they ate and talked, Sienna kept looking at him. His eyes sparkled as he spoke with Audrey and Trisha. Without a doubt, she was completely in love with him. It made her want to weep. She loved him, and he loved her, but she couldn't keep him here with her and that slightly frustrated her. If he said the Lord wanted him to go, then she would not be in his way, no matter how much it hurt.

ELEVEN

The office was dark.

They all crouched at the back of their desks waiting. Audrey shushed two of the officers who were whispering amongst themselves. She looked up and then whispered, "I can hear footsteps. He's coming! Everybody hush!"

They all waited in silence. The footsteps grew louder until the door opened and the lights came on.

Audrey sprang up just as the others did. They all yelled, "Surprise!"

Ken jumped and then laughed. "Guys! What are you all doing here so late?" He looked at the two-tiered yellow cheesecake sitting in the middle of his desk and grinned. There were drinks next to the cake, as well as plastic plates and cups. Above him was a banner with the words, "Farewell to our great police chief, Ken Baylor!'

He faced Audrey. "So, this is why you called me to the office at eleven o'clock at night."

Lieutenant Burns, a middle-aged officer, smiled

at him and said gruffly, "Boss, we are going to miss having you here."

Everyone gave Ken their well-wishes, but Audrey stood to the side, fighting her misery and trying hard to keep the tears away. He was leaving; just when she'd finally fallen in love with her dream man after being single for most of her life.

She finally let out a sigh of frustration. Life just wasn't fair. Ken looked over at her, and she put on a smile for him. I can't be like this today, she told herself. She got herself together and walked over to him. "So, you have to cut your cake now," she said, grinning.

He smiled tenderly at her. "You're the one responsible for all this. How did you plan it all when you were in New York?"

"I already had most of it planned before I left," she said, drinking in his features and committing them to memory. "I actually wanted to do a bigger farewell party for you, but because I had to leave for Sienna's, I couldn't."

"This is the best surprise party ever, and the fact that you were the one who planned it for me makes it even more special." He touched her arm. "Thank you."

She started to feel gloomy once again and instantly pushed it away. I have to be thankful that I at least got to be here before he left.

She clapped and signaled everyone to gather. She said to him, "It's time to cut your cake," and handed him the knife. He moved closer to the cake and his brows lifted. He laughed out loud as he read the words spelled out in blue icing, "Farewell, Boss! From your minions!"

He blew out the candles and beamed as they all sang, "For he's a jolly good fellow!" After that, they shared the cake.

Everyone stood in groups talking and eating. From time to time, Audrey glanced at him as she spoke with a group of officers and him with another. Finally, she couldn't take it anymore. She walked up to him and with a sly smile, she took his face in her hands and kissed him in front of everybody.

The officers sniggered, but she didn't care. None of them had mentioned it, but she was sure they already knew about her and Ken anyway.

When she drew back, his eyes were as round as saucers with shock. And then he grinned. "Wow, Audrey! That kiss was something! But I thought we were keeping it a secret for now," he whispered.

She shrugged. "I just wanted everyone to know that you are mine."

He nodded. "Well then, in that case," he pulled her close and planted a firm kiss on her lips. "I want them to know that you are mine as well!"

They both ignored the snickering and smiled at each other.

For the rest of the party, Audrey talked with Ken and the other officers while she thought about her plans for their final date tomorrow. Since it was a Saturday, they would go to the amusement park in the morning, and then the fair in the afternoon before finally heading back to her house until he left in the evening. At least they would get to spend the entire day together and make the most of what they had.

She watched him laughing and talking and kept her eyes on him until he looked at her. When he did, she saw in his eyes the sadness and sense of loss she felt in her heart. She forced a smile and mouthed, "I love you."

He smiled back and said the same before turning back to his conversation.

*****

At about seven o'clock the next morning, Audrey went to Ken's house and rang the bell.

He opened the door, and she smiled. He looked adorable still dressed in his pajamas, his dark hair messy. He rubbed his eyes and said in a sleepy voice, "I didn't know you were going to come so early."

She pushed his hair back from his face and kissed his cheeks. "You look so cute," she said.

Grinning, he wrapped his arms around her waist and pulled her close. "How are you today?"

"Good," she answered. She stepped into his house, spick and span as always, and sat on the black leather loveseat. He came and sat next to her, and she studied his face. "I love how you look right now." She'd never seen him this early and seeing him like this reminded her of why she was so sad. She wanted to see him this way every morning. And that meant marriage for her. But when would their relationship progress to that once he left? As the saying went: out of sight is out of mind.

She pressed down her concerns and said, "I can't wait to see you like this every day," and then she groaned inwardly. She'd just spoken out her thoughts. She might as well have asked when he planned to marry her. That would be so presumptuous, especially now that he was leaving.

He scrutinized her face, but didn't say anything. For a full minute, they stared at each other.

I would give everything I have to know what's on his mind right now, she thought. He already knew exactly what was on hers, since she had just spoken it out. She broke her gaze at last and said, "Ken, you have about thirty minutes to get ready, so we can head out."

He nodded, stood and left the living room.

She glanced around. The room was very masculine, all dark wood and leather furniture. Involuntarily, she imagined herself living here, adding feminine touches to the place.

Stop it! She chastised herself. She had to stop imagining being married to him . . . for now. Besides, another problem worried her. He wouldn't leave his job in Miami to come and settle here with her. Neither could she leave hers or her dear parents' house to move to Florida.

The new predicament which she had never considered before began to weigh heavily on her. Finally, after some minutes, she forcefully pushed it out of her mind. Today was a day for happy memories to be made, not a day to indulge in a worry fest.

Twenty minutes later, Ken appeared again, looking fresh in a white cotton shirt and brown pants. "I'm ready," he said.

They left in her car. All through their time together at the amusement park, eating ice-cream, going on the rides, she took mental pictures and stored each memory in her heart. When they went to the cinema to catch a movie, she half watched the film and half watched him, studying his face so it would remain with her even when he was gone.

After their long day out, before they entered her house, he caught her wrist. "Audrey, you looked kinda sad today. Even though I'm leaving Rosefield now, we will still get to see each other via video calls."

"It's not the same," she said.

He sighed audibly. "I know. For one, I won't get to do this." He tilted her chin up and kissed her slowly and deliberately. She pressed her body close to him, returning his kiss with fervor, knowing she would not get to kiss him for a long time to come.

At last, she stepped back, slightly unsteadily. He put his hand around her shoulders to support her, and she smiled. "Okay, we need to get in so I can start preparing dinner now. It has to be ready soon so we can eat before your flight. We won't survive for long on only ice-cream and bags of chips."

He grumbled playfully. "Who needs food when we can spend the time kissing?"

"Umm, everyone on the planet." She replied amidst laughter and brought out her house keys from her purse. "Besides, we can't keep standing out here, kissing."

He grinned, wrapped her in his arms and whispered in her ear, "We kiss in public a lot. Maybe it should be our thing; then we can make the neighbors constantly jealous."

Her pulse raced. It sounded like he was saying they would be married and living here soon.

She forced the thought from her mind and pushed him away, laughing.

They cooked together. She gave him directions on how to cut the ingredients for the stir fry while she cooked the rice. They prepared the entire dish in forty minutes and then sat at the dining table, eating and chatting. They reminisced over all they had done together throughout his stay. They talked about their patrols through the city together and talked some more about their past and family members. She threaded her fingers through his, glancing perpetually at the clock, wishing she could stop the time from ticking on.

But the time kept going until the clock struck eleven. It was time for her to take him to the airport.

She heaved a sad sigh as he stood.

"Come here, my love," he said to her.

She went to him, and he hugged her. After a long moment, she pulled back and said, "We have to leave for the airport now, or you'll be late for your flight."

As she drove, he talked about the new buildings that had sprung up in Rosefield within the past few months. She knew he was trying to avoid any conversation about his leaving, but there was no avoiding it. He was leaving, and things would not be the same for either of them.

When they reached the airport, she waited for him to check in.

After he had, he turned to her. "So, this is it then," he said.

She took in a deep breath so she wouldn't break down and then gave him a big smile. "Yep!" she replied almost shouting.

"I'll call immediately when I get to Miami, I promise."

She nodded. "I'll love you forever."

He put his hand on her cheek and said, "I'll love

you always. Remember that."

They held hands until it was time for him to go. She blinked back the tears threatening to spill from her eyes as he walked away.

He turned again and said, "I've loved every minute with you. Remember, we still have many more." He blew her a kiss, turned around again and walked away.

She watched him until he was out of sight and then hurried out of the airport. When she got to her car, she put her head on the steering wheel and let the tears fall down her face.

*****

Sienna stood in front of the camera with her hands propped on her hips. The set for the photo shoot was decorated to look like a plush living room, and she had to use some of the furniture as props. Andy, the photographer, took a shot and then told her to change her pose. She placed a foot on the cream sofa and tilted her head back.

"No. Lean against the wall and look over your shoulder," he said, adjusting his camera for the next shot.

She pursed her lips and turned only slightly, uneasy about fully exposing her backside to the camera. She was wearing barely-there lingerie, and she felt extremely uncomfortable.

Andy gave a loud sigh of frustration and straightened. "What's wrong, Sienna? You've not been following my instructions. "Take a look at this," he said and showed her the camera roll. "You look like you are about to run out of here any minute now." He put his hand on her shoulder. "I love photographing you because you take directions really well. Usually, it doesn't take more than a few hours to get great shots of you. Today, however, you seem out of sorts. Are you sure you are well enough to come back to work?"

She winced as she looked at the pictures. She did look frightened. Nora, the lingerie designer, had paid good money to have her pieces showcased in the best light. None of these pictures came close to doing that. In fact, all of them were unusable.

Sienna shook her head and then asked him, "Can I have a minute, please?"

He looked around the studio. Fortunately, Nora wasn't around today. He nodded. "Okay, but you have to be quick. The shoot is supposed to end an hour from now. This place is already expensive to rent, and Nora will have to pay more if we go over the set time."

Sienna nodded. She shrugged on the silk robe hanging on the sofa, strode to the dressing room a few feet away from the set and sat heavily in front of the mirror. This was the second lingerie shoot she'd had since Bryan left. The first one had been just as emotionally taxing, and she'd gone home feeling awful.

Today, she felt utterly incapable of going on. She exhaled as she began to feel the familiar anxiety start to work its way through her. The condemning voice whispered its usual words of doom, and for a short moment, terror overwhelmed her. And then she whispered the prayer that Bryan had taught her. "The Lord loves me, and I am his," she said.

She spoke it over and over again, letting it

settle in her heart even though everything in her screamed that it was a lie. Gradually, the panic attack and woeful feeling subsided, and she breathed a sigh of relief.

She pressed her lips together and then whispered again, "Lord, I don't think I can do this anymore. I don't want to be a lingerie and bikini model anymore. Please help me find a way out."

She felt trapped. As much as she wanted to honor her contract with the agency, the revulsion she felt every time she had to put on revealing lingerie and pose in front of the camera wasn't going away. It was getting stronger. She had been asking God to help her find a way out of the contract, but so far, her prayers had not been answered.

Andy hollered from outside the dressing room, "Sienna, we need to continue the shoot."

She silently cried out, "Please, Lord, I can't do this anymore. I need your help. What do I do?"

The three-year contract with her agency was unbreakable. Unless the Lord intervened, there would be no escape. As the doorknob turned, she stood, feeling defeated.

Andy came in. "I'm sorry, Sienna, we need to go on with the photo shoot."

She nodded and started to follow him. As she stood in front of the camera again, her heart pounding, she heard a gentle whisper in her heart, "Ask him about it." She blinked in surprise. The voice sounded like it might be the Lord's, but as she had never heard God's audible voice before, she wasn't sure it was.

She considered obeying for a minute and then changed her mind. Andy was just a photographer.

How could he possibly know how to get her out of her iron-clad contract with Surge?

She looked up at him. He was tapping his feet, staring impatiently at her.

What would it hurt if you asked him?

She shut her eyes and exhaled. It was true. What was the worst thing that could happen? He would say he didn't know. That was it.

"Sienna, what are you doing?"

She opened her eyes and looked at him. He was scowling at her. She said, "Andy, do you know how a model can get out of an iron-clad contract? I don't think I want to keep modeling anymore, but I don't know how to get out of my contract with Surge Models."

He looked at her as if she was plumb crazy and then he shrugged. "I don't understand why you would want to get out of modeling when it pays so well."

She shrugged. "I just want out."

He stared at her for a few seconds and then said, "You just said you're signed to Surge Models?"

"Yes."

He raised his brows. "I guess some people aren't cut out for the cut-throat fashion industry. I think I know someone who might be able to help you. I'm not totally sure he can get you out of your contract, but I'll call him. I'll let him know one of my favorite models wants to see him."

She held her breath as he got out his phone from his pocket, dialed a number and waited. He walked away with his phone to his ear while she prayed it would work out.

Andy came back and looked at her. "He says

he'll have to take a look at the contract. He is an entertainment lawyer, and his office is at Hudson Square." Andy got a pen and paper and wrote out the man's name and office address for her. "We can postpone your shoot until tomorrow evening and see if my friend can help you," he said.

She hugged him. "Thank you so much, Andy. I hope it works."

He shrugged. "If it does, I think it'll be such a shame because you are a great model. I wish you the best, though."

*****

The next day, Sienna drove to Hudson Square and found the address Andy had given her.

She stepped into the large industrial building which had several offices in it. Quickly finding the law firm, she entered and told the attractive brunette at the front desk that she had an appointment with the Entertainment lawyer, Chris Peyton. She was glad when the girl immediately led her to the lawyer's office.

She took a deep breath to calm her nerves and silently prayed before she entered. The office was surprisingly modern, completely different from the old building it was located in. It was all glass and steel with two large metallic figurines and a potted cactus.

Chris Peyton, a slightly built man behind a huge desk, looked up at her. "Sienna Gardner?"

"Yes." He motioned for her to take a seat and she did. She said, "It's a pleasure to meet you."

"Likewise," he replied. He looked intently at her.

"Andy told me you want to get out of your contract?"

She nodded and told him about her three-year contract with her agency and about her decision to leave now. When he asked for a copy of the contract, she handed it to him, and he read through it for a minute. He looked up and told her the contract looked inflexible, just like she knew. "I only see one termination clause here, but I hardly think it applies to you."

He shook his head and said, "It states that if you are physically or mentally impaired in a way that absolutely prevents you from continuing your job, you may be released from the contract. But that's subject to an official medical or psychiatrist report. which the agency will have to validate."

His eyes assessed her. "You look pretty healthy to me, so I don't think that will work for you. I think you may be stuck in your agency."

She frowned. "So, in other words, I have to have a life-threatening illness or be straight-up crazy before they let me go?"

"Pretty much." He replied with a straight face.

She remembered the doctor at Benedict memorial, the hospital where she had been taken after her suicide attempt, had given her a referral to see a particular psychiatrist. She had put the letter away, never dreaming of going to see a shrink. Now, maybe she would have to.

She squirmed in her chair, unwilling to talk about her suicide attempt or explore her horrible anxiety attacks again. However, she had no choice. She told the lawyer everything.

After she finished, he nodded, his expression even. He said to her, "If you can get a psych report that proves you are mentally incompetent, and that the anxiety arising from your modeling jobs partly drove you to the suicide attempt, they might let you go."

She pressed her lips tightly together. But it will take such a long time before I'm diagnosed, Lord. I'll still have to go on modeling until then."

A Bible verse popped into her mind. Commit thy way unto the Lord; trust also in Him, and He shall bring it to pass. She exhaled and stood. "Thank you so much."

Once she got home, she emptied all her purses, searching for the referral letter. At last, she found it in an old Marc Jacob's bag and quickly left her apartment again. She drove to Benedict memorial. The hospital was busy with nurses, doctors, and patients everywhere. She found the psych ward, hurried to the reception desk, and told the young lady there that she wanted to see Dr. Samir, the psychiatrist she'd been referred to.

"Please sit," the woman said after she had looked at Sienna's referral letter.

Sienna glanced around the place as she sat. Unlike the main hospital waiting area, which was noisy and overrun with people, this place was quiet. There were only two other patients here.

After about thirty minutes, a nurse waved her into the psychiatrist's office. A slim man with black hair and a bushy beard looked up and smiled at her as she entered.

"Please sit," he said. When she did, he added, "So, why have you come to see me today?"

He listened without interrupting as she told him about her mental and emotional challenges for the past year, leaving nothing out. After she finished, she prayed silently for a quick diagnosis even though it was a long stretch.

He nodded and began to scribble something down. She was surprised but grateful when he said, "Hmm, I had a patient today with almost the exact same symptoms. I think I can safely say you have OCD, religious OCD to be precise. I need to have a few more sessions with you to give you a comprehensive diagnosis, but this is most likely the cause of your severe anxiety attacks." He asked, "When last did you have an attack and how serious was it?"

She thought about the question for a long moment. Since she started confessing acknowledging God's unconditional love for her daily, she hardly ever had the attacks. When she did, it left quickly, as soon as she repeatedly spoke God's word of love over herself. She looked at him. If she told him that, though, would he still give her a diagnosis or declare her now mentally fit?

Trust in the Lord, she heard in her heart. She decided to tell him the truth.

After she did, he said, "You are a Christian."

She slowly nodded.

He grinned. "I am a Christian too. I've seen many people cured of religious OCD through confessions like yours. I use confessions alongside proven medical treatments and medication to help my patients. You are saying you have not had a major attack since you started your confessions?"

She nodded.

"Okay. I'll still give you a general evaluation, but I think you are on your way to getting completely cured."

She decided to tell him about her modeling dilemma. When she finished, he said, "The modeling definitely contributes to your crises. I think you would be right in leaving, especially with your suicide attempt." He smiled. "Don't worry about it. Let me write you a recommendation letter that you can show your agency."

While she watched, he wrote hastily on a long piece of paper that had the hospital's emblem on it. After he finished, he gave it to her.

She read his note; amongst other things, it said,

> ... the patient has a debilitating disorder known as religious OCD. It is triggered by a number of things ... In this patient's case, her triggers include the articles of clothing she has to wear at her job. The patient has tried to hurt herself before. Continuing her present job might lead her to try again. My recommendation is that she discontinues modeling and focuses on getting well ...
> Sincerely
> Dr. SamirMani, Psy.D.

She stared at him, completely overcome with emotion and tongue-tied. The Lord had done another miracle for her using this dear man. "Thank you so much, Dr. Samir," she finally said. "This means a lot to me."

He smiled warmly, "It's nothing. And I think you've reaffirmed my belief in the power of God's word."

She left his office with a huge smile on her face.

TWELVE

Trisha opened the door and walked into Audrey's, fuming. She dropped her purse on the coffee table, cradled her growing belly and lowered herself on the sofa. She kicked off her ballet flats and put up her feet.

Audrey came into the living room. "Trish, you're back from court. How did it go this time?"

Trisha shut her eyes and exhaled, trying to contain her anger. "I am so tired of all this. First, Stan tried evading the divorce papers, and then he contested the divorce. Imagine, he had the guts to contest it, even though he committed adultery repeatedly."

Audrey sat beside her. "So, what is the court saying now that you've filed for a no-fault divorce?"

"Stan!" Trisha spat out. "We've been ordered to go for marriage counseling because according to Stan, 'we have no irreconcilable differences!' As if counseling will help that man. He's sick, Audrey! He can't stop cheating." Trisha snorted. "I don't know why he can't get it into his thick skull that

I'm not budging this time. This divorce will happen no matter what he does."

Audrey shook her head. "He thinks you are still that wide-eyed teenager he married. The one who would let him get away with whatever he does. He's been trying to get you to change your mind since you filed for this divorce months ago."

Trisha sighed, weary of it all. "Can we talk about something less annoying? You spoke with Ken again today, didn't you? Have you guys finally come up with a plan to see each other that works for both your schedules?"

Audrey gave a sad smile. "Not yet. For now, he still has that ongoing homicide case and can't get away from work. And since I was made police chief, I haven't been able to either." Her expression turned wistful. "I miss him so much, it hurts."

Trisha felt a thread of envy go through her. She was happy for her sister, but her own relationship was basically over. She brushed the jealous feeling aside and said, "I know you guys will soon find a way. The reunion will be all that much sweeter when you do."

Audrey replied, "I guess so." The doorbell rang, and she frowned wondering who it could be. She stood and went to open the door.

Trisha turned to see who it was. When Audrey yelled, "You can't come into my house!" and started to shut the door, Trisha blinked, wondering who it was.

"I just want to see my wife! Trish, if you are there, please I just want a minute. Please!"

Trish narrowed her eyes in anger.

Stan!

She stood slowly and went to the door. Audrey and Stan were still struggling. Audrey was pushing the door, trying to get it closed, while Stan stuck his foot and head into it.

"I'll soon arrest you for breaking and entering, Stan!" Audrey said.

"I don't care. I need to see Trish."

Trish put her hand on Audrey's shoulder. "Please let me handle this, Audrey. Thanks."

Audrey looked at her. "Are you sure?"

She nodded. "It's okay, sis, I can handle him."

Audrey glared at Stan and then left.

"Please, I just need a minute," Stan said as he entered the house. He wore on his face his usual woe-is-me expression; the one he had adopted since the divorce proceedings started. She wanted to tell him to get lost, but she shrugged. "Haven't you said enough in court already? What else do you want to say? You've succeeded in delaying this divorce, and you've made it more painful than it needs to be."

"I'm sorry, but I am just trying to do everything I can to save our marriage," he pointed at her stomach, "for our sake and our unborn baby. I think counseling will help us. I know I have not been the best husband, but I have been faithful to you even before you filed for a divorce."

"Congratulations, Stan! You deserve an award for being faithful to your wife for a couple of months."

"I didn't mean it that way. I just . . ."

"What about me, Stan? What about the fact that I have stayed faithful for all the years we've been married?"

He looked down and then looked at her again,

shame plainly written on his face. "It's why we need this counseling. To repair the damage I have caused."

She surveyed him, this man she had loved so much. She said, "I don't even know why you are here. It's not like I have a choice about the counseling since it's a court order."

"I'm here to ask you to please give it a chance, Trish. Please."

She sighed. "I don't know, Stan."

He began to speak again, but she held up her hand and shook her head. "No, please don't make me promise to do anything for you that I don't want to."

He sighed audibly. "Okay." He looked defeated, and she started to feel sorry for him, but she quickly pushed aside the feeling.

"I'll see you at the counselor's office on Monday, then," she said to him, hinting that it was time for him to leave.

He nodded. "Monday." He walked out the door with his shoulders hunched.

She watched as he entered his car and drove away. Anger and resentment churned in her as she stood at the door, looking into the distance. How dare he try to make her the bad guy? He was the one who had ruined their marriage, yet he was making it appear like she was the cold-hearted one who didn't want their marriage to work. She'd been the one trying to save their marriage by all means for years. Tired of doing that was what she was now.

Grim determination entered her heart. Enough. She would no longer entertain any form of guilt concerning what happened. It was time she started to think only about herself and her unborn child. The counseling session was a formality. Their marriage was over as far as she was concerned, and he had to get that into his head.

She shut the door and put him firmly out of her mind.

*****

Ken gripped his cell phone tightly as he looked at Audrey. He smiled as she told him about the antics of some of the Rosefield residents. Even though she was in her uniform without any form of makeup, she still looked very beautiful. He only wished he could actually hold her now and kiss her.

"Why are you grinning like that?" Audrey chuckled.

"Just thinking about holding and kissing you now," he answered. Her bluntness had gradually rubbed off on him. It was great when he was in a conversation with her because it deepened their emotional connection. However, it had led to one or two awkward discussions with fellow officers. "You look beautiful by the way," he added.

"Aww, thanks, baby," she said and continued her story.

He placed his elbows on his desk as he tried to shut out the noise of the other police officers in the station. He put aside his longing for her so he could listen carefully to what she was saying now.

"That man actually thought the entire Rosefield Police Force was his personal bodyguard," Audrey chuckled. "Imagine driving into the station and asking us to accompany him to the game because he thought he was being followed."

Ken laughed.

Soon they changed the subject and talked about how much they were yearning to see each other soon. "How is your work schedule now, Audrey?" Ken asked.

"Still swamped, and you?"

He sighed. "Hectic as ever."

She pursed her lips. "At this rate, we won't get to be together until next year."

"We will find a way to make it work soon," he said.

She didn't say anything. Her look of disappointment broke his heart. "Hey!" He tried to cheer her up. "Chin up. I love you!"

"I love you too, babe." She looked back for a second and then smiled warmly. "Duty calls. I've gotta go. I'll call you in the evening before I go to bed."

After the call ended, he sat back on his seat letting his mind wander. Audrey looked so sad, and frankly, he felt just like she looked. This long-distance relationship thing was harder than he had thought it would be. He just wasn't sure he was cut out for it.

He stood to clear his head and went out of his office. The station was busy as usual with cops everywhere—some booking suspects, others hauling them off to jail, perps with looks ranging from fear to defiance, while others just chatted.

He passed by an office belonging to his good friend, Lenny Stevens, and stuck his head in to say hi.

"What's up, DC!" Stevens said, using the name he'd taken to calling Ken after he was promoted to deputy chief.

"I'm good," Ken answered. A blond woman was sitting in front of Stevens with her back to the door, probably a domestic violence victim. Stevens handled such cases on the regular due to his specialist training. Ken was glad someone other than him was in charge of such cases. He probably would be charged with murder sooner than later if he was.

The woman turned around, and his eyes widened in astonishment. She looked exactly the same as when he last saw her, except for the scar on her left cheek. He gasped. "Lauren!"

At first, shame clouded her features, and then she stood and hurled herself at him. "Ken! Oh, Ken!" She hugged him tightly. "I heard you had been transferred to somewhere in Idaho," she pulled back to look at him and then fell into his arms again. "I'm glad you are here."

He stood rigid in disbelief, and then he held her tight. He rubbed her back to comfort her as she cried, while memories flooded his mind; memories of her in his arms like this, years ago. He held her away to inspect her face and sucked in his breath at how deep the scar on her cheek was. "What, what happened to you?" he asked.

Stevens answered for her, "She was severely beaten by her husband yesterday, and this is not the first time."

Ken gritted his teeth as rage took over him. "Your husband . . . has been abusing you?"

She put her head down, slightly embarrassed, and said, "He gets angry over the smallest things, and then he starts yelling and hitting."

Stevens said, "Jack and I are going over to the

house to arrest him now. Do you want to come?"

Lauren shook her head before Ken could say he did. "Please stay here with me, Ken. Let the others go and arrest Richie." She looked into his eyes, and he saw her pain and her fear. His anger turned to distress, and he wrapped his arms around her, feeling an intense feeling of protectiveness for her. "I'll stay with you, Lauren. Don't worry."

Stevens left to make his arrest while she followed Ken to his office, clinging to him. He sat her down on the sofa beside his desk and looked at her.

She clutched his hand, trembling with fear. "What are they going to do to Richie?"

"Hopefully, they will be able to put him away for a long time, so he'll never lay his filthy hands on you again."

She began to cry. "It's been so hard. My marriage has been filled with fear and abuse. For the first two years, Richie never hit me. He only screamed and threatened to when he got angry. And that was a lot of times. He was always livid whenever I spoke to any guy remotely good looking. At first, I convinced myself that Richie was being a little bit jealous all the time because he loved me so much. But when he started hitting me, I knew instantly that it wasn't love, rather it was his ego . . ."

She cried harder, and he held her again. He spoke words of comfort to her while his emotions raged. Where was the confident, fun-loving girl he'd known years ago? Apart from her beauty, those were the traits that had attracted him to her and caused him to fall in love and consequently ask her to marry him. He had been devastated when she'd broken off their engagement.

As if she could read his mind, she looked up at him with tears streaking down her face and said,

"I'm so sorry, Ken, for breaking your heart all those years ago. I was young and foolish. I thought you were too nice and not exciting enough. I wanted a bad boy." She sniffed. "Turns out bad boys don't make good husbands."

Ken smiled sadly. He could recall clearly the days after they broke up. He had wandered around his house in his pajamas, feeling lost and confused. Work had been his salvation.

She put her head on his shoulder. "If only I had married you instead of Richie. I know now that you would have made a great husband." She raised her head and looked pointedly at his ring finger. When she put her hand on his cheek, he felt slightly uncomfortable. However, he brushed his discomfort aside. Lauren was going through a lot right now. He needed to be there for her. Nothing could happen between them.

He smiled at her.

She must have taken his smile as encouragement because she leaned close and brushed her lips against his.

He gasped and gently drew back from her. "No, Lauren. We can't. I have a girlfriend I love very much." He had let go of all the resentment he felt toward her a year after they broke up. But he had also let go of his feelings. Now, he only felt really sorry for her.

She nodded and her eyes brimmed with tears. "I'm so sorry. I didn't know what I was thinking. Please forgive me. I think it's just from all the stress and then seeing an old friend. It won't happen again, I promise."

He nodded. "It's nothing. I understand."

I sure hope it doesn't happen again.

THIRTEEN

For an unemployed girl, Sienna was exhilaratingly joyful. Finally, she was free from her contract with her agency. Free to do whatever she wanted to. She flopped down on her sofa, holding the letter that had led to her freedom. The agency had given in after they read Dr. Samir's letter. She'd signed release papers after that, and then they'd let her go. Now, she was legally free from her modeling contract.

She shut her eyes, lifted up a prayer of thanksgiving, and then she whooped in excitement. "Finally, freedom!" She got up to make herself a peanut butter sandwich and then carried her plate out to the porch to enjoy the feel of the summer sun on her skin.

She put her sun hat on as she reclined on the couch. She ate her sandwich and hummed a tune to herself. And then sadness tore at her, and she pressed her lips together to hold back a sob.

Bryan.

She'd been super busy for a while now. Busy enough that she could mostly relegate her feelings for him to the back of her mind. But now, it all came back. She wanted to see him again. She ached to see him. If only he were here to experience this freedom with her. It was because of him that she now had this peace in Christ.

She looked up and murmured, "Lord, I miss him so much."

She sighed. His face was on her mind, his bright blue eyes gazing at her. Instead of trying to push it away as she had formerly done, she embraced it and held his image close.

When will I get to see you again, Bryan? Her love for him suddenly felt both comforting and distressing.

After a long moment, she put aside her distress to focus on planning for her life going forward. She had no job and would soon run out of money. Her apartment was pretty expensive. The rent would be due soon, and although she had saved up enough money to pay for this month, she would not have next month's. Plus, she was used to working. Staying idle for an extended period of time would frustrate her; it was not something she could do.

"Umm, so, Lord, I have quit my job . . . just like I believed you wanted me to do. What now? What am I going to do for a living?"

She listened closely but heard nothing. She looked into the distance and thought, if the Lord doesn't show me anything soon, I might have to find a random modeling job.

But not lingerie or swimsuit. Never again. Maybe commercial modeling, like the kind she'd done before she quit and went to the Bible College, she thought.

Her heart suddenly jumped. The Bible College! What if I go back there?

But her heart sank again. Just like Bryan had said, it wasn't God who had led her there the first time. Fear had. And He wasn't the one leading her now.

But what then was leading her toward the school? She knew immediately.

Love was. Specifically, her love for Bryan.

But Bryan didn't think having a relationship with her was a good idea. He'd insisted that it would affect her recovery and growth. But she would love to see him again; however, if he thought that having a relationship with her wasn't for the best at this time, then she would keep her distance because he knew what was best.

But as she retired to her room at night, she tossed and turned, unable to sleep. She kept thinking about the Bible College and Bryan. By the time she woke up she had such a deep longing to see him and to go back to her studies at the school, she actually felt it might be God telling her to go back there. But she knew how thoughts like this could be deceiving. She began to pray about it, asking the Lord to show her what to do.

By the evening of that day, the only direction she'd gotten was a strong feeling that she needed to leave New York to go back to the Bible College. It was like the Bible school had been engraved in her heart. She still wasn't sure it was the Lord, but she knew she couldn't stay in New York anymore. Besides, everyone she loved was in Rosefield, or close to it—Audrey, Trish, and Bryan.

She slept with the same thoughts going through

her mind. When she woke up in the morning, her longing for Bryan had multiplied so much that she knew she would give up everything to see him.

She prayed again, "Lord, I want to go back."

Gradually she felt complete peace in her heart that it was the Lord's will for her to return to Beulah. She also knew she would not return to New York anymore. She had to put some things in order first, including selling her car. It was super flashy. She wouldn't need it for Bible school.

Before the end of this month, she would be ready to leave for the Bible College. She would get to be close to her sisters. Most of all, she would once again see the boy she loved with all her heart.

*****

Trish parked in front of the 'Love and Marriage Renewal Center,' and exited her car. The center was a simple one-story building surrounded by groves of juniper trees. It looked more like a family home than a government-approved counseling facility. Stan's car was parked beside the red Ford Fusion next to hers.

She sighed wearily and shielded her eyes from the sun as she walked toward the building. She passed this place to her bookstore every day. Once or twice, she had considered asking Stan to come here with her just to strengthen their marriage. She'd not known that their union needed more than strengthening and, certainly, she never imagined that she would end up coming here during the last days of her marriage. And there were just days left before the marriage was dissolved, as far as she was concerned. Stan was wasting his time thinking he could change her mind this time around.

His sudden zeal to keep their marriage together at all costs both surprised and angered her. Where was this passion a year, three years ago? If he had not messed up so many times until there was no going back for her, they would not be where they were now—about to get a divorce. Without a doubt, before the end of this year, she would be single again.

As she entered the building, she found Stan sitting on a chair right next to the door. He smiled brightly at her and stood as she sat next to him. She was surprised when he handed her a bouquet of red and pink roses.

"Your favorite, Trish," he said.

Scowling, she took it from him. "Thanks, but where am I supposed to put this now? On such a hot day, they're going to wither before I get home."

He looked at her with a clueless expression, and she knew he hadn't thought about that. It was just like him. He never thought things through, and certainly not about the consequences of his actions.

She looked up just as the receptionist, a middle-aged woman in thick glasses called out their name. "Dr. Peterson will see you now," she said. She gave them directions to the counselor's office, and then turned to another couple who had just come in.

They both went in the direction the receptionist had pointed out. There were several doors in the narrow hallway. They found the one that had the name Dr. Lori Peterson engraved on it in gold letters, and Stan knocked.

A female voice called out for them to come in.

They entered, and the counselor, a forty-some-thing-year-old brunette with flawless skin and a broad smile greeted them warmly. "So," she looked into a file and looked up at them, "you are the Cole-mans, and you are going through a divorce right now, am I correct?"

"Yes," Stan answered.

"So, tell me, what exactly do you hope to take away from these sessions?" she asked.

Stan replied, "We want to try to mend the rela-tionship and see . . ."

"No!" Trisha interrupted him. "I want to end the marriage. I'm only here because he contested the divorce and the court ordered us to go for marriage counseling."

The counselor looked from her to Stan and then back to her. "I would like to see you both separately if you don't mind." She smiled at Trisha and then said to Stan, "Can I speak to your wife first?"

Stan nodded and then left the office.

The woman smiled at Trisha. "Can you tell me, from your own point of view, what led to the breakdown of your marriage?"

Trisha took a deep breath and then began to talk about everything that had happened within the last couple of months in her marriage. She started with her suspicions about Stan's cheating, and then went on to tell the woman how she'd found his mistress's text message while he was showering.

"That was the first time I found out he was cheating on me," Trisha said. She spoke about how Stan had promised not to cheat ever again and how she had foolishly believed him because she'd loved him. But how later he had betrayed her trust yet again. "Our marriage has been full of lies and infidelity," she said finally.

The woman asked her if she thought he was sincere about wanting her forgiveness and about trying to make their marriage work.

"I think he's always sincere about wanting to be forgiven every time he messes up. I just don't think he has the ability and discipline to stay faithful."

They talked at length about her childhood, her parents' marriage, what her hopes and dreams for her own marriage had been on her wedding day. After that, Dr. Peterson spoke for a long time on forgiveness and how a marriage can recover and be much better after infidelity. "That's if both parties are truly willing to put in the required work."

After the lengthy discussion, Trisha still came to the same conclusion—her marriage to Stan was over.

She went out to sit and wait at the reception area while the counselor spoke for about half an hour with Stan. When she was called back into the office, she sat without looking at him. The counselor focused on her and told her that from her talks with Stan, he appeared genuinely repentant and willing to do whatever it took to make their marriage work this time. She asked Trisha if she would consider giving him a chance to prove himself. "If you choose to forgive him and give this a chance, your marriage can actually become better than it ever was."

After talking to them about realistic and unrealistic expectations in their marriage, she sent them away with "a suggestion," which was to Trisha more "an order" because of the court ruling. "I want you both to go on meaningful dates regularly for about a month. You can start this weekend. Stan, you plan the first date, and Trisha, the next. If after all the dates, we can't salvage your marriage, then you can call it quits."

Trish wanted to refuse, but she knew she really didn't have any choice.

"You return here for another round of talks next week, and I'll see how your first date went."

"This is just a waste of time," Trisha muttered. Stan turned sharply to her, and she stood. She went out of the counselor's office with Stan on her heels.

"Trish, wait!"

She turned around. "What?!"

"Won't you please reconsider this divorce," he said his expression remorseful. "For the sake of our child."

She sighed as she studied his face. He looked so miserable, so despondent. For a brief moment, she wanted to say, "Okay, I forgive you," but she remembered what Audrey had said about him cheating on her in the early years of their marriage. Who knew how many other women there were? He talked a good game, but without a doubt, he could not keep his promise of being faithful. If she agreed to call off the divorce, it was only a matter of time before he cheated on her again, and then where would she be?

"I'm sorry Stan, I've just had enough," she said. Before he could say anything else, she turned around, hurried to her car, and drove away quickly.

It wasn't until she was in traffic that she realized she had tears in her eyes. She wiped off the tears with her sleeve, but she couldn't wipe away the image of Stan in her mind, begging her to stay with him.

*****

Audrey sat at her dining table listening to Trisha talk about her counseling session earlier in the day. They'd eaten dinner together thirty minutes ago, and it was all Trisha had talked about. Audrey felt sorry for her. Trisha didn't deserve all the stress, especially now that she was pregnant.

Audrey took a sip of her bitter lemon and said, "Stan is impossible. He's making a simple divorce so complicated. It's not . . ." Her phone began to ring, and she looked down at it. When she saw it was Ken, she smiled. "Excuse me, Trish."

She stood and went to her room. "Hey, babe!" she said as she answered.

"Audrey, how are you?"

"Great, now that I get to hear your voice."

Ken said, "How are things at the office? I miss the simplicity and the easy vibe of that place. Over here, it's one case after another, usually serious ones. It's so unlike Rosefield, where the most serious case I had was that burglary."

"And we've not even had that kind of crime in a really long time." Audrey laughed. "Maybe that burglary was committed just to welcome you to the Rosefield Police Department."

Ken chuckled. "It was a good welcome. If only I had that when I came back here. You don't even want to know what case I was welcomed with."

"I'm so sorry, Audrey said, trying not to laugh.

She had told herself about a week ago that getting constantly depressed because Ken wasn't here was unhealthy. It wasn't like her sadness would help them find a way to be together. They had both decided to make conscious efforts to be upbeat when they spoke with each other. Instead of words of heartbreaking longing, they made fun of their work schedules and specific cases. "All I've had this week are a few traffic offenses and a brawl. So boring."

"Good times at the station." He chortled. "Anyway, I was calling to share an idea with you. I have a week-long vacation coming up, and I was thinking about coming to Rosefield to spend it with you. How does that sound?"

She beamed as her heart soared. "That sounds amazing, Ken! When will your vacation start?"

He said, "Twenty-first of this month."

She shook her head, disappointment stabbing at her. "I have to attend a seminar in Atlanta with some of the guys here."

"Oh," he said, sounding just as disappointed as she felt. She suddenly had an idea. "But it's not so far from Miami. Why don't I fly over after the seminar? It's just for two days, but that means I can only spend two days with you as well. But those two days will be so much fun!" She giggled as she felt excitement running through her veins.

"That is a great idea!" he hollered, and she laughed. "I am so relieved now. The thought of spending my vacation alone was awful. I'll get to see you and even show you around my neck of the woods."

They decided that he would pick her up at the

airport once she arrived. She would already have her hotel booked, and that would be where she would spend her nights. During the day, however, they would be together, out on dates, or at his house chatting and catching up.

Long after the call ended, she couldn't stop smiling. She went to bed, elated. Soon, she would see Ken again. She would actually get to touch him and kiss him. Hopefully, their relationship would then progress toward what she wanted with all her heart—to be his wife.

*****

Bryan raked his fingers through his hair as he sat in his office at the chapel. For the last thirty minutes, he'd been trying to study his Bible in preparation for his sermonette during the evening prayers. But he couldn't concentrate. His mind was consumed with thoughts of Sienna. Since he left her home in New York, he thought of her every single minute of every day; in the morning, as he went through his classes and duties in the chapel; at night as he slept, her face filled his dreams.

Somehow, he'd managed to get through each day in spite of it all, but today, he was finding it really difficult to continue. He covered his face with his hands, weary. "Lord, I miss her so much." He had left her in New York because he was going crazy with longing. He'd wanted to be so much more than just a mentor for her, but what he wanted was not what she needed.

One of his good friends in class suddenly barged into his office, panting.

"Charlie? What is it?"

"I'm just coming from the administration block.

Those 'watchers' have finally gotten what they want. They sent a list of harsh new school rules to the provost some time ago, and he approved it yesterday. Come and see. The list was framed and is hanging on the admin block notice board."

Bryan blinked in surprise. "What list? I didn't hear anything."

"You've been in here since morning. Almost everybody has seen it. You better come and take a look now because I think the rules will be enforced immediately."

Bryan stood from his seat and hurriedly made his way to the admin block.

There was a small crowd of students gathered when he got there, reading what looked like a very long almanac. He inched his way to the front and frowned as he began to read.

The Bible College students' one and only duty is to focus on the Lord and on how to please Him. So, with immediate effect, students caught doing any of the following, unless married, will be expelled:

1.Kissing.
2.Holding hands with a member of the opposite gender.
3.Hugging a member of the opposite gender.
4.Being alone with a member of the opposite gender. Mixed gender groups are allowed.
5.Living off campus with a member of the opposite gender who isn't a relative.
6.Dating—as this is not a place for romance.
7.Sex or other forms of it.
8.Male students are not allowed in the female dormitory.
9.Female students are not allowed in the male dormitory.

Bryan continued reading, his mouth agape in disbelief. After the twenty-second rule, he stopped.

As a school, rules were needed, but most of these were just ridiculous. Expelled for being alone with or hugging a member of the opposite gender is simply insanity!

Bryan began to leave the administration block, his mind reeling. The watchers had always been a sort of menace in the school, laying curses on people who they thought did not fit into their brand of Christianity. He had tried to fight their extreme legalism by confronting them whenever he could and preaching the love and grace of God, but they had the ear of the school administration. The leader of the group was the provost's nephew who happened to hold the same views as he did.

However, for the past few months, they'd become surprisingly quiet, and he thought they had finally put aside their legalistic rhetoric. Now, it appeared they'd only been lying low, waiting for the right time to unveil their masterpiece.

He got to the chapel, went into his office and sat. For a minute, he continued to think about the ridiculous new rules, and then once again his mind went to Sienna. He groaned and picked up his Bible. He began to read, hoping that by so doing he could get her face out of his mind. With these new rules, he knew he had his job cut out for him. He needed to start a series of Bible lessons in the chapel that would show that God's love rather than a set of rigid rules and regulations was enough to keep students on the right path. To do that, he had to fully focus on God's word and not on Sienna.

But he still couldn't get Sienna out of his mind.

He scrubbed his face with his palm. He had to find a way to forget her. She belonged in New York and the fast-paced lifestyle of the fashion world. He belonged here, in this small sleepy town, doing what God had called him to do. That wasn't going to change. Besides, he wasn't even sure she felt the same way about him. Without a doubt, she held him in high regard, but he wanted more. He wanted her to love him just as he loved her.

He sighed loudly in frustration. *Forget about her, Bryan! She isn't coming back here, and it's for the best. You need to focus on what God wants you to do now.*

But instead of forgetting her, his heart filled with agony at the thought of never seeing her again.

He stood with his thoughts jumbled. He had to get to his last class for the day and then come back here for the evening prayers. He gathered his textbook and Bible and then looked up as someone entered the office.

It can't be!

He shut his eyes and opened them again, wondering if they were playing tricks on him. Was she really here or had his mind conjured her up after months of obsessively thinking about her? He whispered her name, "Sienna."

She dropped her bag and fell into his arms before he could decide she was real. She cried, "I've missed you so much, Bryan."

His heart pounded as he wrapped his arms around her, and his voice choked with emotion as he said her name again, "Sienna." He held her tighter, loving the feel of her. "How come you are here?"

She drew back after a minute and looked into his

eyes. "This is where God wants me to be. I didn't tell you when you were in New York, but I can't hold it in anymore. I love you, Bryan. I am crazy about you, and I want to be with you."

His heart raced wildly with joy and wonder. He drew her close again and ran his hand through her hair. He couldn't contain his happiness as he said, "I want to be with you too." He kissed her hair and inhaled the scent of flowers. "I've missed you so much." He kissed her lips, first softly, and then with all the stored-up passion inside him.

She pulled him closer to her as they kissed, and he felt her tears on his cheeks. "I love everything about you," he said when they briefly came up for air. He bent and kissed away her tears. He took her lips again, kissing her slowly, the sweetness of the moment shaking him to his core.

And then a loud voice broke into the magical moment. "Chaplain Bryan, you are violating school rules . . . right inside the chapel!"

Bryan pulled away slightly and looked at the intruder. It was the leader of the watchers.

"I saw you reading the list of new school rules at the admin block some time ago, so you already know about them. I'm going to have to report you."

Sienna looked confused, but Bryan said, "Go ahead, but please leave Sienna out of this. I'm to blame. She didn't know because she just came back now."

The watcher, a boy named Alan, shook his head. "Ignorance does not excuse anyone." He looked at them as though they had stolen a personal item of his and sneered, "The punishment for this is expulsion."

He marched out of the chapel, and Bryan yelled out at him, "Please leave Sienna out of it!"

Sienna's eyes were round with shock. "What was that guy talking about?"

"The new rules in school, Sienna."

"He said something about expulsion?" Sienna asked with a worried look on her face.

"Just leave it to me," Bryan answered. "I will handle it." And he had to try to handle it quickly before it was too late.

Lord, if Sienna gets expelled, I'll never forgive myself.

FOURTEEN

Bryan hurried to the senior chaplain's office, a small separate building at the back of the chapel. He had to get the chaplain to mediate on his and Sienna's behalf before that watcher boy got the provost to expel them. He couldn't let that happen, especially for Sienna's sake. It would be his fault if it happened. Seeing her again and getting to hold her had made him completely lose his senses. He'd totally forgotten about the new rules.

He reached the office and opened the door, his heart pounding with fear. There was a huge chance that Chaplain Lincoln was away on one of his frequent trips. Hopefully, that wasn't the case.

Lord, please let Dr. Lincoln be here.

Hannah, Chaplain Lincoln's secretary, smiled at him. "Bryan, are you looking for Dr. Lincoln?"

He nodded.

"He traveled to Dallas for a Bible conference, but he'll be back on Saturday."

Bryan's heart sank. He took a deep breath and then decided to call the chaplain. If he could get through to him, maybe he could still talk to the provost over the phone. He took out his phone from his pocket and dialed the senior chaplain's number.

His line was unavailable.

"Oh, my Lord, please help me!" he prayed aloud, more in exasperation than a plea.

Okay, what do I do now?

The only option was to go to the provost's office right now and try to defend if not himself, then Sienna. After all, she had no idea about the new rules.

He ran as fast as he could and got to administration block quickly. He hurriedly climbed the flight of stairs to the top floor and entered the provost's office. He told the secretary that he wanted to see the provost and the woman waved him in without a word.

He knocked at the slightly open door and then entered. The watcher, Alan, was there, sitting in front of the dean. He was waving his hand and saying something to the provost, his uncle. The provost, a massive man with a constantly stern visage, looked up at Bryan grimly.

"Just the person we were talking about. Sit down, Bryan."

Bryan sat with his stomach churning and his hands slightly shaky.

"So, Alan was just telling me that you were caught red-handed with a girl in the chapel."

"We were only . . ."

"Stop!" the man raised his hand. "The point is that you broke the school rules even though you knew about them." He glared at Bryan and said harshly, "I expected more from you as the school assistant chaplain. I take it you are here to defend yourself, but it's too late."

Bryan's heart skipped a beat. He wanted to complain about the injustice of the rules, but he resisted. This wasn't the time for that. He had to get himself and Sienna out of trouble. He looked at the man and pleaded. "Umm, sir, the rules were just pasted on the admin board today. We haven't had time to get used to them."

The man shook his head. "Even so, there are some things a Christian shouldn't do . . . like fornication."

Bryan's eyes widened, and then he turned to glare at Alan. He faced the provost again and said, "I can assure you, sir, that Sienna and I have never been intimate in that way. I would never do that."

"Still, you were caught kissing, and you have no excuse for that." The man cleared his throat. "However, because the new rules were just given today, you and that girl will only be suspended for three weeks. But if you are caught again, you won't be so lucky."

Bryan felt his stomach boiling with anger. He blurted out, "You can suspend me! But it wasn't Sienna's fault." He sighed and pleaded in desperation. "She just came back to school. Please don't punish her for what was my fault alone."

The expression on the provost's face remained resolute.

Bryan tried again. "She has to stay because she's a little vulnerable to . . ." he suddenly stopped at the now curious expression on the man's face.

"Vulnerable to what?" the provost asked in a cold voice.

Bryan knew he had said a little too much. Anything he said now might get Sienna in more trouble than she was. He shook his head. "Nothing."

The provost said with finality, "You better go before I change my mind and expel you and that Sienna girl!"

Bryan stood. He'd not succeeded at all. Instead, he'd almost made things worse.

"Go get the girl and come back here in an hour. By then, your suspension letters will be waiting for you. I suggest you pack your things as well before you come here as you will be leaving the premises immediately, as soon as I hand the letters to you both."

Bryan left the office and walked slowly to the chapel. After telling Dr. Lincoln's secretary what had happened so she would pass the news to him, he walked to the female dormitory and stood outside the building. With the new rules, male students weren't allowed inside the female dorm and vice versa. He stopped one of the female students entering into the building and gave her a message to pass along to Sienna Gardner.

"Please tell her Bryan wants her to meet him in front of the chapel as soon as possible."

*****

Sienna ran as fast as her feet could carry her. She knew something bad had happened, she was sure of it. When Bryan told her, he was going to try to 'fix it,' whatever 'it' was because he refused to explain further, she had known something was wrong. She didn't understand fully what that watcher boy was saying about breaking the rules, but she knew it wasn't good.

She got to the chapel and found Bryan right at the door. Her heart thudded at the perturbed look on his handsome face. She tried to take his hand, but he held them behind his back.

Frowning, she said in alarm, "Bryan, what is it?" Why did he refuse to hold my hand?

He led her into the chapel. A few students were there, probably waiting for the evening prayers. He sat at the pew near the window. When she tried to sit next to him, he shook his head.

She became terrified. "What's wrong, Bryan?" What did I do to upset him? He pointed at the pew in front of his. "Can you please sit down there?"

"Why?" she cried. "Why can't I sit next to you?"

He looked into her eyes and said, "I love you with all my heart, Sienna, but I have gotten you in trouble, and I don't want to make it worse."

"What are you saying? What happened?"

He groaned. "They made new rules in school just before you came back. There are a lot of them." He named a few for her. "Most of them are about interactions between members of the opposite sex. We violated the rules by being alone together and kissing."

She gasped. "The watchers! I heard them talking about it months ago, but I had totally forgotten about it."

Bryan had a weary expression on his face. "It gets worse Sienna. The rules come with consequences, specifically expulsion. That watcher, Alan, he reported us to the provost."

Her heart jumped in horror, and she cried, "Have we been expelled?"

"No," Brian said. "Just suspended. The provost wants us to go to his office in about an hour to get our suspension letters. He said we have to leave the premises immediately after that."

"No!" she exclaimed.

"Yes," Brian said. He looked down. "It's my fault. I saw those rules before you came back, but I still kissed you anyway. Now I have gotten you in trouble."

She reached out and laid her hand on his cheek.

He shook his head and said softly, "We can't touch each other, Sienna. It's not expressly written in the rules, but it's implied."

She didn't remove her hand. Instead, she searched his face and said with determination, "I love you, Bryan. I don't care what the school authorities say. No one is going to separate us. If we have to leave permanently to be together, so be it."

"But you told me this was where God wanted you to be. And I told you how God brought me here. This place is where he wants me for now. We can't just quit the school permanently when it's part of God's plan for us."

"But how are we going to be together with the stringent rules? We'll ultimately get expelled if we continue our relationship here."

"I can't let that happen . . ."

"Bryan, no! What are you saying?" For the first time in months, her body began to tremble, and the familiar panic began to bubble up inside her. "Are you saying we should break up when we've just started dating?"

He put his hand on her shoulder, a distressed look on his face. "Breathe, Sienna, that is certainly not what I'm saying. I would never break up with you. I love you way too much."

She tried to smile and took in deep breaths.

He smiled sadly at her. "What I'm saying is that we still have to obey the Lord. We have to find a way to be together without the knowledge of anyone in the school.

"You're saying we should keep our relationship a secret?"

"Yes, we don't have a choice."

"How are we going to manage that?"

"I don't know yet. We'll have to find a way." He looked at his hand on her shoulder and quickly removed it.

She shook her head slowly. "You see. It's easier said than done. It means we can't kiss, hold hands, or even really be seen together unless in a group. Right now, we are violating school rules."

He sighed and looked at his wristwatch. "We need to get to the provost's office soon." For a minute, his eyes stayed glued to her lips, and she knew he would have kissed her if not for the stupid new rules. "I think you better go and get your things," he said.

Her heart soared as she suddenly realized something. "We need to look at the silver lining in this. We'll get to spend some time together uninterrupted before we come back here. You can visit me in Rosefield and stay for some days, and I can go visit you as well."

He smiled ruefully. "Even without the rules, with our attraction to each other, that won't be very safe."

She searched his eyes. "We won't be alone when

you visit. Audrey and Trish will be in the house." She laughed at the look on his face. "Yes, I know they are kinda boisterous, but you told me you liked them."

"I think it's a great idea, Sienna," he said, looking excited.

She nodded, feeling equally excited. "How about we leave together and go straight to Audrey's. You can stay for as long as you like. We will have so much fun together."

"I would love that, but I hope Audrey won't mind?"

"Her house is a bit small, but we will manage. She won't mind, but you'll have to put up with her and Trish's endless teasing."

He chuckled and stood. When she stood up as well, he reached out and took her hand. And then he groaned. He quickly let go of it and said, "I have to learn not to even touch you in school."

"That will be hard."

"Anyway, you need to go and pack your things. I'll do the same. Let's meet here in about twenty minutes. Is that okay?"

"Yes." She gazed at him, longing to kiss him. But she couldn't, she didn't want to put him in more trouble than he already was. She turned away quickly. "I'll see you soon. I can't wait for us to go to Rosefield so I can show you around my town." She almost clapped with glee.

He smiled widely. "I can't wait too."

She skipped away, feeling dizzy with excitement. She would get to spend weeks alone with Bryan, strengthening her bond with him. They would take regular strolls through Rosefield holding hands and stealing kisses at the house. She could already see them now having long conversations on the porch, way into the night.

She reached the dormitory and began to pack the things she would take to Rosefield with her. Her roommate was not around, and it brought back memories of the time she packed up all her things and left the school. She had been broken and confused then. This time, she felt totally different. For someone being suspended, she was in high spirits, just as she'd been when she quit her job.

She finished packing and skipped out again. Reaching the chapel, she found Bryan was already there. They walked to the provost's office together with their bags while she itched to take his hand.

Well, once we are out of here, we can hold hands.

They sat in front of the provost, and she tried not to look so happy. Bryan tickled her hands under the table, and she knew he was trying to hide his pleasure as well.

"Well, here is your suspension letter," the provost said, handing them both white envelopes. "You've all your things with you?" he asked.

"We do," Bryan said.

He looked from her to Bryan, and then his face turned red. He narrowed his eyes. "You know, I feel like you are both enjoying this. You look like you'll leave here and do something even worse."

Sienna's heart thudded. Lord, help us!

"If you are both planning on leaving here together, please put that idea out of your mind. 'Cause if we find out that you both did, you'll be expelled immediately."

Sienna drew in a sharp breath.

Bryan said, "We are not planning on doing anything wrong. It's just that I live a bit far from here and Sienna's . . ."

"Don't even think about it!" The provost barked. He looked at Sienna. "You'll be leaving first today. Bryan, you'll leave tomorrow. And as I said, if I even hear a rumor about you two meeting at some point before you come back here, you'll both be kicked out of the school; do you understand me?"

Sienna turned to face Bryan, her heart sinking in despair.

"I said, do you understand me?"

Bryan's expression held a grim determination. "Clearly, sir!"

"Good! Now Miss . . ." he looked down at her name on the suspension envelope he'd just written, "Gardner, you can leave now. Bryan, you'll wait here until she's out of the premises."

Sienna sat frozen, disbelieving how far this man would go to keep them apart. It was like he had a personal vendetta against them.

The provost narrowed his eyes in anger. "Miss Gardner! You can go now!"

She stood slowly and looked down at Bryan.

He looked at her with helplessness in his eyes and mouthed, "I love you."

With tears flooding her eyes, she whispered, "I love you, Bryan, with all of me."

The provost looked furious. "Go!" he ordered her. "Before I expel you!"

She went out of his office and slowly went down the stairs of the admin block. All the way to the school gate, she refused to give in to the sob that kept threatening to escape her lips. Outside the gate, as she stood to wait for a taxi, she vowed in her heart that nothing anyone did would ever separate her and Bryan. They were going to be together now, no matter how many stumbling blocks the school put in their paths.

FIFTEEN

Trisha put on a simple knee-length black dress for her date with Stan. She had no idea where he was taking her, but he'd called to let her know she was to wear something nice. This was the best she could get herself to do, or wanted to do at this point. She put on a pair of black open-toe flats, took a deep breath and then picked up her purse.

She surveyed her reflection in the mirror. Her hair was held up in a severe pony-tail—to remind Stan that their date meant nothing to her—and her belly had grown so much that her dress rode up her thighs. She put her hand on her bump as she thought about the baby. Her utmost desire had been for her child to be raised in a two-parent home, but it would not be possible now.

She smirked. Unless of course, Stan remarried before the baby was born—which she wouldn't put it past him to do—so he could torment some other unsuspecting woman with his infidelity.

No strange woman is going to raise my daughter. She sat down on the bed for a few minutes, feeling hot in spite of the air-conditioning, and slightly achy. This was one of those weekends when she would have just stayed home, curled up on the sofa with a book. Instead, she had to go out on this sham date.

She exhaled and stood up again. This pregnancy was difficult. Her feet were swollen, and she was continuously out of breath.

She went to the living room. Sienna was there, doing exactly what she'd just been dreaming of—lying on the sofa, reading a novel. Sienna had come back from her Bible college in tears yesterday and had narrated how she was suspended because she'd been caught kissing Bryan. It had sounded unbelievable and almost laughable. And Trisha would have laughed out loud if not for Sienna's tears.

"They can't suspend you both for kissing!" she had exclaimed. "You are full-grown adults for goodness' sake!"

Audrey had added, "I think you should leave that strange Bible school."

But Sienna had refused. "I know that's where God wants me to be right now, and Bryan feels the same."

"Are you okay, today?" Trisha asked, looking down at Sienna on the sofa.

"I'm better." Sienna smiled and put her novel aside. "You look great, Trish."

"Yes, off to my first forced date with Stan." Trisha looked around. "I hope Audrey doesn't come out here before Stan arrives. She'll make his life a living hell, and as much as I don't care for him anymore, I am in no mood for any drama today."

Sienna laughed. "That's Audrey for you. But I

think she's packing for her trip to Atlanta tomorrow."

"Oh, yeah! She told me about that." Trisha chuckled. "After her conference, she'll go to Miami to see her beau."

Sienna's expression suddenly turned sad, and Trisha pressed her lips together.

She misses Bryan. She was clearly crazy about the guy. "Don't worry about it, Sienna. You'll get to see him in school soon. For now, I guess you'll both have to be content with chatting on the phone."

"But we won't be able to have any kind of meaningful relationship there." Sienna put her head down. "It's just so unfair."

Trisha gathered her in her arms. She sighed as the loud beep of a car horn startled her. "I guess Stan is here." She drew back from Sienna and smiled at her. You'll find a way. You've always said God will make a way for you. Believe it now." She stood. "I have to go."

She went out the door waving at Sienna.

Stan was walking toward her, a bouquet of pink and red roses in his hand. She resisted the urge to roll her eyes. Did he think bringing her flowers all the time would make her change her mind, with everything he had done in their marriage?

"Hi, Trish, you look great." He handed her the flowers.

She took the flowers reluctantly, went back into the house and dumped them near the front door. She walked back to him and asked. "Where are we going?"

"Somewhere nice," he replied, smiling slightly.

She shrugged, determined not to ask where specifically they were going, and walked to his car. He opened the door for her, and when she entered, he went around and got into the driver's seat. He drove for a long time, passing her bookshop, the fire station, and 'Satin Dreams'—the popular bridal store where all the brides-to-be in Rosefield shopped. When he raced past the public library on the outskirts of town, she frowned. Turning to him, she asked, "Why are we leaving Rosefield?"

He didn't answer.

He continued to drive while she wondered where he was taking her. Finally, he stopped in front of an old two-story building in Green Valley. She stared at it. It looked really familiar.

And then she gasped. It was the motel they had honeymooned in twelve years ago after they got married. They both had no money then, so just finding a place they could afford outside Rosefield to spend their honeymoon in—even if it was a two-bit motel—was a dream.

She smiled, feeling nostalgic as she remembered how happy they had been at the time, how in love they were. When they were led up the stairs to their rooms, she in her wedding dress and he in his tuxedo, she remembered giggling and holding on to Stan. Once they got to the door, he'd carried her into the room.

She turned to him. "You brought me to Apex Motel?"

He nodded, looking pleased with himself.

She smiled at him. His smug grin was justified. This was a well-thought-out date.

"This brings so many memories of happier days," she said in a whisper. When she exited the car, she looked up at the brown-and white-building. "It still looks basically the same." She chuckled. "Who knew it was still here."

He said to her, "I came and checked it out earlier in the week when I was thinking of what to do for our date. It has a restaurant now where we can have dinner."

Her heart suddenly went into her mouth. He was expecting her to stay here with him; to pretend that they were on another honeymoon. She smiled coldly. "You do know there is no way I'm going to stay in the same room as you. We are not ever going to be together in that way again."

For a few seconds, he looked downcast, and then he suddenly seemed to think he deserved it, so he gave her a small smile. "I know. I just brought you here to bring back memories of happier times; to remember those days when we were madly in love."

"Before you ruined it all," she said.

He sighed loudly. "Let's just go in."

They entered, and Trisha couldn't help smiling. Everything looked the same. From the massive mirror on the wall to the worn-out leather loveseat near the console table, the furnishings in the lobby were older than they were then, but they were still arranged in the same position.

The host, a tall man in a red suit, led them past the lobby to a room she hadn't been to when they came here—a modern-looking restaurant. The restaurant had only a few people in it and was moderately quiet. He sat them at a table with a huge spherical urn as a centerpiece and a waiter came to take their orders. He handed Trisha a menu, and she perused it. After she told him what she wanted and Stan reeled out a list of unhealthy carbs, the waiter left.

Trisha looked at him from across the table. "Stan, I'll have to admit that this is a really nice gesture."

He smiled. "Remember that old woman in the room next to ours? She was so fascinated by the fact that we were honeymooners that she wouldn't leave us alone."

Trisha chuckled. "At first I thought she was a nice old woman who was just curious. When she kept knocking on our door every single hour, I knew she was nuts."

He shook his head. "That was pretty crazy."

They kept reminiscing until the waiter brought their food. As they tucked in, they laughed and chatted about their honeymoon experiences and then about the first few weeks of their marriage. Trisha couldn't remember the last time she and Stan had such a great time together. Bringing her here was the best thing he could have done. It was a pity he hadn't done it before their marriage disintegrated.

They finished their meals, and Stan winked at her.

She shook her head slowly. "I know that wink, Stan. You are up to something." She looked intently at him, curious to know what he had on his mind.

"Do you remember our room number when we stayed here?"

She raised her brows. "No, that was such a long time ago. How am I supposed to remember that?"

"I do," Stan said with a smirk. "Do you want to see it . . . just to know if it still looks the same?"

She sighed. "Stan?"

He shook his head. "No, not for that, just to see it."

"Really, you expect me to believe that you just want me to see the room?"

"What are you afraid of, Trish? It's not like I can force you to do what you don't want to. And you are pregnant. I'm not even thinking about that right now."

She scowled at him. "Well, thank you for letting me know I'm completely undesirable!"

"Umm, no, it's not . . . if you want to, I'm not saying I won't . . ."

"Stan! Stop it!"

He smiled sheepishly. "I'll be a perfect gentleman, I promise."

She waited while he collected the keys to the room from the lobby. When he came back, she stood and followed him out of the restaurant and up a staircase. As she climbed the stairs behind him, holding on to the rails, she chided herself. You know where this is going to lead, don't you?

She paused for a brief moment to catch her breath and then tentatively continued up.

They reached the top of the stairs, and as they walked down a vaguely familiar-looking hallway, her worries increased. They stopped in front of a door, and Stan unlocked it. She entered the room after Stan did and glanced around. It looked delightfully familiar with the gaudy red and gold décor. She smiled, forgetting her concern and flopped on the bed. "Just like it was back then."

He grinned at her. "I knew you would like it."

She got up and went to look out the window. Memories of their time here flooded her mind. She looked back at Stan and pictured him as he was back then. She remembered the morning after they arrived here. He'd ordered breakfast in bed before she'd woken up. Beside her was the usual bouquet of roses.

She sighed with regret. If only he hadn't gone and destroyed it all. She looked into Stan's eyes and saw he was gazing at her. Her breath caught in her throat as she recalled that look. That was how he'd looked at her on their wedding night, right here in this room.

She blinked in surprise when he said, "Are you ready to leave?"

For a long moment, she didn't answer. With the way he was looking at her, his question was the last thing she'd expected. She forced a smile and nodded.

He doesn't want you because you are now fat.

She suddenly felt self-conscious and put her hand on her swollen belly. Even though she didn't want him either, she still felt a little sting of rejection.

And then, almost immediately, she pushed her insecurities away. He had told her he would be a perfect gentleman, and he was honoring his word. She smiled at him and then walked out of the room.

As they got back into his car to drive home, she turned and said to him, "Thanks, Stan. I had a great time. It was really thoughtful of you to bring me here."

He nodded but didn't smile this time.

As he drove home, she couldn't help gazing at

him. She kept recalling different significant points in their marriage, all they had been through to-gether, the good and the bad times. As she thought about it, she realized that the good times definitely surpassed the bad.

Do I really want to throw it all away? She thought ruefully.

SIXTEEN

Ken felt excitement bubbling up inside him as he answered Audrey's phone call. Before long, she would be here in Miami, and they would finally be together again. He stretched out on his leather couch and said, "Hi Audrey. Where are you now?"

Audrey answered, "I'm at the airport in Atlanta. My flight is in about thirty minutes. So, in about two and a half hours, I'll be at the airport in Miami."

Ken smiled. He looked at his wristwatch and saw it was almost noon. "Okay, I'll set out for the airport in about an hour and a half." He gripped his phone tightly. "I can't wait to see you, baby!"

"Can't wait to see you too," Audrey replied, her voice filled with excitement.

After the call, he stood and went to the bathroom to lightly trim his beard. Audrey liked running her fingers through it, and he wanted it to look nice for her.

As he trimmed the beard while looking at the mirror, he continued to think about Audrey. He felt partly nervous and partly exhilarated, as he was planning to ask her to marry him at the end of her stay here. He was so tired of being apart from her.

However, one thing troubled him—their living arrangements. He couldn't leave his job and move to Rosefield, but Audrey wouldn't want to leave hers either. She finally had her dream job. He couldn't ask her to abandon it and move here with him after they were married.

She might just refuse to marry me if I even mention it, he thought in self-mockery as he finished trimming his beard and got into the shower. That meant they were soon to be at an impasse.

He finished showering and went to his room to put on a black T-shirt and a pair of blue jeans. As he walked to the kitchen to fix himself some lunch before leaving for the airport, the doorbell rang. He frowned, wondering who it was. Walking to the living room, he opened the door, and his eyes widened in surprise.

"Lauren!"

"Ken, I'm so sorry to bother you." She sniffed.

He frowned. She had been crying.

She entered his house, glanced around and gave him a sad smile. "I haven't been here since we broke up, but it still looks the same."

He winced when she suddenly broke down.

"What is it?" he asked. He hadn't seen her since the day she'd gone to the police station, choosing to stay away deliberately. After she'd tried to kiss him, he had decided it was for the best, especially when he heard that her husband had been put in jail. She was safe, or so he'd thought. From the way she looked now, it appeared that the wretch had been let out of prison. "Is it your husband?" Anger churned in him. "Did they let him out?"

She nodded. "The court reduced his offense to a misdemeanor, and he was released from jail after paying a fine."

Ken raked his fingers through his hair, anger and frustration raging in him. How could they let out that beast?

"He came to the house threatening me, and I tried to defend myself. That incensed him." She pulled up her blouse slightly, and he saw a bandage wrapped around her waist.

He spat out, "That guy did this to you? I am going to kill him if I ever lay my eyes on him."

She shook her head and sobbed. "I don't feel safe, Ken. My home isn't safe, and I have nowhere to go. Can I stay with you, just until I find somewhere else?"

He laid a hand on his forehead as his mind roiled with conflicting emotions. Audrey might be a strong woman and open-minded, but she wouldn't understand why Lauren was staying at his house instead of finding somewhere else to stay. He felt torn. On the one hand, he wanted to protect an old friend, but on the other, he needed to preserve his present relationship.

Lauren looked into his eyes. "Please, Ken. I feel safe with you, and I really have nowhere else to go."

You could go to a shelter.

As if she read his mind, she said, "You know I can't bear shelters after what happened to my mom and me when I was a child."

He thinned his lips as he recalled something she had told him about that. He exhaled and then nodded. She was terrified of shelters. Plus, he couldn't just turn her away with all she had been through. "Okay, Lauren, but I hope you'll find somewhere soon. My girlfriend will be arriving in Miami today, and I need to explain to her that you are only staying here temporarily."

Lauren nodded. "I will, I promise."

He glanced at his wristwatch. He really had to get to the airport. Lauren would stay here while he went and picked Audrey up. The plan was that he would drop her off at her hotel to rest and freshen up. Two hours later, he would go back to the hotel, pick her up again, and bring her here. He had to explain Lauren's presence in his house before he did. He looked at her again. "Are you sure you don't have to go to the hospital?"

"No. I've been there already."

"There has to be a way to get that monster behind bars again. He can't be terrorizing you like this."

"He was ordered to attend anger management classes some weeks ago, but I don't think it's helping."

Ken snorted. "He doesn't need anger management classes. What he needs is jail time! Anyway, Lauren," he sighed, "I have to go now. Are you sure you will you be all right on your own?" He held his breath, hoping she wouldn't say no. It's not like I can take her with me.

She nodded. "I'll be fine."

She looked a little scared, and he loathed leaving her now, but there was little he could do.

He scolded himself. Stop worrying. She will be safe here.

He went in to get his cell phone and car keys,

and then his ears suddenly perked up. There was a strange scraping sound coming from the back of the house. His eyes flashed as a loud crash sounded from his living room. He opened his drawer and grabbed his gun.

Slowly, he made his way to the living room, careful not to make a sound. He paused behind a wall before he reached the room and stuck out his head slightly. His eyes widened in horror. A burly man he guessed was Lauren's husband had one hand tightly wrapped around her waist and the other covering her mouth.

Her eyes bulged with pain.

"Let her go!" Ken walked out and pointed the gun at the burly bully.

The man gave Ken a murderous look. "She's my wife, not yours! I know you are her ex. You are trying to steal her away from me!"

Ken ignored the man's rant. He came closer, the gun aimed at the man's head. "I said let her go right now!"

The man swore loudly and then threw Lauren down. He cursed her and ran out of the house.

Ken roared as his body shook with rage. There was nothing he would have wanted more than to hunt that maniac down, but Lauren was thrashing on the floor, hurt. He bent down and tried to pick her up, but she groaned in pain.

She shut her eyes and said haltingly, "I think . . . I think my leg is broken from the fall."

Ken grimaced. There was blood on her shirt, seeping from the wound on her waist. The brute had opened up her wound. He got up and rushed to the phone on the mantel. "Hang on. Let me call 911."

Ten minutes later, the paramedics placed her on a stretcher, and Ken followed them in the ambulance. All through the ride, he held her hand while she sobbed.

"You'll be fine, Lauren," he continuously assured her. But he knew she wasn't crying because of her physical injury. It was from the emotional and mental ordeal she'd just faced; the ordeal she was still going to face with her lunatic husband at large.

They got to the hospital, and he watched helplessly as they rolled her away. One of the paramedics had told him on the way here that her wound would have to be stitched up as soon as they got to the hospital.

And then he gasped as he remembered Audrey.

He reached into his pocket, and then immediately recalled he hadn't taken his phone. Audrey would probably now be trying to contact him. He asked the nurse at the reception desk if he could use the phone. When the woman agreed, he dialed Audrey's number.

There was no answer.

He dialed again, but she still didn't pick up.

He groaned. Where are you, Audrey?

*****

Ken called a taxi using the hospital phone. After that, he went to sit in the waiting area beside Lauren, who had a hand on her waist, wincing in pain. Her wound had been stitched up and bandaged and her leg put in a cast. She'd been given instructions on how to care for her stitches and to stay off her leg until it was fully healed. He said to her, "Our ride will be here very soon."

She nodded, and he looked away into the distance. The hospital was packed with patients and medical staff, but the only person his mind focused on was Audrey. He had called her again and again with the hospital phone, but he still hadn't been able to reach her. He sighed with worry and got up. "Just a minute Lauren." He walked to the reception desk again, and the middle-aged nurse eyed him.

"I'm sorry," he said to her. "Just one more time."

She turned away, and he picked up the phone. He took a deep breath and let it out slowly to release his anxiety. He figured Audrey would already be in her hotel now. She would wonder why he hadn't come to pick her up and would have called him a dozen times. Was that why she wasn't answering her phone? Was she angry with him?

The phone rang, but again, there was no answer. He huffed in frustration and then returned to his seat next to Lauren.

"You're worried about your girlfriend?" Lauren asked.

He gave her a small smile. "Umm, she's a big girl. I know she's fine. It's just that I left my phone in the house, and I'm worried she may have been trying to reach me for hours without success."

"Hopefully, you'll get through to her once you get to your phone."

He nodded and glanced at his watch. "The cab driver said he'll be here in about ten minutes. Let me go out and see if he is." He went out and waited until a taxi stopped in front of him. After he'd confirmed the taxi was for him, he said to the driver, "Please hold on," and then went to get Lauren.

She stood and began to hobble with her crutches while he put his arm around her shoulder for extra support. Once outside, he helped her into the car and got in beside her.

When they got home, he lowered her down onto the couch and smiled at her. "Can I get you anything?" he asked.

She shook her head. "No, thank you so much, Ken. I don't know what would have happened if you didn't come to rescue me from Richie. He's turned into a monster." She bit her lip. "Thank you." She started to rise from the couch, but he shook his head.

"No, Lauren. Lie down."

She leaned back and then groaned. "Oh no! I think I have opened up my stitches again."

His eyes widened in concern. "I hope not. Let me see." He raised her blouse and saw the stitches were still intact. "They are fine," he said, smiling with relief as he put her blouse down again.

*****

After taking a quick shower, Audrey hurriedly put on a knee-length polka dot dress and wore a pair of flat gold sandals. She picked up her purse and quickly left her hotel room. Ken had not shown up at the airport, and she was worried. She had waited and waited, but he still didn't come. Unfortunately, her phone had gotten lost somewhere between the Atlanta airport and Miami. She tried to call him with a pay phone, but he didn't answer any of her calls. After a few hours of waiting and worrying, she'd finally decided to go to her hotel on her own, check in, and then take a cab to his home address.

She quickly found a taxi, gave the driver Ken's written home address and entered. Her heart pounded with worry as they drove through traffic. She felt something might have happened to Ken. Ken always kept his word, and this was totally unlike him to ditch her without any word or explanation. Everything in her told her something had definitely happened to him.

Or he has suddenly lost interest in you.

She brushed away the weird thought. That was unlikely, considering he'd sounded very eager to see her just a few hours ago.

That left the only possible reason she could think of—something had happened to him. But what could it be? Maybe he was ill. The thought left her feeling faint.

She looked out the window as the driver drove into a quiet suburban neighborhood. The long street was lined with acacia trees, and most of the houses were similar-looking one-story homes. The whole area was lit like it was Christmastime, and she could see into some of the houses. The driver finally stopped in front of a house with a police car parked in the driveway. That meant Ken was home, but in what state?

She stepped down from the taxi, her heart beating fast with dread. If something had happened to him, how would she be able to go on?

After paying the driver, she began to walk slowly to his front door, afraid of what she would find when she got to his house. Was he hurt or sick? She prayed fervently in her heart that he was fine.

But if he is, then why hasn't he been answering my calls?

When she saw his curtains were open, showing

his brightly lit living room, she made a beeline for the window instead. And then she blinked.

It can't be!

She moved closer, and her eyes widened in horror. Ken was hunched over a blond while the woman lay on his couch. Audrey felt nauseated as he laid his hand on the woman's back. When he raised her blouse, she couldn't watch anymore and quickly turned away.

She ran down the street as fast as she could, tears blurring her sight. So that was why he hadn't come to pick her up from the airport or answered her calls. He was busy with that blond.

She couldn't stop running until she reached the end of the street.

She leaned against a tree and bent her head as she let the tears pour down her cheeks.

How could Ken do this to me?

She should have known. The relationship was too good to be true, and they had been moving way too fast. Perhaps the long-distant relationship had proven way too hard for him to handle.

She took a deep breath and dashed at her tears. He had no right to cheat on her! The distance was just as hard on her as it was on him. She exhaled and flagged down a taxi. "The Renaissance Hotel," she said. She got in and shut her eyes, feeling completely numb. As the driver drove back to the hotel, she vowed never again to give her heart away.

*****

Ken woke up early, made pancakes for Lauren, and hurriedly prepared to go to Audrey's hotel. He had no information about her room number, but he would check every single room in the hotel if he had to.

He had tossed and turned throughout the night, worried about her. With everything in him, he longed to go to the hotel and find her, but he couldn't leave Lauren in the house alone at night. He'd decided to postpone to this morning and tried to force himself to go to sleep, without success.

He carried the pancakes and syrup on a tray and went to the guest room where Lauren had slept. Quietly, so as not to wake her up, he set the meal beside her bed. In spite of his stealth, she stirred and then sat up.

"Hi," he smiled at her. "Did you sleep well?"

She smiled back and combed her hair with her fingers. "I was in some pain during the night and had to take the meds the doctor gave me. Apart from that, I slept quite well." She looked at the pancakes he had set on the bedside table. "You made me breakfast?" she smiled sadly at him. "Always such a gentleman." She looked like she wanted to say something else, but she didn't.

Ken shrugged. "Lauren, I need to go out for a short time this morning, but I'll be back soon." He didn't want to leave her, especially after what had happened with her husband yesterday, but he had to go find Audrey.

She looked up at him with a mixture of fear and disappointment in her eyes. "Okay," she replied.

"Make sure you don't open the door for anyone. I'll call you when I get back so you can let me in."

She nodded, and he smiled reassuringly at her. From the expression on her face, she was clearly scared, even though she was trying hard to be brave.

He left the room, walked out of the house and locked the door. He glanced at his phone to see if he had any recent missed calls but found none. Yesterday, after they'd returned from the hospital, he saw several missed calls on his phone from a number he didn't know. When he called the number, no one had answered.

He had called an acquaintance of his who worked at the airport to help him find out if Audrey's plane had landed safely. The man had gotten back to him with reassuring news. Her plane had indeed landed in one piece. Which meant that she was fine and probably the person who had tried to reach him with the strange number.

He drove off to the Renaissance Hotel, strode into the lobby and walked up to the receptionist. "Hi, I'm looking for a Miss Audrey Gardner. I think she checked into this hotel yesterday."

The receptionist, a friendly-looking woman, smiled and asked him if he knew Audrey's room number. When he said he didn't but would like her to find out for him, the woman shook her head. "I'm so sorry. We don't give out our guests' room numbers, no matter what."

He sighed, brought out his police badge, and held it out to her. "MPD. I'd like you to check for her room number for me, please."

She lifted a brow and then looked down at her computer. "Just a second." A minute later, she looked up at him. "Miss Gardner checked out this morning."

He blurted out, "To where?"

"I'm sorry, sir. I don't know."

"Did she leave a message or something?"

"No, she didn't."

Ken shut his eyes for a second, bewildered. He opened them, exhaled and then left the hotel, determined to get a hold of her.

SEVENTEEN

Bryan was counting the days before he would be reunited with Sienna. He had been lying in bed in his family home reading a book, but he put the book away after he'd spent almost an hour staring absentmindedly at the same page. He stared at the ceiling, thinking.

There were eight days left before he could finally get to see her again in person. They talked on the phone, and he got to see her during their video chats. But it wasn't the same, and it wasn't enough.

For the last two weeks, he'd been at his parents' house in Green Valley. He enjoyed spending time with them, as he hadn't done so in quite a while. However, he would rather be with Sienna now. Their phone calls and video chats were great, and he knew she was in good hands since she was with her sisters. But he just wanted to get back to school so he could finally be with her in person. He wanted to be able to hold her, to run his fingers through her hair and kiss her.

But you won't even be able to do all that in school.

He sighed and sat up on his bed. Just seeing her in person would have to do. How they could have a relationship without ever being alone with each other or being able to express their love for one another, except maybe by text, was a mystery right now.

But they would find a way. They had to. He would graduate the beginning of next year. Even if they had to wait until she graduated two years from now, then they would. He would wait because he loved her deeply.

He prayed, asking the Lord to give him the strength to not mess things up when they got back to school. Any attempt he made to try to see her privately would probably result in disaster. Those watchers were without a doubt now going to be spies for the provost, looking out for anyone who would break the new rules and telling on them.

For the umpteenth time, he thought about just leaving the school so they could be together, but he knew they couldn't do that. The Lord had explicitly told him to come to the College, and He hadn't told him to leave. Sienna also felt the Lord wanted her in the school. As long as it was God's will for them to remain there, they would have to stay and find creative ways to continue their relationship.

He suddenly felt an overwhelming urge to call her again, even though they had chatted on Skype the evening before. He dialed her number and waited for it to connect.

Her face appeared on the screen, as beautiful as ever. She said chirpily, "Hi, sweetie!"

"Hey, babe! How are you today?"

"I'm good." She smiled at him. "You look handsome as always. I wish I were there with you."

"We will soon be together," he said. "I've been counting the days. We have eight days more."

She shook her head. "It'll be worse when we get back to school, Bryan. I doubt we will be allowed to even video chat. We can talk in a group in public, but we have to vet our words."

He moaned. "We need to come up with a plan, Sienna. And we need to do that as soon as possible." He looked away for a second and then he looked back at her. "I've been thinking about it, but I haven't been able to come up with anything yet."

"Me neither."

He rubbed his chin thoughtfully. A plan had been niggling at the back of his mind for days, but it had been vague until now. It suddenly became clear what their best course of action should be, but he decided not to tell her about his idea for now.

She smiled softly, and the angelic glow it brought to her beautiful face made his heart drum. "What are you thinking about, love?"

He nearly told her, but he managed to hold it back. He diverted her attention by telling her about his older brother who lived in L.A. After that, they talked about school, about their forced break and how they were spending it. Sienna told him about her sisters, who apparently were in the process of breaking up with their significant others.

"I'm so sad for them," she said. "Especially for Audrey. Ken seemed like a nice guy, but I guess he wasn't."

After the call ended, Bryan ran his plan through his mind again. It was simple, but he knew it would be effective. It would shut the mouths of those watchers and everyone like them. Most of all, it would ensure that he and Sienna could spend as much time as they wanted with each other without fear of punishment.

*****

The stars were starting to peek out of the dark sky when Stan drove Trisha home after another date. This time it was a picnic at the Rosefield Park, which they'd frequented for months after they got married. He knew she would enjoy the date, and she had.

Trish turned to him and smiled warmly. "Have I told you I had a great time?"

"Yes," he grinned, "several times already."

From the corner of his eye, he saw her gazing at him. When her eyes were still on him five minutes later, he turned and grinned at her. "I've loved spending these weekends with you, Trish." He turned back to the road.

She sighed loudly. "I have too. I just wish you had put this amount of work into our marriage years ago. We probably wouldn't be where we are now, in the middle of a divorce, if you had."

He pursed his lips and then gave her a grim smile. "I know, I messed it all up, but I'm trying to fix it, and I will. I love you, Trish. I don't want our marriage to end."

"I didn't want it to end either, but I can't keep putting up with your infidelities."

"I haven't looked at another woman since you filed for a divorce."

"Still . . ." She didn't say anything more.

They drove in silence until he stopped in front of Audrey's. He quickly exited the car and went to open her door. He held her hand as she stepped out of the car, and he didn't let go until they were in front of the door.

"I can't wait for our next date," he said, looking deep into her eyes.

She gave him a rare grin. "I suppose you are taking me somewhere from our past again? Won't you tell me where we are going next?"

"Hmm, I'm not telling you anything. It won't be a surprise if I do, will it?"

She chuckled. "Okay then. I will be looking forward to it."

He smiled and then tentatively reached out and touched her baby bump. He bent down, his lips almost touching her belly, and whispered, "We'll tell you all about how we saved our marriage when you are old enough, champ," he said.

She giggled. "You know she's a girl, Stan."

"I know. A girl can be called 'champ' too."

She shrugged, and he searched her eyes. "Do you know something else I can't wait for?" he asked.

"What?" she asked softly, her eyes locked on his.

"I can't wait to hold our daughter in my arms." He straightened and looked Trish in the eye. "I promise to spend the rest of my days loving you and our beautiful child. It'll be the most special thing in the world."

She seemed overcome as her eyes shimmered with tears.

He carefully drew her to him. When she didn't resist, he took her face in his hands and then gently kissed her. When he pulled back, tears were running down her cheeks.

He wiped them away with his thumb and said, "I'll see you later."

She nodded.

He walked to his car, but he could feel her eyes on him. Once he was behind the steering wheel, he waved to her and drove off. About seven minutes later, he got home and immediately brought out his cell phone from his pocket. He dialed a number and waited.

"Hello, Stan! What news do you have for me?"

Taking a deep breath, he answered, "Everything is going according to plan."

*****

Ken redialed Audrey's number and waited. It rang and rang, but she still didn't answer. He groaned in frustration as it stopped ringing and put his hand on his head. He yelled, "Why aren't you answering your phone, Audrey?"

Lenny Stevens popped his head into Ken's office. "Are you okay, DC?"

He forced a smile and nodded. "I'm good, Stevens." But he was far from it. He'd been trying to call Audrey since the day he found out she'd abruptly checked out of the hotel. Every time he dialed her number, it rang and rang without an answer. He'd called her sisters to try to reach her through them, but they also never answered his calls. He had even called a few of the guys at the police station in Rosefield to find out if she was fine, and to ask her to call him, but they always came back with, "She's good, but she never responds when we pass your message along."

Stevens looked at him as though he didn't believe what Ken had said, but he shrugged and left.

Ken ran his hand through his hair and heaved a frustrated sigh. *Lord, why won't she speak to me?* Unfortunately, he couldn't go to Rosefield to see her now as he was swamped with work. He was in charge of two ongoing cases that were very sensitive, plus Lauren was still in his house, under his protection. He couldn't just leave her like that. She had mostly healed physically, but her husband was still on the loose and could attack her again.

He called Audrey's number once more, knowing she wouldn't answer and waited as it rang. When there was still no answer, he moaned and resisted an overwhelming urge to fling his phone across the office.

There is no way I can do this anymore.

He had to act now before he lost forever the woman he loved. Obviously, she had something against him, and he had to find out what exactly that was and try to fix it somehow. Case or no case, and Lauren or no Lauren, he had to go to Rosefield.

He left his office and walked over to his boss' office. Eric Renner, the chief of police, looked up when Ken knocked. "Can I come in, Eric?" he asked, standing at the door.

Eric looked up at him and shrugged. "You are already in, Ken." He pointed at the chair across from him. "Take a seat."

Ken came in and sat.

"What's on your mind? The drug trafficking case?"

"Umm, it's a more personal matter." He threaded

his fingers together, slightly anxious. Telling his boss he had to go to Rosefield now to win back his girlfriend had sounded great in his head. Sitting across from Eric's intimidating stare now, he realized how it would sound. Still, it was the single most important thing he had to do. He brushed aside his reservations and said, "I need to go to Rosefield . . . to see a friend. It's imperative that I go."

Eric scowled. "We are in the middle of two intense cases, and you want to leave?"

"I'll only be gone for two days. No more. I really need to do this. I'll lose someone I love very much if I don't go."

Eric shook his head. "Unless that someone is at the point of death, I'll have to refuse."

"Eric, sir, I need to do this. Patrick can handle the case just for two days until I'm back. He's been eager to prove himself, and this is his chance."

"Patrick can't even tie his shoelaces!" Eric shook his head slowly and looked up, his expression thoughtful.

Ken held his breath.

At last, he looked at Ken again. "Okay, but only for two days. We need you here, Ken. You know that."

"I promise I'll be back in two days."

"When do you want to leave?"

"As soon as I can . . . probably tomorrow."

"Okay, then."

Ken smiled and thanked the police chief before returning to his own office.

Now I need to find a safe place for Lauren to stay and recuperate until I'm back.

But where could he take her? Lauren didn't like

shelters because of her childhood experiences, and he couldn't think of a place where she could go now.

For a few minutes, he sat thinking about it, and then he gave up and went back to work. Half an hour later, as he pored over the narcotics case file, his cell phone rang. He glanced at it and saw the call was from Vince Burns, one of the police officers he'd asked to check up on Audrey. He picked up his phone and answered eagerly. "Hi, Vince. Have you got anything for me?"

"Umm, I don't know how to say this, but I heard Chief Gardner speaking with someone on the phone; I'm not sure who exactly it was. She said she saw you with a blonde in your house."

Ken nearly dropped the phone. "What? A blonde . . ." And then it immediately hit him. "Lauren!"

"Who?"

"Never mind. Thanks, Vince. I appreciate your help."

"It's nothing."

Ken ended the call. He stared at the wall in rueful amazement as the pieces began to fall in place in his mind. Audrey had probably come to his house on the day he was to pick her up or the next day. Somehow, without him seeing her, she had spotted Lauren in his home and had understandably misunderstood their relationship.

He felt like kicking himself. If only he could redo it all. But still, it wasn't like he'd had a choice. He couldn't have turned Lauren away after what happened with her husband.

He glanced at the ceiling. Now that he knew why she wasn't picking up his calls, it was even more crucial to go to Rosefield as soon as possible and try to iron things out. First, though, he had to figure out where to take Lauren. He couldn't leave without doing that.

That evening, as he drove home from work, an idea gradually filtered into his mind. It was risky, but it was the best thing he could do. And it would kill two birds, or maybe three, with one stone.

He got home and found Lauren lying on the couch in the living room watching TV. She sat up painfully when she saw him and smiled. "Hi!"

"Hi, Lauren. How was your day?"

"Good, but boring."

He sat on the sofa across from her and said, "I need to leave town tomorrow. I want to go to a small town called Rosefield; that's where my girlfriend lives."

Her eyes filled with fear and she bit her lip.

He shook his head. "I'm not going to leave you here, Lauren. I'm taking you with me."

She gave him a nervous chuckle. "I don't think your girlfriend will like that very much."

He looked her in the eye. "I need to confess that I have two . . . or three reasons why I want you to come with me. The first reason is the obvious one. I don't want to leave you here alone. The second reason is that I need your help. Audrey, my girlfriend, somehow saw you here and now she's not answering my calls. I need you to personally tell her nothing is going on between us."

Lauren's brows knitted together, and for a long moment, she didn't say a word. And then she nodded. "You really love this girl. I'm a little jealous, but I'll help you. How could I not after all you've done for me?"

"Thanks." He heaved a sigh of relief. "There is one more thing. You know you can't stay here forever and just as you said, my girlfriend won't be happy about it, but I cannot leave you to your fate when your husband is still a threat to you. I think you'll be safe in Rosefield, for now . . . until something is done about him."

"You want me to go stay in a small town that I have never heard of?"

"Yes. I lived there for some months. It's a very safe place, and I know a husband and wife who wouldn't mind taking you into their home."

Lauren pressed her lips together and then nodded. "If you say it will be the safest place for me to stay for now, then I trust you." She smiled sadly at him. "Thanks, Ken, for everything. You are one of the kindest people I know. After how I treated you, breaking off our engagement, you've still been nothing but kind to me. The world needs more people like you."

He smiled. "I don't know about that, Lauren, but thanks."

"So, when do we leave?"

"Tomorrow."

*****

Audrey just wanted to forget about Ken, but he wouldn't stop calling her. He had taken to sending her messages through the other officers at the station; messages she completely ignored. Even though she had tried her best to push him out of her mind, she still missed him terribly. His constant calls and messages made it even more difficult for her to forget him. But she had to. He had betrayed her. And to add insult to injury, he kept calling her, as if he'd not cheated on her. He didn't know that she had found him with another woman, in the act.

She might still ache for him every day, but she had come to terms with the fact that it was over. She wasn't like Trish who kept forgiving Stan's inconceivable indiscretions. She glanced at the clock on her office wall, saw it was almost five p.m. and exhaled.

About time. She hadn't been able to concentrate on work at all, so she might as well go home now. She picked up her knapsack and purse and left the station.

Driving home from work, she began to crave some ice cream. She turned to the right and drove to Xavier's where they sold the most decadent chocolate caramel ice-cream. She bought three large tubs. Except for Trisha, who seemed annoyingly ecstatic since she'd begun her dates with Stan, the house had been miserable for weeks. She and Sienna had been moping around the house. Well, no more pining over guys! They would have an ice-cream party today.

But as she drove by the house where Ken had lived when he was in Rosefield, she suddenly burst out sobbing. She scolded herself as she cried, but she couldn't stop. Since she'd met Ken, she'd turned into a blubbering fool.

The tears blurred her sight as she drove, and she kept wiping them with the back of her hand. She got home, at last, exited her car and brought out a tissue from her bag. She didn't want Trish or Sienna seeing her looking like this. Wiping her tears thoroughly, she took a deep breath before she walked up the stairs. She opened the door and then froze.

What is this?

She stared in disbelief. Ken was seated on her couch, and that blonde chick she'd seen him with was beside him. He had actually brought her to her home. The nerve of him!

She slowly dropped the ice cream on the coffee table and said coldly, "What is happening here? Who let you two into my house?"

Ken stood. "Audrey, I'm sorry! I wanted to stay outside, but Sienna let me in."

She barked, "Then find your way out with that . . . thing!"

The girl stood, and Audrey glared at her.

"I came to explain everything, Audrey," Ken said, looking intently at her. "If you would just listen, please."

"Umm . . . no! Ken, I don't know what you think you are doing, bringing this woman here, but you better leave now!"

"I brought her here so she can explain what really happened . . . since I know how stubborn you can be."

"How dare you!"

"We are not together, lady!" the blonde said sharply.

Audrey bristled and then spat out, "Are you crazy? Leave my house right now, or I'll be forced to arrest you for trespassing." She sneered, "Or I might just decide to shoot you."

The woman appeared unfazed.

"Audrey, just listen!" Ken ordered. She turned to look at him, and he added, "Please!"

For a few moments, Audrey looked away, trying to contain her anger. She finally exhaled and then said, "Make it quick."

The blonde said, "Ken is an old friend of mine. My husband has been physically abusing me, and I had to go to the police station. Some days ago, because of my husband's abuse, I came to Ken's house, as I was afraid to stay in my own home. Richie, my husband, attacked me again in Ken's house, and Ken rushed me to the hospital. I've been staying at his place because I have nowhere else to go and I'm afraid for my life."

Audrey felt a flush creeping up her face. Had she misjudged the situation she saw? She turned to Ken. "But, I saw you with her." The image still stayed firmly in her mind, even though she had tried hard to expunge it. "She was on the couch . . . and . . . you . . . you lifted her blouse."

"This was why," the blonde said. She lifted her blouse and Audrey gasped. A long scar ran across her waist. "My husband did this. The day he came, he opened up the wound that had already been stitched. It had to be stitched back up at the hospital. I was probably showing it to Ken the day you saw us."

Audrey held back a sob. She looked at Ken, feeling so embarrassed. "Was that why you couldn't come pick me up?"

He nodded. "I left my phone at home, but I tried to reach you with the hospital telephone."

"My phone was lost while on the trip to Miami," she said slowly." She covered her mouth. "I'm so sorry, Ken! I should have trusted you instead of jumping to conclusions."

Ken held out his hands to her, and she went to him. He folded her in his arms, and she hid her face in his shirt.

"I'm sorry," she apologized again.

"It's okay. I probably would have acted the same way if I were in your shoes." He rubbed her back soothingly. "I've missed you so much."

She smiled sadly. "I've missed you terribly." If only she'd come into his house that day, she would have found out the truth, and it would have saved them all the heartache of these last few weeks. The shame tore at her, and she did the only thing she knew would bring her comfort. She lifted her face up for his kiss.

He kissed her forehead, her chin, and her nose. Finally, he kissed her lips slowly. He started to draw away after a few seconds, but she held on to him. She kissed him again, a kiss that expressed, she hoped, how sorry she was and a hope for a future between them. "I love how you are so good to me in spite of everything," she said to him.

He grinned. "And I love the taste of your lips." He kissed her again.

Someone cleared their throat behind her, and then she remembered the blonde woman was still in the room. She had totally forgotten about her.

Ken brushed his nose against hers and then turned to the woman. "I'm sorry, Lauren."

"It's okay."

Ken said, "I told Lauren she could stay in Rosefield for now. Maybe with the Gibsons."

"They will be happy to have her. The last girl they had in their home was also a domestic abuse survivor. She's finally moved to her own house."

"I thought they would," Ken said. "You hear that, Lauren? There is a nice couple not far from here who would be happy to have you. I'll drive you there later this evening." He looked at Audrey. "You can come with us, Audrey, if you want to."

Audrey smiled at him. "No need. You drive her. I'll be waiting here when you get back."

He kissed her cheek, and she held on to him. And for the first time in weeks, she felt whole again.

EIGHTEEN

Sienna sat up on her bed, clicked the answer button on her phone and smiled when Bryan's face appeared on the screen. Her stomach filled with butterflies as it always did whenever she saw him. "Hi, handsome," she said. "I'm so glad you called now."

Bryan grinned. "Hey, gorgeous! How are you today?"

"Better, now that I see your handsome face."

He beamed at her, but then lost the smile after a few seconds. "So, Sienna, I have something really important I want to tell you."

Her heart raced as she gazed at him. He had a solemn look on his face. "What is it?"

"About the rules in school and how we can be together without breaking them. I have an idea."

She blinked rapidly. "What?"

The serious look on his face faded, replaced by a nervous one, and she wondered what that was about. He always seemed so sure of himself.

"What is wrong, Bryan?" she asked worriedly.

"Umm, I've been thinking of this for a while. My

idea was to ask you after I graduated from the Bible College next year."

"What do you want to ask me, Bryan? You are making me nervous."

"I'm sorry, I didn't mean to alarm you," he said. He turned away for a second and then turned back to face her again. "I know this is not as romantic as you would want it to be and certainly not how I pictured asking you, but right now, I have no choice." His laptop moved, and she lost sight of him for a few seconds. When he reappeared on the screen, she gasped. He was on his knees.

He moved closer until only his face was on the screen once again. "Sienna Gardner, you don't even know how much I love you . . . and words are not enough to tell you . . . but I hope this does." He brought out a small box from behind him and then took a ring from the box. He lifted the ring to the screen. It was a rose gold ring encrusted with small oval diamonds.

She immediately began to weep, overcome with emotions.

"I love you, Sienna, with everything in me. Next to the Lord, you are my life and all that I dream and hope for. Will you marry me and stay with me forever?"

She wanted to answer his question immediately, but she couldn't stop sobbing.

"Sienna?"

She finally managed a nod.

"Are you saying yes, sweetheart?"

She croaked out a "yes" as her heart soared.

He whooped. "I wish we could seal it with a kiss!"

She wiped her eyes, puckered, and pressed her

lips to the screen.

He did the same.

"Now we've had a virtual kiss," she said, smiling. The moment felt surreal like she was in a sweet dream she didn't want to wake up from. She giggled and said, "Am I in a dream, Bryan? 'Cause if I am, I never, ever want to wake up!"

He laughed. "I feel the same, so I guess we are both in the same dream."

She giggled again and said, "I love you, Bryan. Thank you for asking me to be your wife."

"And thank you for saying yes," he said softly. "Now, that brings me to the next phase of my plan."

"Oh, there's more?" she asked.

"Of course there is more. This might be the tricky, and quite frankly, crazy part, but it's the only thing I could think of to solve our problem."

She instantly guessed where he was going and a feeling of exhilaration surged through her. She held her breath, waiting for him to continue.

"The new rules in school state that members of the opposite sex are not allowed to date, kiss or be together alone; but it also clearly states—'unless they are married'. If we get married before we return, we will be able to be alone together without fear of being expelled." He gazed anxiously at her. "What do you think about that, sweetie?"

Her pulse raced, and she felt like she was about to burst with joy. There was nothing she wanted more than to marry him now so he could be hers completely and she, his. Feeling giddy with anticipation, she nodded. "I would absolutely love that!"

He heaved a huge sigh of relief. He had half expected her to tell him his plan was crazy and unrealistic.

She squealed, "Imagine, Bryan! I'll be your wife in no time, and we can finally live together!"

He laughed. "Where are we going to live?"

"Can we live on campus?"

"Umm," he looked thoughtful. "I don't think so. I don't think any married couples live on campus right now." He shook his head. "That won't even be possible as there are no mixed gender accommodations there."

"Then we can live off campus," she said.

"Yes, we'll have to find accommodation as soon as we get married. This brings me to the third phase of my plan."

She chuckled. "Your plan has a third phase? Well, if it is as exciting as the first two, I can't wait to hear it."

"So, I've also been thinking about how we will get married. Because we have to get married quickly, we might not be able to invite anyone right now. I'm thinking of a small church at . . ."

She interrupted him. "No, Bryan, what about school?"

"Ugh?"

"What if the senior chaplain can wed us in the school chapel? That would be perfect since everyone, including the authorities, will know we are now married. That's what we want, isn't it?"

His whole face lit up. "Sienna, that is perfect! I'll call Dr. Lincoln and tell him. I'll have to do it now so that he'll make space for us in his schedule. I hope he'll be available to wed us as soon as we return." He winked at her. "You'll make such a beautiful bride."

She giggled, imagining herself in white while pledging her life to him. "And you will make a beautiful groom."

"Beautiful? Isn't it supposed to be 'a handsome groom?'"

"Yes, but also beautiful."

They continued to talk about plans for the wedding. They had to first get a marriage license, but the chaplain would handle the other documents for them. They both agreed that for now, they would not invite anyone. When they were married and settled in an off-campus apartment, they would have a bigger wedding and invite their families.

"I wish I had money to get you a beautiful dress," Bryan said. He looked a little sad. "All my savings from my chaplain's allowance will be going towards getting us an apartment. And even that won't be what you are used to."

She frowned, worried that his lack of finances was bothering him. "Don't worry about any of it. I have lots of beautiful dresses and quite a large amount of money saved from my modeling jobs."

He started to shake his head, trying to protest, but she cut him off and said, "Bryan, it's okay. We won't lack anything, and as I said, I have lots of dresses to wear for the wedding."

"But you don't have 'a wedding dress.'"

"I'll wear something white. It doesn't matter what I'm in, as long as I get to marry you."

"Sienna?"

"Yes, Bryan?"

"Is it possible to be so in love you feel like shouting it out to the whole wide world?"

She giggled again. "I feel like I'm about to explode. I love you so much."

After the call ended, she lay on her back and stared dreamily at the ceiling. She felt like she was floating on clouds and sighed in contentment. In a few days, she would be married to the love of her life. No feeling in the world could compare.

*****

Stan came home late from work, went up to his bedroom, and removed his tie. He tossed it carelessly aside and then hurried downstairs to get some dinner for himself in the kitchen. As he passed by the living room, the doorbell rang.

He frowned. Who can it be? Maybe it's Trisha.

She'd come to the house yesterday for the intimate dinner he had planned for both of them. The date had gone really well, and he was expecting her to terminate the divorce and move back in any minute now.

He walked to the front door and opened it. And then his eyes widened in surprise.

"Hi, Stan! Have you missed me?"

"Carla!" He gaped at the tall, willowy brunette who he'd had an affair with for a few months. She was in a red dress that clung to her every curve. He drew in a sharp breath. Usually, he was more discreet with his extra-marital affairs, but he'd been so taken with her that he had been completely reckless. He had left his phone carelessly on the bed. It was how Trisha had found out. He'd broken up with her in order to focus on Trisha and make sure she canceled the divorce. Now, here she was, on his doorstep, looking more beautiful than he'd ever seen her.

What if Trisha comes here now?

Panic gripped him. "You can't be here, Carla!"

"Won't you ask why I came all the way from New York?"

"I know why you came, but it's not gonna happen."

She slithered into his house, her red lips in a pout. He swallowed as she closed the door behind her. "Are you saying you don't want me?"

He nodded slowly. "I don't!"

"It's not true, and you know it." She started to unbutton his shirt. "I can see it in your eyes; you still want me, Stan."

"No, Carla, I don't. I'm trying to patch things up with my wife."

"Exactly, you are only going to patch things up. Admit it, Stan, you can't stay away from me for too long. We are bound together."

He shook his head slowly.

She cupped his face in her hands and kissed him firmly. "You can't resist."

He felt himself sliding and falling as she wrapped her arms tightly around him and kissed him passionately. His mind screamed, begged for him to push her away, but he couldn't.

Trisha could come here any moment from now.

He finally mustered up a little strength and weakly pushed her away. But she came back, pressed herself against him and kissed him even harder.

At last, he found he couldn't resist anymore and succumbed. Even as she held his hand and drew him up the stairs and into the bedroom, he cursed his weakness. Like Trish had said to him before, he was a sick man, a compulsive philanderer. If she found out about this, everything he'd planned with Derrick would be ruined.

*****

"What do you mean you don't want to get a divorce anymore, Trisha?" Audrey asked, a look of utter disgust on her face. She was still in her pajamas, as it was still very early. She stood up from the sofa and glared down at Trisha. "After just a few dates, Stan has succeeded in turning your head. Do you actually think he's changed just because he said so?"

Trisha sighed. She'd known telling Audrey would be like this, but she had not been able to resist. She told her sisters everything. She turned to Sienna who was lounging on the couch in a silk negligee, hoping to get her support.

Sienna shrugged. "I kinda side with Audrey on this, Trish. That guy mistreated you for years, and I don't think he's going to change. Maybe you can wait for some time to see if he truly has before you drop the divorce."

Audrey shook her head. "I actually don't see any reason to keep waiting. Just go forward with the divorce and be done with Stan for good."

Trisha looked at Audrey and then at Sienna. "You two don't understand. You are not . . . ."

"Don't say it!" Audrey cut in. "Just because we aren't married doesn't mean we don't know right from wrong. A leopard can't change its spots."

"But he has changed," Trisha said.

"How do you know that?"

"From the way he has treated me since these dates started." She stood and smoothed down her mustard shirtdress. "Anyway, my mind is made up. I want to stay married to Stan, especially because of the baby."

Audrey laughed harshly. "Don't come crying to me when he hurts you again."

Sienna, sweet as always, glanced up at her with a look that said she was sorry to disagree but couldn't help it.

Trisha huffed. "Well, I'm going to see him before I head to the bookstore."

"So early," Sienna said. "He's probably still asleep."

"I want to tell him what I have decided before he goes to work. He'll be super excited." She grabbed her purse from the couch. "I'll see you guys in the evening."

Sienna said goodbye, but Audrey turned away. Trish rolled her eyes, and then went out to her car. Audrey was so harsh. She was conditioned to be that way as a policewoman, but she carried it into all her relationships. That was why she had treated Ken so badly. She'd jumped to conclusions, believing he was cheating on her and had ignored his calls.

Well, I'm not going to be like Audrey. I'm going to give Stan another chance.

Trisha got into her car, smiling, imagining Stan's face when she told him she was calling off the divorce. He would be so happy. All his hard work had paid off. All the dates he'd planned had been great, and she'd had a blast on each of them. Plus, she'd enjoyed his company tremendously. Most of all, she had come away with total confidence that she still loved him and wanted to remain married to him.

She got to the house and parked beside his Ford Fiesta. Getting out of her car, she walked to the door, found it was unlocked, and pushed it open. She came in and looked around. The house was as clean as when she'd left it, but she wasn't surprised. Stan was mostly never at home. Hopefully, that would change once she moved back in.

"Stan!" she called and then began to climb the stairs. He was definitely still asleep, but he would want her to wake him up for this news.

I can't wait to see the expression on his face.

She exhaled at the top of the stairs, walked to their bedroom door, and opened it.

And then her eyes widened in horror. She swayed on her feet and put her hand on her belly as a wave of nausea went through her. Lying beside her husband, with her body wrapped around him, was another woman. For a minute, she stood, trying not to throw up all over the floor, and then she yelled out his name, "Stan!"

He jerked up, and his expression went from fear to horror as he looked at her.

She finally made herself move just as the other woman stirred. She didn't want to see the whore's face. She heard Stan's footsteps behind her and forced herself to move down the stairs faster so he wouldn't catch up with her.

She reached the bottom of the stairs, marched to the door and jerked it open.

Stan came up behind her. "Trish! Please!"

She turned around with rage. "Are you serious, right now, Stan? What could you possibly say for yourself now?"

He stared sheepishly at her, clearly unable to defend his abominable behavior.

"I didn't think so." She regarded him with loathing and her heart filled with hatred. "Tomorrow, I'm going to start to do everything I possibly can to speed up this divorce. I never want to lay eyes on you. Never again!"

"Trish, please . . ."

She ignored him and got into her car. She drove away and then stopped the car some distance away from the house. She put her head on the staring wheel and shut her eyes. Why didn't I listen to Audrey?

She started her car again and drove straight to the house rather than the bookstore.

Audrey and Sienna were still in the living room when she got in. She swept past them and rushed into the bathroom.

They followed her, worry clouding their faces. "What's wrong, Trisha?" Sienna asked.

Audrey laid a hand on her shoulder. "What did that dog, Stan, do now?"

Trisha couldn't answer any of their questions as a mixture of rage and embarrassment surged through her whole being. She knelt and bent over the toilet and threw up all the oatmeal she'd had earlier. And then she fell into her sisters' arms and sobbed.

NINETEEN

Stan sat in his study and covered his face with his hands. Since the day Trisha had stormed out after finding him in bed with Carla, he had been postponing making this call to Derrick. However, he couldn't delay any longer. He had to tell Derrick what had happened.

He scrubbed his face with his hand. Derrick will have my head.

He reached for the phone, and then his hand stilled on it. Clearly, he began to recall the day when Derrick had come to the house to make him an offer. He'd been away for a week on business and had taken the girl he was seeing at the time along with him. Somehow Derrick had found out about his affair. He'd paid him a visit, and they had sat right here in the study.

"I have a proposition for you that you would love," Derrick had said as he sat back on the stuffed leather chair across from Stan's. He looked his usual slick self in a bespoke navy-blue suit, his fingers threaded together.

Stan had thought it was about the affair he was having. In a way, he didn't really care if Derrick told Trisha about it. His marriage had lost all the excitement, and he was considering filing for a divorce. He told Derrick, "As my future brother-in-law, I know you think it's your duty to keep me on the straight and narrow, but . . ."

Derrick cut in. "I don't care about your little affair. I'm here for something bigger . . . much bigger."

Stan had raised his brows, extremely curious. "What is it?"

"It's about an inheritance. The Gardner's inheritance to be specific. A will left by the sisters' late father."

"I thought you already distributed their inheritance as their father's executor?"

"There was another will. The day before he died, Phil Gardner led me into his home office, unlocked the bachelor-chest and pulled out a secret compartment. He brought out another will for the girls and showed it to me. He said it was to be read only after he and girls' mother had died. He left them a fortune."

Stan laughed. "Phillip Gardner didn't have that kind of money. He was just a poor high school teacher."

"No, he wasn't. You know how much he trusted me when he was alive. I was like the son he never had, and he told me a lot of things. One of the things he told me was that his late father, John Barrel, was very wealthy. He said that throughout his life, he didn't want anything to do with his father or his money because of how the man treated his mother. That's why he took his mother's maiden name,

Gardner." Derrick leaned forward and said, "In the will he gave me, he states that he has bequeathed Barrel's Fortune to his daughters and their future husbands."

Stan's ears perked up. "Okay, so how much are we talking about here?"

"His father was worth an estimated six hundred million dollars. He was a widower who had no children except for Phillip Gardner and left everything he owned to him."

Stan's heart fluttered at the thought of all that wealth. He said, "So, if the money is supposed to be for the husbands as well, why didn't you tell the girls and then wait until you could marry Sienna to get your hands on your own share of the money?" He smiled and held up his hand. "Don't tell me. You wanted it all for yourself."

Derrick smiled. "Why go after just a fraction of the wealth when you can have it all?" He shrugged. "Anyway, the will also says, and I quote, 'They will understand what and where Barrel's fortune is.'"

Stan's hands had trembled with excitement. "So only the girls know where their father's fortune is?"

Derrick nodded. "Yes. But they obviously don't know about this second will. I planned to get one of them to fall for me and then find out what and where Barrel's fortune was without tipping my hand. I started by asking Audrey out, but she was immediately suspicious and a bit too, well, perceptive. I had to move over to Sienna, since you and Trisha were already seriously dating. That wasn't a tough choice to make as she is beautiful, but the problem was that she was only fifteen. Being ten years older than her, I had to wait until she was older to show my interest."

"You are a patient man. You waited for three years before you made your move, but you played her well."

"She wasn't that easy. I thought I could get the information from her without having to marry her, but every time I hinted at it, she found a way to change the subject. I eventually had to ask her to marry me just so I could keep her interest and find a way to coax the information I wanted out of her."

"That was why you left your job here and moved to New York to be near her, wasn't it?"

Derrick nodded mischievously. "I told myself that if I ultimately didn't succeed in getting the info out of her, I would marry her, reveal the will's existence, and at least get some of the wealth, but she ran away."

Stan had rubbed his hands together with glee. "I take it you want my help now and are willing to share the money with me once I deliver?"

"Yes," Derrick said. "Since I didn't succeed in discovering the location of the inheritance from Sienna before she ran off, I need you to find out from Trisha."

"And I'll get fifty percent of the wealth, or I talk."

Derrick sighed. "Thirty."

They'd finally agreed on forty percent.

Just before Derrick left, Stan had scrutinized his face and said, "There's just one thing niggling at the back of my mind. The Gardners died a few days after you were shown the will." He gave Derrick a cold suggestive smile. "Did you kill them?"

Derrick shook his head. "Of course I didn't. You know they died in a car crash, right?"

Stan had searched his eyes. Derrick's face looked impenetrable; he couldn't tell whether he was telling the truth or if he was just a very good liar. Stan didn't know whether to believe the man or not.

He came out of his reverie and sighed. I can't keep postponing this call. He picked up the phone and dialed Derrick's number.

Derrick answered on the first ring. "Yes, Stan, what do you have for me?"

"I . . . I failed."

"What do you mean you failed? You called me not long ago to say it was all going according to plan, so what do you mean you failed?"

Stan put his hand on his face. "I . . . umm . . . Trisha caught me with another woman. She says she never wants to see me again." There was silence on the other line for a full minute, and Stan began to think the man had hung up on him. "Are you there, Derrick?"

"Stan! Really! Your lack of self-control is astounding. So you couldn't wait until you discovered what Barrel's fortune is before indulging in your favorite pastime?"

"It wasn't planned. The woman Trisha found me with just appeared at my door and . . ."

Derrick interrupted. "As titillating as I'm sure your story is, I am not in the mood to hear it. You've destroyed our carefully thought-out plan."

Stan laughed harshly. "Well, you didn't succeed in keeping any Gardner girl either. You failed with both of them."

"Audrey is an annoying know-it-all. Not even the saintliest man can abide by her many rules."

"Well, she is dating someone right now. I think

they are pretty serious, so you just didn't know how to handle her," Stan scoffed, pushed to justify himself because of Derrick's haughtiness. "Even Sienna out-maneuvered you."

"Sienna is weak-minded, and you know that. She ran away not because of something I did. From the moment I found out about the fortune, I played my cards right. I would have married her if not for that 'thing' she told me about. I should have taken it seriously when she did."

"Who is boring who with long stories now? Listen, we agreed that if I failed and Trisha went on with the divorce, you would find Sienna. I suggest you find her now and somehow get her to marry you. Trisha told me she's madly in love with some other guy. They might just decide to get married any moment now."

Derrick sneered. "Okay then. I'll come to Rosefield right away and find Sienna. I know what her weaknesses are, and I think I've figured out how to play on them. I'll show you how it's done." He didn't say anything for a few seconds, and then he added, "And, Stan, you can't tell anyone that I'm on my way. I want to surprise my dear little Sienna."

*****

Sienna quickly put on a white one-shoulder chiffon dress. She accessorized with gold chandelier earrings and bracelet and then wore a pair of gold heels. Her stomach fluttered in nervous anticipation. She'd already packed her things into a suitcase in preparation for the wedding. She was thankful Audrey and Trisha weren't home. They knew she was going back to school today but didn't know she was getting married. They would have insisted on throwing her a big wedding if they knew and she didn't want that now. All she wanted was to marry Bryan. Later on, she would surprise them with the news.

She smiled broadly. I cannot wait to be his wife.

After she finished with her makeup, she studied herself in the full-length mirror beside her bed and smiled, liking what she saw. She picked up her beaded gold purse from the bed, grabbed her duffel bag and went down the stairs.

She sat in the living room to await the taxi she had called to pick her up. Before she left for work, Audrey had volunteered to drive her to the college. She had immediately refused as she didn't want to be seen in her dress. "Go to work, Audrey. I'll find my way," she'd said.

A car horn sounded outside, and she stood up. Must be the taxi. She rolled her suitcase to the door and opened it. And then her mouth fell open with shock.

"Derrick! What are you doing here?" Panic began to work its way through her as the images of their last time together came flooding back. This was the man she had promised to marry but had left at the altar. Guilt took hold of her.

Derrick looked at her and then his eyes grew watery. "You look beautiful, Sienna. Where are you headed?"

Sienna couldn't speak.

Derrick said, "Sienna, I came here to ask you to come back to me. We belong together."

She blinked and then choked out, "I can't, Derrick. I'm marrying someone else." The guilt tightened its grip on her until she felt dizzy, like she was going to pass out. She understood how it looked. She'd jilted him, and now she wanted to wed another man. What could be more heartless than that?

He looked devastated. "You can't, my darling. You promised your life to me. And remember what you used to tell me, about doing God's will no matter what. Would God want you to build your happiness on someone else's misery?"

She shut her eyes as her heart began to race with anxiety and shame. She whispered, "I'm sorry."

"You left me at the altar heartbroken. I couldn't eat or sleep for months. I did nothing but replay the sad events of our wedding day over and over again. I have been a broken man since that day. That was why I came here, to ask you to return so I can be whole again. I've tried everything else, but nothing will do until you come back to me."

Sienna felt herself swaying on her feet. She held on to the door as waves and waves of guilt and sheer panic went through her. Already, Bryan would be waiting in the chapel. Soon, he would begin to wonder where she was and probably start thinking she had abandoned him at the altar too. She had to get to him quickly.

She opened her eyes and looked at Derrick. But was it fair to him? She had been the cause of his misery. How could she skip away to find happiness while leaving him to his despair? How would she be able to live with herself if she did that?

"I need you back, Sienna," he said in a broken voice.

Her pulse began to race as her emotions roiled.

She took a deep breath to try to calm herself and managed to say, "I can't."

"Yes, you can. You can't just leave me like this. I loved you. I still love you with all my heart. I can't live without you. It's why I came."

Tears welled up in her eyes, and her heart ached. Lord, please help me, she silently prayed. She bit her lip after the prayer. Would God really help her now, knowing she'd done such harm to this man?

And then Bryan's face appeared in her mind. If she left on their wedding day in order to repay a debt, she would also be breaking his heart. He would be devastated. She took another deep breath and said softly, "Derrick, I'm sorry for all the pain I've caused you; for all that I might cause in the future. But I can't leave my Bryan. I can't do that to him. He and I were made for each other." She sighed as she looked at Derrick. Even though she had just clearly added to his pain with what she had said now, there was nothing she could do about it. She added, "I know you'll find someone else soon. I'll specifically pray about that every day." It was the least she could do.

His expression suddenly turned furious, and she backed away as he snarled, "You'll pray for me? Really, Sienna, think about it." He sighed loudly, and then the angry look faded. He gave her a small smile and said, "I know you always want to do God's will. Isn't God just? You left me first, and so I think in God's eyes, I am the one you are supposed to marry." He took a step toward her. "And as someone who wants to always do God's will, are you certain God wants you to marry that Bryan?"

Sienna sharply sucked in her breath. Oh Lord,

maybe he's right. I never asked if you wanted me to marry Bryan. I'm probably just following my own lustful desires. Tears slipped down her cheeks as her heart twisted in pain. No, I love Bryan. I love him so much.

A voice whispered in her mind, But is your love for him from God or is it really just lust? Are you totally sure God wants you to marry Bryan after jilting Derrick?

Her heart stopped. All the awful anxiety and shame that had left came rushing back, threatening to suffocate her. It felt just as bad as the day she nearly killed herself. She doubled over, grasped her throat and began to hyperventilate.

Derrick came and held her. "Breathe, Sienna. Breathe. You only need to do the right thing, and it will go away."

She began to breathe in and out, over and over again, but the panic didn't leave.

"Will you come with me?" Derrick said.

"Lord, I just want to do your will," she whispered.

Derrick said, "Marrying me is God's will. And remember, your father trusted me. He would have approved of us if he were alive."

She trembled as he said that. He was right. He'd been her father's right-hand man when he was alive.

Maybe he is God's will for me, and I would be disobeying the Lord if I married Bryan.

"Will you come with me, and marry me?" Derrick asked again.

She nodded, and he held her hand and led her into his car.

TWENTY

Bryan glanced again at his wristwatch and gritted his teeth. He paced the chapel, anxiously running his fingers through his hair.

Where are you, my dearest Sienna?

She was more than an hour late now. Chaplain Lincoln was already complaining. He had a seminar in Chicago, and he had to leave for the airport soon.

Bryan walked to the door and looked out. He walked back to the altar and sighed heavily.

Dr. Lincoln said, "Bryan, I'm sorry. I have to leave now!"

"Please, Chaplain, she will be here soon." He took out his cell phone from his suit pocket and redialed her number. Her phone rang, but as usual, there was no answer. He let out a loud sigh laden with anguish. He would go look for her, but if he left, Chaplain Lincoln would go, and they would not be able to get married. Only God knew when next the chaplain would be back.

He sat down in the front pew, trying to rein in

his jumbled-up emotions. Why wasn't Sienna here yet?

Chaplain Lincoln said, "Bryan, have you considered the fact that she may not come at all?"

Bryan shook his head. "She'll be here," he said. But the chaplain's words haunted him.

What if, like her former fiancé, she's left me on our wedding day?

He shook the thought away. She would never do that. They loved each other. A more troubling thought immediately replaced it. Knowing she would never leave him at the altar, what if something terrible had happened to her, like an accident? What if she was lying dead somewhere?

He put his hand on his head, trying to shake away the terrible thought that had gotten hold of his heart. He had to think positively. He couldn't afford to entertain any more of these negative thoughts.

He gathered himself together and whispered, "The Lord will bring her here safely." But after he said it, he looked at his watch again, and all the fear returned. It was an hour and a half past the time they'd agreed to meet here. What could possibly delay her from being here now except something really dire?

He covered his face with his hands and prayed fervently that God would keep her safe.

*****

Sienna tried to stop hyperventilating as Derrick drove her out of Rosefield. In her heart, she kept crying out to God for help, over and over again. But instead of relief, she felt like her whole body was about to explode. Bryan's face stayed in her mind. What would he be thinking now? How would he feel?

She knew how he would feel; the same way she felt now— like she was being stabbed multiple times in the heart with a sharp knife. "Lord, how can I live without Bryan?" she cried out.

But if this was what God wanted her to do, what her father would have wanted . . .

"Sienna, relax!" Derrick said harshly.

Sienna winced, and tears poured down her face. "Bryan," she whispered. "Lord, please help me!"

Love is enough!

She jerked her head up. That voice! It was clear, clearer than even Derrick's beside her. It came from within her but also from outside of her.

Was that the Lord's voice, and if it was, what exactly did He mean? Was He saying His love was enough through this trying time or . . . ?

Her eyes widened as she realized what the Lord was saying. Derrick's was the voice that fed her guilt and shame. Before she started going out with him, he'd told her that her father would want them to be together. She remembered that even when she had tried to end their relationship just before they got engaged, he had used her father's supposed wish to guilt her into staying with him. Now, he was doing the same thing, feeding on her anxiety to make her return to him.

But Bryan hadn't coerced her. Rather than feed on her fears, he'd helped her out of them. He truly loved her. Derrick didn't. If she chose love, she chose God's will. She turned to Derrick and whispered, "Love is enough. I choose love."

He frowned. "What did you say?"

"I choose Bryan," she shouted.

His face twisted into a mask of rage. "No, you don't! You are going to marry me!"

"No, I'm not! I want to get out of the car now. I'm late for my wedding."

The look on his face became menacing, and he snarled at her, "You will marry me and tell me what Barrel's fortune means!"

She didn't know what he was talking about and she didn't care. "Stop this car right now, Derrick!"

He drove faster instead, like a crazy drunk.

"Stop the car!" she screamed at him.

He increased his speed again.

She bit her lip in fear as she looked at him. He had a crazed look in his eyes that let her know her life was in danger. She glanced out of the window. She could barely make out the trees as the car tore down the road at breakneck speed.

They began to approach an intersection. Cars zoomed by in different directions. Sienna took a deep breath. She had to do something now or be killed, as it didn't appear Derrick was going to slow down.

She discreetly loosened her seat belt and then turned to him. "Derrick, if you just slow down, I'll willingly go with you."

He turned sharply to her, and she was afraid they were going to get into an accident if he didn't face the road again. She forced a smile, praying he would.

He did and slowed slightly.

Just before they reached the intersection, he slowed a little more. A police vehicle was parked on the side of the road, its doors open.

This might be my only chance, she thought.

Without thinking any further about it, she took a deep breath as her heart drummed, opened the door, and jumped out of the car. She rolled and tumbled for what seemed like forever, and then stopped a few feet from the police car.

Derrick's car screeched to a stop a foot away from her. Sienna grimaced as he came out of the car, his face red. A policeman got out of the police vehicle and ran to her, and she looked up at Derrick. He gave her a death stare, got back into his car and raced away.

"Are you okay?" the officer asked.

"I'm good." She tried to get up, but it seemed her legs didn't want to move.

"Hold tight," the man said. He radioed for help and then looked down at her. "Why did you jump out of a moving vehicle?"

"That man . . . tried to kidnap me?"

"Do you know his car number?"

She remembered Derrick's number clearly from when they were a couple and dictated it to the policeman. He radioed again, this time calling for backup.

"I need to get to my wedding," she said, her legs throbbing and her heart in the same painful condition. She knew Bryan would be heartbroken. He would think she had left him at the altar just like she'd left Derrick. She couldn't let that happen.

The officer shook his head. "I'm sorry, ma'am. You have to stay here until the paramedics arrive."

"I have to get to my wedding!" she yelled, and then she sighed. "I'm sorry. Please, can you help me?"

The paramedics began to pull up, and she told them the same thing. They ignored her and began to check to see if her legs were broken. After a few minutes, one of the men said to her, "You are lucky. It doesn't appear that it is, but you need to stay off it until . . ."

She cut him off, "I can't! I have to get to my wedding now!"

His eyes widened in surprise as he couldn't tell if she was crazy or not, and the policeman said to her, "Okay, ma'am. Are you really serious about getting to your wedding now, or are you just delirious from the fall?"

"I am serious!" She told the man her fiancé was waiting for her at their college chapel. "I hope he isn't gone by now!" she cried, tears welling up in her eyes.

"Calm down!" the officer said, and then sighed loudly. "Okay, I'm a sucker for love, so I'll help you."

The tears spilled down Sienna's face, and amidst the tears, she smiled in gratitude. "Thank you so much."

The policeman carried Sienna into the car and sped off. All the way to the Bible College, Sienna prayed, asking the Lord for one thing—that she would still be able to marry Bryan today.

*****

Bryan pleaded with the senior chaplain, "Please, sir, just a few minutes more. She'll be here." He looked at the clock. She was more than two hours late. Something had definitely happened to her.

Or she has left you at the altar just like she left

her ex-fiancé? a voice in his head mocked him.

He felt like weeping, but he held himself in check. *She wouldn't leave me at the altar. I know she loves me.*

The chaplain shook his head and picked up his briefcase. "It's time for my flight. I have to go."

"Please, just a minute more."

"I can't. I have no choice." He walked away.

Bryan held his head in his hands and sat on the steps of the altar, his emotions raging. *She couldn't have just left him waiting here. Why won't she answer my calls?*

He called her again and groaned when she still didn't answer. "Lord, please . . ." His head jerked up as he heard a loud commotion outside. He stood and hurried out the door. A police car was parked right in front of the chapel. On the lawn and a policeman was helping a girl out of the car.

His heart soared. "Sienna!" And then he saw she was walking with a limp. Her dress was torn, and her hair was in a mess. He ran to her and frowned. "What happened?"

A small crowd of students had gathered around the entrance of the chapel, watching and whispering. He held her hand and ran his fingers over her hair, worriedly gazing at her. He was breaking the rules, but he didn't care.

She shook her head. "I'll tell you about it all later. Let's just get married." She pointed at the chapel. "Is Dr. Lincoln still there?"

Bryan shook his head sadly. "He left. Just now." He held her right arm while the policeman held her left. Together, they took Sienna into the church. After she was sitting in the front pew, Bryan said,

"Let me go see if I can still catch up to Chaplain Lincoln and get him to come back."

He ran to the college parking lot as fast as he could. As he ran, a voice in his mind kept telling him he was wasting his time. Even if Dr. Lincoln were still at school, he would probably not agree to wed them today as that would mean canceling his flight.

I have to try, Bryan told himself as he ran.

He got to the car park and spotted the chaplain getting into the back of his car. Moving as fast as he could, Bryan reached him just as the senior chaplain's driver started to reverse the vehicle. He waved for the car to stop, but it didn't. He yelled, but the car sped off.

Bryan's heart sank, and then the car began to back up.

His heart soared again.

The chaplain stuck his head out of the window as his car stopped beside Bryan. "What is it?" Chaplain Lincoln asked.

Bryan told him that Sienna had finally arrived. He explained that she was late because she had been in an accident. "Her leg is broken, sir," he said, "but she still came because she really wants to marry me. And I really want to marry her." He held his breath as he looked pleadingly at the chaplain, hoping he would reconsider and agree to marry them.

Dr. Lincoln sighed loudly and then said, "Fine. Since you are both so determined to get married now. Who am I to stand in the way of true love?"

Bryan whooped and thanked the man, excitement surging through his body.

They got back to the chapel, and Bryan's eyes

widened in surprise. The place was packed with students. He walked down the aisle, looking at them. He and Sienna had invited no one, but it seemed as if almost all the students in the school were here. He sighed as he bent to kiss Sienna and said, "Well, at least we have more than two witnesses to our wedding."

She smiled and brushed her nose against his.

The chaplain began the wedding with a prayer and then a short sermon on love. Bryan's heart skipped with excitement. He looked down at Sienna who was sitting on a slipper chair beside him. Even though her dress was now dirty and torn, she was glowing. She smiled up at him.

Chaplain Lincoln asked them to repeat the marriage vows after him while they exchanged the wedding bands. After the traditional vows, he nodded at Bryan. Bryan had told him he and Sienna wanted to declare their love for each other at the altar to seal their marriage. He had considered writing his declaration down, but had decided against it. Instead, he'd chosen to speak words that spontaneously came from his heart.

He took Sienna's hands and began: "Sienna, I didn't know it was possible to love someone as much as I love you. I think about you all the time, and when we are apart, I can't wait to be reunited with you. You've become a huge part of me, and I can't live without you. I'll love you forever and thank the Lord for bringing you to me every single day of my life."

He ended and smiled at her. Tears were shimmering in her eyes.

She looked deep into his eyes and said, "I don't

even know how to express just how much I love you, but I'll try. This past year has been one of the most trying times of my life, but also the sweetest because I met you. I was a mess, but you loved me through it all . . ." she stopped for a moment, her voice choked with emotion. She continued again. "Because of you, I now know how much God loves me. Next to the Lord, you are my very best friend. I love you with every breath in me, and I can't wait to start my life with you."

Bryan wiped the tears from his eyes, over-whelmed by her declaration of love. He smiled and mouthed, "I love you."

Chaplain Lincoln looked at both of them and said, "Now, by the power vested in me by God and the state of Idaho, I now pronounce you husband and wife." He turned to Bryan. "You may kiss your bride."

Bryan leaned in and gently kissed her. He beamed at her, his heart bursting with joy.

"I love you so much," she whispered.

"I love you more," he said.

Dr. Lincoln said, "Everyone, I present to you, Mr. and Mrs. Larson."

Bryan turned around with Sienna, and the students clapped and roared. He held her hand as they exited the chapel. When they were outside, he took her in his arms and kissed her passionately. He drew back and winked at her. "Now, the whole school knows we belong to each other, we can kiss whenever we want to."

She giggled and then kissed him again. "I can't wait to grow old with you," she said.

"Nor can I," he replied.

TWENTY-ONE

As Audrey drove back from work, she inhaled and then let out her breath slowly. It had been a long day at work, not to talk of a very eventful week in the house.

Sienna had visited a few days ago with a limp and with her boyfriend, Bryan. Only he wasn't her boyfriend anymore. Sienna had surprised her and Trisha by announcing that she and Bryan were married.

In addition to that, Audrey found out that Sienna's ex, Derrick, had tried to kidnap her after he went raving mad. He was in custody now at the police station, continually whispering something about Barrel's fortune. She'd decided to discontinue interrogating Derrick and was making arrangements for him to be moved to a psych ward as he had clearly lost his mind. But as crazy as the guy was those words, Barrel's fortune, sounded strangely familiar to her.

Trisha had gone the opposite direction as Sienna. She had gone ahead with the divorce proceedings, thank God. She'd also taken over the house she'd shared with Stan while he moved out.

With Trisha back in her own house and Sienna in school, Audrey felt a little lonely now. Plus, her sisters now had at least a measure of what they both wanted. While Trisha might be ending her marriage, she was soon going to have what she had always desired—a child. Sienna, of course, was now married to the guy she was crazy about, and she and Bryan looked ecstatic when they visited. She was the only one who didn't have her heart's desire. The man she loved lived a million miles away.

She sighed again. The regular phone calls and video chats weren't enough anymore. She wanted to be near him, to be married to him and to wake up beside him every day.

She heaved a sigh as she got to her house. She stepped out of her car, climbed the stairs and stepped onto her front porch. Opening her purse, she dug out her keys, unlocked the door and then jumped. In the middle of her living room was Ken on his knees, holding out a ring to her.

She covered her mouth and held back a sob. "Ken! What . . . when . . . how are you here?"

He laughed and then, ignoring her multiple questions, said solemnly, "Audrey Gardner, no, Police Chief Gardner, I love every single thing about you. Even how stubborn you can sometimes be."

She grinned at him.

He continued. "Will you marry me, Audrey?"

She bit her lip as she looked down at him. She tried to speak, but felt too overwhelmed to say a word.

"Wow, Audrey! Have I just left you speechless?"

Ken raised his hand with a triumphant smile and shouted, "I left Audrey Gardner speechless!" She shook her head at him, and he chuckled. "You still haven't answered my question."

She cried, "Of course I'll marry you! I've been waiting forever for you to ask me!" She smiled as her heart flooded with love for him.

He chuckled. "That's the girl I know." He slipped the ring onto her finger, stood and kissed her.

A chorus of voices suddenly yelled, "Surprise!" and Audrey jumped again. "What . . . where did you all come from?" She smiled at all of them. Sienna and Bryan, Trisha, a bunch of people from the police department, as well as most of her friends were here.

"I invited them," Ken said. "Trisha let us in with her keys." He turned to them. "She said yes, everyone."

They all hollered and clapped.

Audrey grinned and kissed Ken. "Thank you."

He smiled and nodded.

Everyone soon separated into groups, chatting, eating and drinking. Ken had ordered snacks and drinks, which had been delivered to the house half an hour ago.

Audrey stood near the dining table, chatting with a group of police officers. She saw Sienna at the other end of the living room, tilting her face up to kiss Bryan, and she smiled. Sienna looked so happy. She didn't look at all like the girl who had earlier in the year fled from her own wedding, frightened and confused, and almost taken her life. Bryan's love had changed her entirely. Most of all, God's unconditional love had transformed her life.

She turned toward the direction Trish was. She was talking to some of the guys from the police station. One of them in particular followed her every move with his eyes. She could see Frank was taken with her, but he'd loved her since they were kids. Unfortunately, she had married that idiotic Stan. Well, good riddance now.

She found Ken's eyes from across the room and mouthed, "I love you," and he did the same.

Her heart soared again. Finally, I'm going to marry him.

Sienna walked up to her and said, "So, Derrick is still in custody?"

"He is, but I think he's better off in a psych ward."

Sienna frowned. "When he was taking me to God-knows-where, he said something about Barrel's Fortune."

Audrey blinked in surprise. "He's been saying it over and over again at the station."

"He was yelling at me, saying I had to tell him what it meant." Sienna looked up with a thoughtful expression. "At the time, I didn't care about that; all I wanted was to escape him. But it's been on my mind for days now. Do you know what it means?"

"It does sound familiar. Let's ask Trish. Maybe she will know."

They called Trish aside and asked her about it. She shook her head and said she didn't know what it meant.

They went out and sat on the porch, still talking about it. Audrey looked into the distance and said, "Why can't I place it? It kinda reminds me of Dad; something he said, but I just, I just can't . . ."

She gasped as she suddenly recalled her ten-year-old self sitting on a swing outside their house, while their father pushed her higher and higher. She was giggling and he, laughing. He finally stilled the swing and told her he enjoyed their father-daughter relationship. Unfortunately, he never had one with his father, he'd said.

She asked him about his dad, and he told her that the man's name was John Barrel. He had decided to keep his mom's maiden name because his father didn't care about him or his mother growing up.

She looked at Sienna and Trish and told them all she remembered.

Sienna asked, "Can you remember anything else? Derrick said Barrel's fortune."

Audrey pressed her lips together. "I remember Dad saying his father was wealthy so, maybe that's what Derrick was talking about. John Barrel must have left Dad a fortune. I'll find out more when I interrogate Derrick tomorrow."

They went inside again.

As Audrey talked with the guests and then later drove Ken to Hattie's Bed & Breakfast, she thought about the Barrel's fortune mystery. When she stopped in front of Hattie's, Ken took her in his arms. He kissed her until every single thought, except for one, fled her mind. The only thing that remained was how much she loved him.

"I'll see you tomorrow," he said when he finally got out of the car.

She waved to him and drove home, feeling giddy from their kiss and the surprise engagement. As she lay in bed, she stared at the diamond ring he'd bought her until she fell asleep.

But the next day, as she drove to work, her

thoughts returned to Derrick's rant about Barrel's fortune.

At the station, she sat in front of Derrick to interrogate him, but it was clear he was totally out of it. She started to rise, but she sat down when he mumbled something about Barrel's fortune and another will Mr. Gardner had left before he died. When she asked him about it, she was surprised when he said, "You don't believe me, do you? I have the will in my possession, but you have to tell me what Barrel's fortune means."

She wondered how much of what he was saying was real as she stared at him. His eyes were red and wild-looking. When she started to get up, he screamed at her, and she sighed. In spite of everything, she felt sorry for him.

Poor Derrick. He was so intelligent and proud, now he's reduced to this.

She went to the detective directly in charge of the case. "Can I have those things we just recovered from the suspect's vehicle?"

The man gave her a lot of things that were useless to her, but a brown envelope stuck out. It had the initials P.G, on it, which she guessed stood for Phillip Gardner. She took it back to her office, but decided not to open it until she got home. She would call Trish and Sienna, and they could open it together.

She sat at her desk, called each of them, and asked them to meet her at the house in the evening. Sienna promised to leave school early since she said the meeting was crucial. Trish was already planning to visit in the evening anyway.

*****

That evening, the three of them sat together on the couch in Audrey's living room. She held the envelope in her hand while her heart drummed. She had told them already that Derrick had said something about a new will their father had left them.

She took a long, deep breath, let it out slowly and then started to open the envelope carefully.

Trisha said, "You know what this means. Dad left us a lot of money."

Audrey shrugged. "I don't know. Whatever is in the envelope, if we can't remember what Barrel's fortune means, it'll probably be useless."

Once the envelope was opened, she drew out a folded letter. She unfolded it and straightened the official-looking letter. At the bottom of the letter was their father's signature. She traced it, her heart aching. "Dad!"

Trisha and Sienna shifted closer, their hot breaths on her face as she started to read the will.

THE LAST WILL AND TESTAMENT OF PHILLIP GARDNER.

I appoint my mentee, Derrick Fisher, as executor of my will. If he is unwilling or unable to serve as executor, I appoint my daughter, Audrey Gardner, to take his place.

Audrey continued to silently read the document in tears. She could hear Trisha and Sienna sniffing beside her. And then she came to the part they'd been waiting for. She read it out loud:

. . . I give and bequeath Barrel's fortune to my daughters, Audrey, Trisha and Sienna, and their future spouses, after my death and their mother's. They will understand what and where Barrel's fortune is . . .

Trisha stood. "Audrey, you have to remember more. Dad said we will, but I can't recall him telling me anything about Barrel's fortune."

Sienna said, "I can't either. Maybe because we were too young. But Audrey you should. Please try. Dad said we would know what it meant and where the fortune is. He wouldn't say that if none of us even understands what it means."

Audrey shut her eyes, feeling dizzy from the pressure on her to recall conversations that took place years ago. "I've already told you guys what I remember," she said. "I can't remember . . ." her eyes snapped open. "Wait!" Something was niggling at the back of her mind. She focused, trying to bring the elusive thought to light. She said, "Barrel was grandfather's name and . . ." Her eyes widened. "Fortune was the name of the street Dad said he'd lived with his mother growing up. The number of the street was simple, so I always remembered it. Two-seven-one-seven."

Sienna suddenly sprang up. "Dad once showed me a portable safe he said his father had given him before he passed on. I was about seven." She glanced up at the ceiling. "I think he kept it hidden somewhere in our old room, probably to divert attention from it. Maybe two-seven-one-seven are the digits that can open the combination lock."

Audrey shook her head in astonishment. "It's in

my room? I have never seen a safe there."

They all scrambled to Audrey's room and opened the closet. They all started searching different parts of the closet. Audrey searched the top compartment, jam-packed with old clothes she had never bothered going through. Her hand suddenly found something hard and cold, and she pulled it out. It was a small steel safe.

"Is this it?" she asked Sienna.

Sienna nodded. "Has to be."

They sat on the bed, and Audrey put the small safe on her lap. She tried to open the lock using the street numbers she'd remembered. Lord, please let it work.

When it suddenly snapped open, they gave a collective gasp.

Audrey held her breath as she lifted the lid. And then she blinked. There was nothing in it but a small envelope and the foam covering the bottom. She brought out the envelope and shook out its contents. A white folded paper fell out.

"That's all?" Sienna asked, her voice heavy with disappointment.

Audrey tried to brush aside her own disappointment and picked the letter up. "A letter in Dad's handwriting," she said and perked up again. If their father had gone to such great lengths to keep this letter secret, then it had to be important.

She began to read it out loud:

My dearest daughters,
If you are reading this, then it means that your mother and I are gone.

A shaft of pain went through her and tears fell down her cheeks. She looked up at Sienna and Trisha. They were crying too. She continued.

I hope you are all doing well. I wanted you to only get this when your mother and I are gone because I don't want your mother to ever know. She trusted me fully, and I am ashamed of how I betrayed her trust. I concealed what I knew, but it has been bothering me for years, and I need to get it out.

It was before you all were born. I was newly married to your mother then and only twenty-two. I had just gotten my teaching job at Rosefield High School. An opportunity to travel to Spain came through a teachers' exchange program. Young teachers were sponsored abroad to teach students English. Since I could speak some Spanish, another teacher and I were picked to go. I was overjoyed as I had always dreamt of going to Europe. Unfortunately, your mother couldn't go. I went without her, and there, I met a woman. One thing led to the other, and she had a child, my son.

"No . . . Dad!" Trisha cried. "It's not true! He loved Mom so much. He couldn't have cheated on her."

Sienna shut her eyes and shook her head slowly.

Audrey's hands shook as she went on reading.

. . . but I couldn't claim him as mine because the thought of telling your mother and consequently breaking her heart was unthinkable to me. Anyway, you have a half-brother. My only desire is for you to please find him. As soon as you can!

And one more thing; your grandfather left everything he owned to me, and now I'm leaving it all to you girls and to your spouses. Remove the foam at the bottom of the safe where you found this letter. You will find all the documents you need to claim the inheritance. You will also find more information about your brother that will help in your search for him. Please use the resources available from your inheritance to find your lost brother.

I love you girls dearly,
Dad

Audrey looked up at her sisters. Their faces were wet with tears, and they looked shell-shocked, just like she felt. Not even in her wildest imagination had she ever thought her father would have a secret like this. She said to them, "Well, as heartbreaking and crazy as this is, we have to find this half-brother somehow."

She held her breath, knowing Trish and Sienna might object. The father they had thought was without fault had had an affair and a love child. However, it wasn't the boy's fault, and maybe he might want to know who his father was. Plus, she felt, as she sat looking up at her sisters, a strong desire to find this long-lost brother.

Sienna nodded, but Trisha pursed her lips.

"I agree," Sienna said. "We need to find him. It's Dad's last wish."

Audrey looked at Trisha. "What do you say, Trish. Let's find our brother. That's what Dad wanted."

Trisha was silent for a minute and then she sighed loudly. "Okay, then. We will start as soon as possible."

Audrey wiped her tears and then tore out the bottom of the briefcase as their dad had instructed. Some documents were there, just as their father had said. One by one, she opened and scanned them. Her eyes grew big as she read each financial document. Trisha and Sienna were looking over her shoulders, poring over them too.

After they finished reading all the documents, they sat in silence. None of them was able to speak; Audrey knew that just like her, neither of her sisters could fathom the amount of wealth they had been left.

Trisha was the first to break the silence. She said with a teasing smile, "So, what are you guys going to do with all that money?"

Audrey found her voice and croaked out, "What else but a family trip to Europe? You heard what dad wrote in the will. We are to find our brother as soon as possible."

Trisha said, "Well, I agree with you. If we are going to Europe, we need to go now." She placed her hand on her belly. "Soon, I won't be allowed to fly anymore."

They agreed to meet on the weekend again, and Trish and Sienna left.

Shortly after, Ken came over. Audrey told him about her half-brother and also told him she might be going to Europe soon.

For a few minutes, he sat looking at her with a stunned expression. And then he gathered her in his arms. "I'll support you through whatever you plan to do. Before you leave though, we will have our wedding."

She looked at him like he was crazy and then said, "First of all, that's obvious. I can't wait to marry you." She smiled as he beamed at her. "Secondly, you are coming with me. Do you think I want to stay that long without seeing you?"

He shook his head. "But I can't get off work now . . ."

She interrupted him. "You can, Ken, if you have everything you need and don't need to work."

He lifted his brow. "What do you mean?"

"I mean that the money dad left us is a lot . . . a whole lot."

"How much is it?"

"About two hundred million dollars . . . for both of us. Enough to live off of without needing to work ever again."

Ken put his hand around his neck and coughed. His eyes grew round as saucers, and then he laughed. "Okay, then. I'll start packing right away."

But instead of packing, he wrapped her in his arms and kissed her passionately. He drew back, and said, "You know what the best thing about this news is?"

She shook her head.

"It's not the money. It's the fact that we don't have to worry anymore about being apart because of our jobs. After we get married, I might just quit and move here with you."

Audrey beamed at him. "I was so worried about that, but I didn't want to mention it. I love my job, but if I don't need to work, then I'll quit too, so I can live in the same place as you." She snuggled closer to him and said, "I can't wait to start my life with you, babe."

"Neither can I," he responded.

She shut her eyes and sighed in contentment. At the beginning of the year, she had thought she would spend the rest of her life alone and that her job would be her only companion until she grew old. Now, it was almost the end of the year, and suddenly she had all the money she could ever imagine. Best of all, she had a fiancé; a loving man who would be her true companion for life. God had given her all her heart's desire in less than a year. She was truly blessed and loved beyond measure.

*****

Sienna came back from her classes, threw her purse on the coffee table and flopped down on the sofa, tired. She looked at the time, saw it was almost eight and sighed happily. Bryan would come in at any moment from now.

Since they got married, they had begun a daily routine. After she came back home, she waited for him in the living room as he usually came back late from his classes. They had dinner together, and then they'd sit and chat, basically just enjoying each other's company, and then retire to bed together. Today, their routine would be slightly different as she didn't know if they would be able to sleep after she told him her news.

She glanced around the living room furnished in white and brown. She had chosen white drapes, throws, and a white center rug, while the sofas, coffee table, and other wood furnishings were brown. The two bedrooms in the house were furnished in the same color scheme.

She was deliriously happy, and life with Bryan was better than she imagined it would be. Only one thing had put a damper over her happiness, their happiness. Their money had been running out at an alarming rate. Bryan's meager chaplain's income wasn't enough for their needs. Her savings, used for major expenses like the rent for their apartment, were depleting fast. They had both begun to worry about meeting their daily needs, but now, with the inheritance from her father, they wouldn't have to worry anymore—ever again. She couldn't wait to see the look on his face when she told him.

She heard the door open, and her heart soared with joy. She brushed her fingers through her hair and turned to face the door.

He smiled at her as he walked in and said, "How is my favorite person in the whole world doing?" When she told him she was doing great, he walked over to her and kissed her. "I can't believe I am married to such a beauty," he whispered in her ear.

As usual, he looked amazing in blue jeans and a plaid shirt. Butterflies fluttered in her stomach, and she giggled. "How were your lectures today?"

He nodded. "Fine."

She looked him in the eye. "You know how we've been worrying about money? About how we are going to survive. Well, we don't have to worry anymore."

"How come?" he asked, a bit surprised.

She told him about the will and her long-lost brother, everything. When she finished, he searched her face, a look of wonder on his face, wondering if she was joking. "Sienna, I can't believe it. Are you serious?"

She nodded.

He got up and paced the living room while she smiled. At last, he came and snatched her up in a huge hug.

She laughed and then said, "We have to find a way to get out of school soon so we can travel together."

"It's nearly Christmas. What about then?"

"No, our father wanted us to look for him now. And Trisha soon won't be allowed to fly."

"So, we have a new adventure to start and all the money we will ever need." He whooped, picked her up and spun her around.

She laughed and then planted a kiss on his cheeks when he put her down. She said to him, "When I told you at our wedding that I couldn't wait to start a brand-new adventure with you, who knew that it would be an actual adventure?"

He chuckled. "I did. I knew that life with you would be like a brand-new adventure every day. The money will allow us to spend time together without ever worrying again about how to pay our bills," he said to her. "But whether we have lots of money or little, we will always have each other and the Lord."

She grinned, her heart overflowing.

He kissed her again, a long lingering kiss this time. When he drew back, she asked, "So, are you ready to go on this wild adventure with me and find my long-lost brother?"

He nodded. "I can't wait," he said, and then kissed her again.

A LOOK AT: QUEST FOR LOVE

Newly married, Sienna is compelled to start a family of her own, but longs to solve the final piece of the puzzle; a missing brother she never knew she had. Her sister, Police Chief Audrey, is preparing to marry the man of her dreams—but as her feelings grow stronger, honoring her vow of chastity becomes increasingly difficult to maintain. The perfect solution? Joining Sienna on an adventure to discover their long-lost sibling, and hopefully close a chapter of their lives that's been shadowed by shame and secrecy.

Thirty, pregnant and alone, Trisha follows Audrey and Sienna's contentment and excitement with more than a little longing. She's always been the one to play it safe, and now the time has come to start making her own rules.

Meanwhile, the brother who holds his sisters' hopes and dreams is battling some demons of his own. The women long for a happy reunion, but will soon learn they've invited a traitor into their hearts.

COMING JANUARY 2020

ABOUT THE AUTHOR

Like the characters in her stories, Emma Easter juggles a range of identities.

In the low-income community where she works, Easter is known as a family medicine physician who treats patients of all ages and backgrounds.

College friends see her as an accomplished musician, having studied and mastered five classical instruments—but behind closed doors, she's just as comfortable rocking an air guitar to Creed. And when she isn't giving her heart, soul, and sanity to her three young children she's indulging in her most secret identity of all: meeting new characters, crafting fresh plots, and exploring every corner of her imagination.

Across all these different roles, one cohesive thread has tied everything together: her faith and love of Jesus Christ.

Find more great titles by Emma Easter and Christian Kindle News at https://christiankindle-news.com/our-authors/emma-easter/

www.ingramcontent.com/pod-product-compliance
Lightning Source LLC
Chambersburg PA
CBHW060558030726
47498CB00005B/1447